D0842611

5·19 **DATE DUE**

JUL 23 2019

EVEN THE DEAD

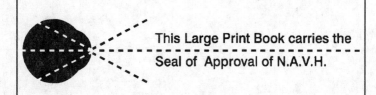

A QUIRKE NOVEL

EVEN THE DEAD

BENJAMIN BLACK

THORNDIKE PRESS
A part of Gale, Cengage Learning

GALE
CENGAGE Learning

Farmington Hills, Mich • San Francisco • New York • Waterville, Maine
Meriden, Conn • Mason, Ohio • Chicago

Copyright © 2015 by Benjamin Black.
Thorndike Press, a part of Gale, Cengage Learning.

ALL RIGHTS RESERVED
This is a work of fiction. All of the characters, organizations, and events
portrayed in this novel either are products of the author's imagination
or are used fictitiously.
Thorndike Press® Large Print Crime Scene.
The text of this Large Print edition is unabridged.
Other aspects of the book may vary from the original edition.
Set in 16 pt. Plantin.

LIBRARY OF CONGRESS CATALOGING-IN-PUBLICATION DATA

Names: Black, Benjamin, 1945- author.
Title: Even the dead : a Quirke novel / Benjamin Black.
Description: Large print edition. | Waterville, Maine : Thorndike Press Large Print,
    2016. | © 2015 | Series: A Quirke novel | Series: Thorndike Press large print crime
    scene
Identifiers: LCCN 2015045995| ISBN 9781410484673 (hardback) | ISBN 141048467X
    (hardcover)
Subjects: LCSH: Pathologists—Fiction. | Murder—Investigation—Fiction. | Dublin
    (Ireland)—Fiction. | BISAC: FICTION / Mystery & Detective / General. | GSAFD:
    Mystery fiction.
Classification: LCC PR6052.A57 E94 2016 | DDC 823/.914—dc23
LC record available at http://lccn.loc.gov/2015045995

Published in 2016 by arrangement with Henry Holt and Company, LLC

Printed in the United States of America
1 2 3 4 5 6 7 20 19 18 17 16

EVEN THE DEAD

1

One glorious morning in the middle of June it occurred to David Sinclair that he was in the wrong profession. He was thirty-four now; after spending eight years training for the job, he was in line for the post of chief consultant pathologist at the Hospital of the Holy Family, succeeding his boss, Quirke, who was on extended and, if there was any justice, permanent sick leave. In those eight years, so it seemed to him, he had not once stopped to ask himself if he really wanted to be a pathologist. Nor could he recall deciding, in his school days, that this was what he would spend his life doing: slicing into the bellies of dead bodies, clipping their ribs and sawing through their sternums, his nostrils filled with their awful smells, his hands gummy with their congealing blood. What was it Quirke used to say? *Down among the dead men.* Was that really the place to spend a life?

The pathology lab was a windowless basement cavern. Banks of fluorescent lights in the ceiling gave off a faint, relentless hum that today was making his temples ache. Outside, he knew, the morning sun was shining. Girls in summer dresses were walking by the river, and there were swans on the water, and flags were rippling in the warm breeze, and in Grafton Street there would be the rich brown smell of roasting coffee beans from the open doorway of Bewley's Oriental Café, and paper boys would be calling out the latest headlines, and there would be the sound of horses' hoofs on cobblestones, and the cries of the flower sellers at their stalls. Summer. Crowds. Life.

The body on the slab was that of a young man, early twenties, slight build. It was badly burned, and smelt of petrol and scorched flesh. At first light that morning, in the Phoenix Park, three members of the Fire Brigade had been required to lift it carefully out of the still simmering wreckage of a motorcar, a Wolseley, that had crashed into a tree just off the main road through the park and burst into flames. A cycling enthusiast out early on his racer had come upon the scene; by then the fire had died down, but a thick column of black

8

smoke was still rising from under the car's gaping bonnet.

A suicide, according to the Guard who had come in with the ambulance men. Over the previous year there had been three similar instances of desperate young men deliberately driving their cars at high speed into highly resistant obstacles; unemployment was steadily rising, and it was a hard time for the young. The Guard himself was young, hardly into his twenties, and looked shaken, despite his offhand pose. Sinclair guessed this was the first dead body he had been called on to deal with, or certainly the first one in this scorched state, clothes burnt off save for a few blackened tatters, the flesh as crisp as fried bacon, the eyeballs bursting from their sockets.

"Any identification?" Sinclair had asked.

The Guard shrugged, pushing his cap with the shiny black peak to the back of his head. He had fair hair and blond eyelashes. "We're on to the City Council, tracing the registration number." He couldn't seem to take his eyes off the dead man's groin and the shriveled black thing there, like a crooked little finger. "Poor bugger," he said. "I hope he was knocked out before the fire started."

"Yes," Sinclair said.

Now, two hours later, the Guard long gone, Sinclair stood frowning at the dead man's singed, leathery skull and the deep indentation above the left temple.

Knocked out. Yes?

The trees on Ailesbury Road seemed to throb in the sunshine, great bulbous masses of leaves shimmering inside a penumbra of grayish heat mist. Quirke stood to one side of the tall sash window, gazing down into the street. These days there were times when his brain clanked to a halt, like a steam train stopping, at night, in the middle of nowhere. He knew it wasn't possible not to think, that the mind was always active, even in sleep, at no matter how subdued a level, but at the end of these blank episodes, when the poor old engine started up again, he would try to grope his way backwards to that dark halting place and find out what had been going on there, often with little success.

Philbin, the brain specialist, had said these latest lapses were probably the result of his general inaction and enervation, combined with nervous tension. In other words, Quirke thought, I'm under pressure and I'm bored. Takes a specialist to spot that, all right.

For months he had been suffering from

hallucinations and what Philbin would later call absence seizures, before giving in at last and going to see if something could be done about his state. By then he was convinced he had a brain tumor, but Philbin had shown him the X-rays, which were clear. Philbin's guess was that there was a lesion on the temporal lobe; hence the mental blanks and the momentary delusions. It was probably an old scar, Philbin said; as old, Quirke supposed, as the slight limp he still had from a bad beating he was given one wet winter night years before by a couple of hired thugs. How the past comes back to haunt us.

"Rest," Philbin had said, nodding sagely. "Just rest, try to relax, stay off the hard stuff, you'll be right as rain."

Philbin had a long narrow head, the top of which was a slightly flattened, shiny curve, like the crust of a loaf. He was entirely bald save for a fringe of suspiciously black hair — did he dye it? — at the back of his skull. When he dipped his head, a little lozenge of silvery light slid over that pale, polished dome, a faint, falling star. He and Quirke had been at college together but had never been friends. Quirke didn't go in for friends, much, even in those early days.

"What about work?" Quirke asked. "When

can I go back?"

Philbin had fiddled with the papers on his desk, his eyes gone vague. "We'll have to see about that. For now, just take it easy, as I say, and stay sober."

He had done what he was told, had taken it easy, and rested, and drunk only wine, and only at dinnertime. He had pills to make him sleep, and other pills to keep him calm when he was awake. And so the days trickled past, each one much the same as all the others. He felt like Robinson Crusoe, grown old on his island.

Mal, his adoptive brother, and Mal's wife, Rose, had urged him to come and stay with them for a while, to convalesce, and he had agreed, against his better judgment. He didn't think of himself as a convalescent, but on the other hand he knew he wasn't well, either. His mood swung like a defective pendulum. One minute he was sunk in despondency, the next he was fizzing with impatience to be back in the world, back in his life. Yet when he thought of the hospital where he had worked for the past twenty years in an airless room below ground, his heart quailed.

What would he do if he didn't go back? Even at this distance he could almost hear his assistant, Sinclair, rubbing his hands at the prospect of stepping into his shoes.

He was fond of Sinclair, in a muted sort of way, but he was damn well certain he wasn't going to let him take his job. No, he would bide his time, and one of these days he would take a taxi to the Hospital of the Holy Family and march down those broad marble stairs to the lab. He would hang his hat on the hat stand and sit down in his chair and put his feet on his desk and shove his assistant firmly back into his box.

He heard the door behind him opening. He didn't turn. He knew by her step who it was.

"You look like a man standing on a ledge and about to jump," Rose said.

Now he did turn. Rose was no longer young, but she was still a handsome woman — slim, sleek, straight-backed, with a cool smile and a mocking eye. They had gone to bed together once, just once, a long time ago. And now she was married to Mal. Quirke still considered it the most unlikely match. But then, to Quirke all matches seemed unlikely.

Rose came and stood opposite him on the other side of the window, and together they looked out at the broad, sunlit street. "What about a stroll?" she said in her smoky drawl; the side of Rose that was a southern belle

13

would never age. Quirke shook his head. She frowned at him. "You don't go out enough," she said. "Don't you ever get cabin fever?"

"All the time. Especially when I'm out."

"Oh, you!" she said, and laughed.

She crossed to the fireplace and took a cigarette from an ormolu box on the mantelpiece. Quirke watched her. He had always wondered about her life with Mal, and since he had been staying with them, the mystery had deepened. When husband and wife were together, at lunch, for instance, or sitting in the drawing room of an evening, they spoke in what sounded to Quirke like strained, superficial phrases, never seeming to say anything. Giving them the benefit of the doubt, he thought perhaps it was the effect of the house and its stultified atmosphere — it had been an embassy before Mal and Rose bought it. And there was his own presence, which was bound to be a constraint. Maybe when they were alone together they behaved entirely differently, in ways that Quirke could hardly begin to imagine. He tried not to speculate on what they did in bed. Mal and Rose embracing, the two of them naked in a sweat of passion — no, he couldn't picture it, he just couldn't. The prospect was too bizarre, too sad, and too funny.

"How are you feeling today?" Rose asked; it was what she asked every day. "I see you've stopped going about half the morning in that awful dressing gown."

"Awful? I always thought it gave me a certain Noël Coward look, no?"

"No, Quirke, I'm afraid it doesn't. The certain look it gives you is of an old alcoholic drying out — or taking the cure, as you say here."

Rose was never one to pull her punches.

"It's not drink that's my trouble this time," Quirke said. "This time, they tell me I'm sick."

"Oh, you're not sick. People like us have no business being sick, Quirke."

He turned to the window and the street again. Rose, smoking her cigarette, stood with one arm folded, regarding him with a fondly skeptical eye. "But go on, tell me: how are you, really?"

"Really, I don't know. Half the time my brain seems dead."

"And the other half?"

He said nothing for a moment. He took out his own cigarettes and lit one. "I seem hardly alive," he said. "I'm stalled, as if something in me had run down."

"The doctor said you'd get well, yes?"

"To tell you the truth, I don't in fact think it's the damage to my brain, I don't think that's the trouble. Something has happened to me, something has — gone out."

"Maybe you should go somewhere, for a holiday."

He looked at her. "Oh, Rose," he said, "come on."

Stung, she took an angry drag on her cigarette and lifted her chin and expelled a thin, quick stream of smoke upwards. "You're impossible, Quirke, do you know that?"

"*You* find me impossible? Think what it's like for me, stuck with myself."

Rose stamped her foot, stabbing her heel into the Persian rug she was standing on. "You make me so impatient," she said. "Sometimes I'd like to shake you."

"I'm sorry," he said. "I was trying to be funny."

"Funny? You? Please don't bother."

He sketched a little bow, conceding the point. "I shouldn't have let you persuade me to come and stay here," he said. "I knew it wouldn't work — kind though the invitation was, of course," he added, not without a sharp edge of irony.

"Then why did you accept?"

"Because it was you who asked me."

They looked away from each other, and were silent. Old things that had once been between them stirred and flashed, like fish in a deep, shadowed pool.

Rose sat down on the arm of a brocaded chair, balancing an ashtray on her knee.

"Mal is in the garden," she said, "pretending to be a gardener. Have you seen his new sun hat? It makes him look like a cross between a coolie and a standing lamp." She paused, casting about her with an impatient frown. "Maybe *I* should take a holiday. Let's get in the car, Quirke, just the two of us, you and I, and drive down to — oh, I don't know. Monte Carlo. Marrakech. Timbuktu." She paused again. "Don't you ever get tired of this one-horse town, this one-horse country?"

He chuckled, wreathing himself in cigarette smoke. "All the time."

"Then why do you stay?"

"I don't know. My life happened here, such as it was."

"My sweet Lord, Quirke, must you always talk in the past tense, as if everything were over and done with already?"

"Or as if it never began."

She narrowed her eyes. There was a lipstick stain on the end of her cigarette.

17

"What would you do if I walked over to you now and told you to kiss me?" He turned his head slowly and stared at her. "Well?" she said, with an angry quiver.

He looked out onto the street again.

"The last time I was in St. John of the Cross, *drying out,*" he said, "there was a fellow there, not young, about my age, whose wife used to come and visit him every day — every day, without fail. She wasn't young either, a bit dowdy, a bit scattered, you know the type. They were just an ordinary couple. But every time she came into the cafeteria, which was where we all went to greet our visitors, the first thing she'd do, every time, was grab his face between both of her hands and kiss him, full on the mouth, passionately, as if they were a pair of young lovers and hadn't seen or touched each other for weeks."

He crossed to where she was sitting and ground the butt of his cigarette into the ashtray on the arm of the chair beside her.

"That's a nice story," she said, looking up at him, sounding not angry now but wistful instead.

"The strangest thing was the effect it had on the rest of us."

"What was it?"

"We were embarrassed, a little, and

18

amused, scornful, you know, all those things. But what we mostly felt was sadness. Just that, just sadness. It wouldn't have been the case if in fact they had been young, and good-looking — then we'd have been jealous, I suppose. But no, we were sad." He stood by the fireplace with his hands in his pockets, his eyes on the rug. "What it was that we saw in them, I think, this couple in their forties, standing there kissing, was a reminder of all we'd lost, or never had — all of life's possibilities that were passing us by, that we'd let go past, without even putting out a hand to stop them, to hold on to them. Don't misunderstand me, it wasn't a strong feeling, this sadness. It was like a — like a wisp of mist blowing against us on a hot day, making us shiver for a second and leaving us colder than we were before." He fell silent for a moment. "Sorry, am I being melodramatic? I hear myself talking sometimes and think it must be someone else saying these things. Maybe my brain *is* turning to porridge."

He frowned at himself, dissatisfied and cross. Rose stood up from the chair and went to him and lifted a hand and laid it against his cheek. He didn't raise his eyes.

"Oh, Quirke," she said softly, shaking her head, "what are we going to do with you,

you poor man?"

There was a tap at the door. Rose left her hand where it was, caressing him, and said, "Come in."

It was Maisie the maid, a rawboned, pink-faced girl with red hair. She stared at them for a second, the two of them standing close together there in front of the big marble fireplace, then quickly composed her face into an expressionless mask. "There's a person here to see Dr. Quirke, ma'am," she said.

Rose at last let her hand fall from Quirke's cheek. "Who is it, Maisie?"

Maisie blushed and bit her lip. "Oh, I'm sorry, ma'am, I forgot to ask."

"Maisie, Maisie, Maisie," Rose said wearily, and closed her eyes and sighed. "I've told you, I've told you many times, you must always ask, otherwise we won't know who it is, and that could be awkward."

"I'm sorry, ma'am."

Rose turned to Quirke. "Shall I go down?"

"No, no," Quirke said, "I'll go."

David Sinclair was standing in the hall. He wore crumpled linen trousers and a sleeveless cricket jersey over a somewhat grubby white shirt. His hair was very black, smoothly waved, and a strand of it had fallen down above his left eye. He was Phoebe's boyfriend. Phoebe was Quirke's daughter. Quirke didn't know what being her boyfriend entailed and didn't care to speculate, any more than he had cared to speculate on the bedroom doings of Mal and Rose. He wished Sinclair wasn't in line for his job. It made the already complicated relationship between them more complicated still.

"I'm sorry, turning up like this," Sinclair said, not looking sorry at all. "I couldn't find the phone number of the house, and the operator wouldn't give it to me."

"That's all right," Quirke said. "What's the matter?"

Sinclair glanced about, taking in the antique hall table, the big gilt mirror above it, the elephant's foot bristling with an assortment of walking sticks, the framed Jack Yeats on the wall, the discreet little Mainie Jellett abstract in an alcove. Quirke had no idea what Sinclair's social background was, except that he was a Jew, and that he had people in Cork. The cricket jersey was an Ascendancy touch and seemed an anachronism. Did Jews play cricket? Maybe he wore it as a sort of ironical joke.

"I wanted to ask your advice," Sinclair said. He was holding a battered straw hat in

21

front of himself and twirling the brim between his fingers. "A young fellow was brought in early this morning. Wrapped his car around a tree in the Phoenix Park, car went on fire. Suicide, the Guards think. The corpse is in pretty bad shape."

"You've done the postmortem?" Quirke asked.

Sinclair nodded. "But there's a contusion, on the skull, just here." He tapped a finger to the side of his own head, above his left ear.

"Yes? And?"

"There are wounds, too, deep ones, on his forehead, where he must have hit the steering wheel when the car went into the tree. They're probably what would have killed him, or knocked him senseless, anyway. But the bruise on the side of his head — I don't know."

"What don't you know?"

Quirke was gratified to find how easily and quickly it had come back to him: the tone of authority, the brusqueness, the faint hint of lordly impatience. If you were going to be in charge, you had to learn to be an actor.

"I don't see how he could have come by it in the crash," Sinclair said. "Maybe I'm wrong."

Quirke was looking at their reflection, or what he could see of it, in the leaning mirror, his own shoulder and one ear, and the sleek back of Sinclair's head. It was strange, but every time he looked into a mirror he seemed to hear a sort of musical chime, a glassy ringing, far off and faint. He wondered why that should be. He blinked. What had they been talking about, what had he been saying? Then he remembered.

"So," he said, putting on a renewed show of briskness, "there's a contusion on the skull and you think it suspicious. You think it was there before the car crashed — that someone did it to him, that someone banged him on the head and knocked him out?"

Sinclair frowned, pursing his lips. "I don't know. It's just — there's something about it. I have a feeling. It's probably nothing. And yet —"

If you think it's nothing, Quirke thought irritably, you wouldn't have come all the way out here to talk to me about it. "So what do you want me to do?" he asked.

Sinclair frowned at his shoes. "I thought you might come in, take a look, tell me what you think."

There was a silence. Quirke felt a twinge of panic, as if a flame had touched him. The thought of going back into the hospital, after all this time away from it, made his mouth go dry. Yet how could he say no? He gave his assistant a narrow stare; did the young man really want his opinion, or was he checking if perhaps Quirke was never going to come back to work and the way was clear for him to lay claim to his boss's job?

"All right," Quirke said. "Have you the car?"

Sinclair nodded; it was not, Quirke decided, the answer he had wanted to hear.

Rose Griffin appeared on the landing above them, leaning over the banister rail. "Is everything all right?" she called down.

"Yes," Quirke replied gruffly. "I'm just going out, back in a while."

Rose was still staring as they walked off along the hall and pulled the front door shut behind them. Quirke had hardly ventured out of the house in the two months he had been staying here. Rose, who had never been a mother, felt as if she had just seen her only son set off on the first stage of a long and perilous journey.

2

Sinclair's car was a prematurely aged Morris Minor. It had suffered a lot of rough treatment, for he was a terrible driver, sitting bolt upright and as far back as the seat would allow, his elbows stiff, seeming to hold the car at arm's length, stamping haphazardly on the pedals and poking around with the gear stick as if he were trying to clear a blocked drain. Along the south city's leafy streets the car flickered between pools of shadow, and each time it emerged the sunlight glared on the bonnet and crazed the glass of the windscreen.

The quays when they got to them stank of the river; farther up, there was the heavy, cloying fragrance of malt roasting in Guinness's brewery. They hadn't exchanged a word since leaving Ailesbury Road; they never did have much to say to each other. Quirke had a genuine if wary regard for Sinclair's professionalism, but he didn't quite trust him, not as a doctor but as a man, and he suspected the feeling was mutual. They rarely spoke of Phoebe — even her name they hardly mentioned, these days.

When Quirke entered the hospital, his palms were damp and his heart was thumping. It was like the feeling he used to have at the end of summer when the new school term loomed. Then he caught the familiar smells, of medicines, bandages, disinfectant, and other, nameless things. A new girl at Reception took no notice of him but smiled at Sinclair. Their footsteps rang on the marble stairs, going down, and now here were the known corridors, the walls that were painted the color of snot and the toffee-brown rubber floor tiles that squealed underfoot. His office reeked of stale cigarette smoke and, he was glad to note, of him, too, even after all this time. He touched the back of the swivel chair behind his desk but felt too shy to sit down in it yet. He tossed his hat at the hat stand but missed, and his hat fell down at the side of a filing cabinet. Sinclair retrieved it for him.

A big window gave onto the dissecting room and a shrouded form on the slab.

"All right," Quirke said, taking off his wrinkled linen jacket, "let's have a look."

He needed no more than a few seconds, turning the corpse's drum-tight skull to the light, to see that Sinclair's suspicions had been well-founded. The dent above the left ear was the result of a deliberate and savage blow. He didn't know how he knew, and certainly there was nothing scientific about the conclusion; like Sinclair, he just had a feeling, and he trusted it.

"Did you say the car crashed before it went on fire?" he asked.

"Ran into a tree."

"Going at what speed, I wonder."

"The Guard didn't say. You think he could have been knocked on the head and put to sit behind the wheel with the car in gear and then let go?"

Quirke didn't answer. He stood gazing down at the charred and twisted body, then turned away. Sinclair put the nylon sheet back into place. Even down here they could sense the sunlight outside, heavy as honey. The bulbs in the ceiling hummed. In the distance there was the sound of an ambulance bell, getting nearer.

"Come on," Quirke said, "you can buy me a cup of tea."

On the way out they met Bolger, the porter, in his washed-out green lab coat, a cigarette with half an inch of ash on it dangling from his lower lip. He greeted Quirke without warmth; there was no love lost between the two men. Bolger's ill-fitting dentures whistled when he spoke; in the winter he had a permanent sniffle, and in the mornings especially a diamond drop of moisture would sparkle at the end of his nose.

"Grand bit of summer weather," he said in his smoker's croak, deliberately looking past Quirke's left shoulder. Bolger stole bandages and spools of sticking plaster and sold them to a barrow boy in Moore Street. He thought no one knew of this petty thieving, but Quirke did, though he could never summon up the energy to report it to the matron. Anyway, Bolger probably had a gaggle of kids to feed, and what were a few boxes of dressings now and then?

In the fourth-floor canteen, a haze of delicate blue cigarette smoke undulated in the sunlight pouring in at three big windows in the back wall. A plume of steam from the tea urn wavered too, and there was a smell of cabbage and boiled bacon. A few of the tables were occupied, the patients in dressing gowns and slippers, some sporting a bandage or a scar, their visitors either bored and cross or worried and teary.

Quirke sat at a corner table, out of the

sun. Sinclair brought two thick gray mugs of peat-brown tea. "You take yours black, right?" he said. He was opening a packet of Marietta biscuits. Quirke took a guarded sip of the tea; it was not only the color of peat, it tasted like it, too. He took a biscuit, and as the dry, fawn paste crumbled in his mouth he was immediately, for a second, a child again, astray in his blank and fathomless past.

"So what do you think?" Sinclair asked. "Are we imagining things?"

Quirke looked out the window at the rooftops and the bristling chimney pots, all sweltering in the sun.

"Maybe we are," he said. "No mention of a weapon being found, I suppose?"

"Your well-known blunt instrument?" Sinclair said, and snickered. "I told you, the Guard who came in was sure it was a suicide. Not that he'll say so in his report. Amazing the number of people who drive into trees or stone walls by accident in the middle of the night, or fall into the Liffey with their pockets full of stones." He lit a cigarette. "How are you feeling, by the way?"

"How am I feeling?" Quirke, annoyed that Sinclair should ask, was playing for time. He took out his cigarette case and lit one

29

for himself. "I'm all right," he said. "I still get headaches and the odd blank second or two. No hallucinations, though. That all seems to be past."

"That's good then, yes?"

Sinclair was not the demonstrative type, and his tone was one of polite inquiry and nothing more.

"Yes, it's good, I suppose," Quirke said, feeling slightly defensive. "It's the fuzziness that gets me down, the sense of groping through a fog. That, and the uncertainty — I mean, the uncertainty that I'll ever be any better than I am now. And how do I even know if how I am isn't just how everyone else is, the only difference being they don't complain? You ever see things, or wake up out of a trance and realize you have no memory of what happened in the past half hour?"

"No," Sinclair said, dabbing the tip of his cigarette on the rim of the tin ashtray on the table between them. "Maybe that just means I'm not very imaginative. Also I don't drink the way you do —"

He broke off abruptly, his forehead coloring.

"Don't worry," Quirke said. "You're probably right — probably there's nothing at all the matter with me except that I've been a soak for so many years that half the brain cells are dead."

"I'm sorry," Sinclair said awkwardly, looking down. "I didn't mean —"

Quirke sat forward and ground his half-smoked cigarette into the ashtray, clearing his throat.

"About this poor bugger in the car," he said. "Let's face it, we're both convinced he was hit on the head and shoved in the car and the car was then run into a tree to make it look like an accident, or suicide."

"Did you notice the strong smell of petrol?"

"Yes, but what of it? Petrol explodes — car fires always smell of it."

"That strongly? It was as if he'd been doused in petrol himself."

Quirke thought for a moment, tugging at his lower lip. "Someone definitely wanted him dead, then."

Sinclair tasted the tea, grimaced, pushed the mug aside. Quirke offered his cigarette case and Sinclair brought out his lighter. Simultaneously they both expelled a cone-shaped stream of smoke towards the ceiling.

In a far corner of the room a middle-aged woman with a bandaged leg began quietly to cry, though not so quietly that she could

31

not be heard. Everyone carefully ignored her. The young man with her, who must have been her son, glanced about quickly, looking anxious and embarrassed.

"So, what do we do?" Sinclair asked.

Quirke smiled. "There's an old friend I think I'll drop in on," he said.

Inspector Hackett was at his lunch at a sunny table in the front dining room of the Gresham Hotel. It was a treat he occasionally indulged in. He had often promised himself that this was how he was going to live when he retired: lunch at the Gresham, a stroll down O'Connell Street to the river and then right, onto the quays, to browse through the book barrows, or left towards the docks to spend a half hour watching the boats unloading. If the weather was inclement, he would drop into the Savoy Cinema and doze in front of a war picture or a Western. He had never much cared for the pictures, finding the stories unbelievable and the characters unreal, but he liked to sit in the velvety darkness, in a nice comfortable seat, and let himself drift off. He always sat near the back, where the sound of the projector was a soothing whirr and the courting couples were too engrossed in each other to distract him with their chatter.

Then when the picture was over he could walk over to the Prince's Bar in Prince's Street, or the Palace farther on, and drink a quiet pint before boarding the bus for home and his tea.

Idle dreams, idle dreams. Retirement was a long way off yet — and a good thing, too. There's life, he told himself, in the old dog yet.

To eat he had a bowl of oxtail soup that turned out to be a bit too thick and heavy, a plate of cold ham with cold potato salad — made with genuine Chef Salad Cream; he had checked with the waitress to make sure — and, to follow, a bowl of fruit cocktail with custard. He liked especially the coldness of the tinned fruit against the warm, silky texture of the custard. With the food he drank a glass of Jersey milk, for the sake of his lungs — TB was still on the increase — and, at the end, with his cigarette, a cup of strong brown tea with milk and four lumps of sugar — four lumps which, had his wife been there, would have been strictly forbidden.

In fact, he was spooning up the hot sweet sludge the not-quite-melted sugar had left in the bottom of the cup when he heard his name spoken and looked up guiltily — but it wasn't May, of course it wasn't — and saw a familiar figure making his way towards him across the room.

" 'The dead arose and appeared to many'!" he exclaimed, with a broad smile. "Dr. Quirke — is it yourself, or am I seeing things?"

"Hello, Inspector," Quirke said, stopping in front of him and smiling too, though not so broadly.

"Do you know what it is," Hackett said. "When I saw you I nearly swallowed the teaspoon, I was that surprised. 'Tis fresh and well you're looking."

Quirke was pleased to see his old companion-in-arms, more pleased than he had expected he would be. He was amused, too: he had noticed before how Hackett, when he was startled or unsure, fell at once into his stage-Irish act, lisping and winking, bejapers-ing and begorrah-ing, all his usual stealth and watchfulness shrunk to a gleam in the depths of his colorless little eyes.

"May I sit?" Quirke inquired. It was always the way: when Hackett started Syngeing, Quirke's response was to turn into Oscar Wilde. Well, they were a pair, no doubt of that, though what they were a pair of, he wasn't sure.

He sat down.

"What will you have?" Hackett asked. "A

glass of wine, maybe, or a ball of malt — or is it too early in the day for the juice of the barley?"

"I'm afraid it's always too early, these days," Quirke said, putting his hat on the floor under his chair.

Hackett threw himself back with an exaggerated stare of amazement. "What? You're not telling me you're after taking the pledge?"

"No, of course not. I have a glass of dry sherry at Christmastime, and on my birthday a snipe of barley wine."

The Inspector laughed, his paunch heaving, and flapped a dismissive hand. "Get away with you," he said, "and stop pulling my leg. Miss!" He waved to a passing waitress, who veered towards them. "This man," he said to her, "will take a glass of the finest white wine you have in the shop — am I right, Dr. Quirke? A nice Chablis, now, if I remember, would be your lunchtime preference."

Quirke smiled at the waitress. She was tall and fair with pale pink eyelids and pale blue eyes. "Tomato juice," he said. "With Worcester sauce and —"

"Is it a Virgin Mary you're after?" she said tartly.

"The very thing." A Virgin Mary, no less!

He wouldn't have thought such a drink was known on this side of the Atlantic. What next? Gin slings? Whiskey sours? Highballs? Maybe the country was changing, after all.

Hackett was still regarding him with his broadest frog grin, the arc of his mouth stretching almost from ear to ear. He seemed to have, of all things, a suntan — below the line of his hat brim, anyway, above which his high, flat forehead was its accustomed shade of soft and faintly glistening baby pink.

"Have you been away?" Quirke asked.

Hackett stared. "How did you know?"

"The bronzed and fit look."

"Ah. Well. Now. I was off," he said, his pale forehead flushing and even his tan darkening a little, "in a place called Málaga, down in the south of Spain. Have you been there?" Quirke shook his head, and Hackett, glancing to right and left, leaned forward conspiratorially. "To tell you the truth, Doctor," he murmured, "it's a terrible place. People rooking you right and left, and all the women half naked on the beach and even in the streets. I couldn't wait to get home. Mrs. Hackett" — he gave a discreet little cough — "Mrs. Hackett thought it was grand." He poured cold tea into his cup and

36

took a slurp of it. "And what about your-self?"

"Oh, I was away too," he said. "Not in the sunny south of Spain, however."

Hackett frowned. "You weren't off again in — in that drying-out place, I hope?"

"John of the Cross?" The Hospital of St. John of the Cross was where Quirke had sequestered himself on more than one occasion to give his liver a chance to recover from the alcoholic insults he had been subjecting it to for more years than he cared to count. "No, not there. I was in a cottage hospital, out beyond the Strawberry Beds. Small, quiet, nice. Very restful."

The Inspector was still regarding him with concern. "Nerves, was it?"

"Sort of. It seems my brain took a bit of a bashing that time those two knocked me down the area steps and kicked the stuffing out of me."

"But sure that was years ago!"

"That's the past for you: it comes back to haunt."

The waitress brought Quirke's drink, and Hackett asked her if he could have a jug of boiling water to revive the tea leaves in the pot. She offered to bring a fresh pot, but he wouldn't hear of it. " 'A pot of tay will take two goes' — that's what my old mother always said."

Quirke smiled, covering his mouth; Hackett by now was well on his way down the Old Bog Road. The eyes, though, were sharp as ever.

"By the way," Hackett said, when the waitress had gone, "how did you know where to find me? Or was it just a happy coincidence?"

"I went round to Pearse Street. Your man, Sergeant Jenkins, whispered to me that you might be here. He made me swear not to tell you it was him gave you away, so not a word, right? I must say, you do yourself well. Lunch at the Gresham, no less!"

"Ah, now you're teasing me, Dr. Quirke, I know you are."

The hot water came and he slopped it into the pot. Quirke was always fascinated by Hackett's clumsiness, which, mysteriously, tended to come and go, depending on the circumstances. Did he put it on, as a diversionary tactic, or was it a sign of mental agitation? No doubt he was itching to know just what it was that had brought Quirke here to seek him out. Right now he was watching Quirke over the rim of his refilled cup, those little eyes glinting.

"I came to consult you about something," Quirke said. "There was a crash in the

Phoenix Park early this morning. You heard about it?"

"I did. Some poor young fellow, ran into a tree and got burnt to a crisp. Suicide, by the look of it, my fellows are saying."

He put down his cup. No clumsiness now.

"Well, my second-in-command," Quirke said, "and probably soon to be commander in chief, young Sinclair, came to see me earlier."

"Did he go all the way out to the Strawberry Beds?"

"No, no, I wasn't in hospital. I'm staying for the moment with my — with Malachy Griffin and his wife, at their place on Ailesbury Road. They very kindly offered to take me in and look after me while I convalesced from whatever it is I'm supposed to be convalescing from."

"Ah, right. And how is Dr. Griffin? Is he enjoying his retirement?"

"I don't think so."

"Do you tell me? That's a pity, now, a real pity."

"He has taken up gardening," Quirke said.

"Gardening, is it! That's a fine pastime. Will you give him my best regards? He's a decent man, the same Dr. Griffin."

They eyed each other in silence for a moment. Mal Griffin had not always been the decent man he had since become, and for a long time had covered up things that should not have been covered up. Old water, Quirke thought, under old bridges.

"Anyway," he said, taking a sip of his glutinous, brownish-red drink, "what Sinclair had come to talk to me about was this poor chap who hit the tree up in the park."

"Is that so?" Hackett said mildly, looking into his cup. Cautious, now, Quirke thought, cautious yet keen, an old dog sniffing blood on the air.

"There's a contusion on the side of the skull, just here." He pointed to a spot behind his temple and just above his ear. "Sinclair thought it seemed suspicious, and called me in to have a look at it."

"And did you?"

"I did. And I agreed with him."

Hackett leaned back slowly in his chair, with his lips pursed and his chin lowered. "Suspicious in what way? In a way that made it seem the poor fellow didn't come by it due to his unfortunate meeting with that mighty oak?"

"Exactly."

Now Quirke leaned back too, and they reclined thus, watching each other. A strong shaft of sunlight through the window beside them had reached a corner of their table and was striking down through the polish and into the wood itself. Like a trout pond, Quirke idly thought, heather brown and agleam, the grain in the wood like underwater weeds drawn out in streels by the slowly moving current. A fish flashing, white on the flank, a fin twirling. Stones, small stones, washed small over the years, the years. Connemara, a sun-struck noon. Lying on the bank, trying to tickle a trout, the fish torpid in the midday heat, its tail fin barely stirring. Then a call, a far shout. *Run, Quirke — Jesus, run!* And then Clifford, Brother Clifford, dean of discipline, so called, pounding towards him in his big boots, over the heather, his soutane flying.

What?

"I'm sorry," he said, blinking. "My mind — my mind was wandering. What were you saying?"

"I was asking," Hackett said, speaking slowly, as if to a child, "if we know the identity of the unfortunate young man, the one with the bump on his head."

"I thought maybe you might know. Someone said your people were tracing the registration number of the car."

Hackett sat forward and wiped his mouth with a linen napkin. "Well, if you'd care to accompany me back to the station, we can

41

make inquiries and see what the tirelessly laboring hordes have been able to turn up."

He signaled to the tall pale waitress and asked her to bring the bill. While they waited for her to return with it, they looked about vacantly. At a nearby table a woman in a hat with a half veil of black lace smiled at Quirke, and he marveled, as so often, at how women could smile like that, with such seeming openness and ease. Was it a trick they had learned? Surely not. It seemed spontaneous, and always touched something in him, a deeply buried seam of wistful longing.

Hackett paid, and gave the waitress a shilling for herself. Quirke groped under the chair for his hat. He hadn't finished his tomato juice; it was the color that had put him off.

Outside in the street the air was blued with the smoke of summer, and there was a smell of fresh horse dung and petrol fumes. They walked side by side along O'Connell Street, breasting their way through the throngs of shoppers. All the women seemed to be wearing sandals and sleeveless summer dresses, and trailed behind them heady wafts of mingled perfume and sweat. Quirke, housebound for so long, felt dizzy in the midst of all this sun-dazed bustle.

What was it that had made him suddenly think of Brother Clifford, after all these years?

Clifford, a cheerful sadist, had ruled with merciless efficiency over Carricklea Industrial School, where Quirke had endured some of the most terrible years of his childhood. It was Clifford who had come after him and two other boys that day they went mitching out on the bog, the day he had almost caught the trout, lying on his belly on the bank beside the little brown river, the sun hot on the back of his neck and the prickly heather tickling his knees. Who were the two that were with him? Danny somebody, a mischievous runt with carroty hair and freckles, and fat Archie Summers, who had asthma and was blind in one eye. Clifford and three or four prefects had rounded them up and marched them back to the gray stone fortress of Carricklea, where Clifford beat them with a cane until their backsides bled. Many years later Quirke had spotted a paragraph in the *News of the World,* giving an account of a court case in which an Irish Christian Brother by the name of Walter Clifford had been found guilty of stealing ladies' underwear from a department store in Birmingham and was fined ten pounds and given a severe caution. Sometimes there was justice, after all, Quirke reflected, or a modicum of it, anyway.

In the Garda station it was stuffy and hot, and the air smelled, as it always did, mysteriously, of parched paper. Quirke sat on a bench and waited while Hackett went off to talk to Sergeant Jenkins. A drunk wandered in from the street and began to tell the desk sergeant an intricate and confused story of an attack on him in the street by an unknown assailant, who had knocked him down and kicked him and stolen his mouth organ. The sergeant, a large, mild man, listened patiently, trying and failing to get a word in.

Quirke read the notices pinned to the bulletin board. They were the same as always: dog license reminders, an alert against rabies, something about noxious weeds. There was to be a dress dance for members of the Force on the twenty-seventh, tickets still available. Forged banknotes were in circulation, in denominations of ones, fives, and twenties. A men's retreat was to be held at St. Andrew's Church, Westland Row, to which all were welcome.

And my brain is damaged, he thought.

Inspector Hackett returned, picking his side teeth with a matchstick. He sat down on the bench next to Quirke and leaned his head back against the wall and sighed.

"Well?" Quirke said.

The Inspector closed his eyes briefly.

"The car was registered to a chap by the name of Corless," he said, "Leon Corless, aged twenty-seven, a civil servant in the Department of Health. Resident at an address in Castleknock village."

"Corless," Quirke said. "Why do I know that name?"

"Leon Corless is, was, the son of Sam Corless, leader and, it would seem, sole member of the Socialist Left Alliance Party, known to the gentlemen jokers of the press as SLAP. Mr. Corless senior, as no doubt you know, was recently released from Mountjoy Jail, having served a three-month sentence for non-payment of taxes. The latest of many brushes with the law. Mr. Corless makes a point of being awkward."

The drunk, having run out of complaints, was being escorted to the door with the desk sergeant's large square hand firmly on his shoulder. In the street outside, a bus backfired, and from the direction of Mooney's pub came the sound of trundling and thudding beer barrels being unloaded from the back of a dray.

"I didn't know Sam Corless had a son," Quirke said.

"Well, he hasn't, anymore, since someone, according to you and your assistant, is after bludgeoning the poor fellow to death and leaving him to roast in his burning car."

3

Phoebe Griffin loved her office. It wasn't *her* office, strictly speaking, but that was how she thought of it. Directly in front of her desk, two tall sash windows looked out over the tops of the trees to the houses on the other side of Fitzwilliam Square. Throughout the day the light on the distant brickwork changed by subtle, slow gradations. In the morning, when shadows still lingered, it was a sort of soiled purple, but by noon, when the sun was fully up, it would become a steady, dazzling white blaze. Late afternoons were best of all, though, when the bricks seemed smeared with a glaze of shimmering, molten gold, and all the windows were yellowly aflame.

She had left her job at the Maison des Chapeaux, with only the smallest twinge of regret, and was working now as secretary and receptionist for Dr. Evelyn Blake, consultant psychiatrist. Quirke had known

Dr. Blake's husband slightly, and had put in a word for her when she was applying for the job. This was a fact she didn't care to linger on, for she was an independent-minded young woman and liked to think that she was making her own way in the world. There was a compensation, however, in that Dr. Blake also was a woman, and therefore unique in her profession, in this country at least. It pleased Phoebe to imagine that she and her employer were joined in an unspoken conspiracy against the male-dominated world in which they were forced to live and work.

Before taking up the job, Phoebe had worried that she would have to spend her days dealing with crazy people. On the contrary, however, Dr. Blake's patients all seemed, so far — Phoebe had only been in the job a matter of weeks — not mad at all, and were nearly always polite and respectful. It was true that some of them gave off an unsettling air of barely suppressed excitement and tension; pop-eyed and tremulous, they seemed constantly on the point of jumping up and breaking into shouts and gesticulations, though they never did. Others were timid, watchful, worried.

A large proportion of the patients, she had noticed, were nail biters. It could be disturbing, listening to them as they sat there gnawing away like squirrels, as if they were trying to get at the sweet, crisp core of themselves. Sometimes they spat fragments of nail on the carpet, though discreetly, watching her out of the corner of an eye. One of them, a youngish man with enormous ears and so thin it seemed he must be starving himself to death, not only bit his nails but also, on occasion, sucked his thumb. She tried not to look at him, sitting there sucking away, like a big, emaciated baby.

There was never more than one patient waiting; that was Dr. Blake's rule. Her consulting room had two doors, the one behind Phoebe's desk and another one, on the far side of the room, where the patient could exit unseen when the session was at an end. No sounds ever came out of that room. The door had been specially installed, and was extra thick, and Phoebe found uncanny the fraught, unbroken silence always at her back.

She was happy enough in the job, though at times she was bored. In the shop the customers were normal — most of them, anyway — and used to chat to her, talking about the weather and stories in the news, and gossiping about well-known people

49

misbehaving themselves. Here, at Dr. Blake's, there was a feeling sometimes of being in church; she might have been an assistant outside the confessional, monitoring the penitents as they silently waited their turn to slink into the shadowed chamber and tell their shameful sins.

David Sinclair teased her about her job. "How were the head cases today?" he would ask, crossing his eyes and letting his tongue hang out. She was displeased. Usually he was sensitive and didn't mock people. Maybe, being a doctor himself, he felt threatened by psychiatry, this strange, almost mystical practice that the church kept trying to ban and forbade its members from having anything to do with. Freud was a Jew, however, and so was David, which surely should have made him have sympathy with, or at least understand, the thinking that psychiatry was based on. But maybe that was a foolish assumption.

Today was slow, so far. The thumb sucker had been in first thing, with his aggrieved and accusing stare. Then there had been a harassed woman with her feral ten-year-old son, then a shady man in his sixties who, although he was dressed in slacks and a sports shirt, had the definite air of a priest — why did priests, when they tried to disguise themselves in ordinary clothes, always give the game away by wearing white socks? It was as if, through old habit, they had to have some sign of sanctity about their persons. Now it was nearly lunchtime, and the next patient who was due, Mr. Jolly — that really was his name — hadn't appeared yet, although he was down in the appointments book for twelve-thirty. Mr. Jolly liked to chat and had told Phoebe all about his problem, which was that he couldn't resist beating his wife, even though he claimed to love her dearly. There had been occasions when Phoebe felt Mr. Jolly wouldn't need to bother going in to see Dr. Blake, since he had already poured out all his most intimate troubles to her, here in the waiting room.

In the end Mr. Jolly didn't turn up, and at one o'clock Dr. Blake came out and told Phoebe that since there were no more patients due today, she could take the afternoon off. It was not unusual for Dr. Blake to let her go like this, which was another nice thing about the job. The doctor was in her early middle age, a large, handsome woman with untidy hair, prematurely flecked with gray, which Phoebe was convinced she cut herself, as no hairdresser would have let her leave the salon looking like that, like a ragged and tipsy page boy. Her husband, a surgeon, had died not long ago in a car crash on the Naas Road. She was taciturn but not unfriendly, and she rarely smiled, though when she did she was transformed. She had a broad, soft face and strikingly large, almost black eyes. Her manner was slow, and she had an air of faint melancholy that Phoebe guessed was congenital and not due to her recent bereavement. She wore tweed skirts and floppy silk blouses and sensible flat shoes. She was what Phoebe imagined she herself would be, one day, except, she hoped, for the hairstyle.

Phoebe put the plastic cover over her typewriter, wondering if Mrs. Jolly was getting an extra beating today, and if that was what had delayed her husband. In fact, she suspected there was no Mrs. Jolly, except in Mr. Jolly's fevered imaginings.

The day was hot but there was a cool breeze coming down from the mountains, the pale outlines of which she could see far off past the end of the street. She walked along by the green railings of the square, savoring the smell of cut grass — the petrol mower had already been going when she arrived at the office that morning. At the bottom of the street she turned left and walked along Merrion Row to St. Stephen's Green.

She hadn't been to the Country Shop since Jimmy Minor's death; it was the place where she and Jimmy used to meet. Now as she went down the steps she recalled fondly how he would come rushing into the café and fling himself down at the table and launch straight off into a scurrilous story about some politician or businessman, heedlessly dropping ash on the table, while his tea got cold and his sandwich began to curl at the corners. Poor, dear Jimmy, beaten to death one dark night and flung into the canal like a dog.

She sat at a table by the window and ordered tea and a ham sandwich, in Jimmy's honor. She took out her packet of Gold Flake and her lighter and put them on the table. She had taken up smoking again, she wasn't sure why, on her last day at the hat shop. She wasn't a real smoker, and hardly inhaled at all. She just liked the image of herself sitting on her own at a café table with a cigarette and a book, looking mysterious, or at least interesting. She had always been solitary, and was so still, despite the fact that she was going out with David Sinclair. He was solitary, too. The result was that they were never really together, only side by side, like two trees growing close by each other in a forest.

The waitress brought her order. She was a plump, friendly girl with a wen on the side of her nose who had been working here for as long as Phoebe could remember. "Oh, and miss," she said, "there's this for you." She handed Phoebe a folded slip of paper. "A person asked me to give it to you."

It was a half sheet torn from a copybook, like the copybooks they used to use for shorthand practice at the agency when she was doing her course there. The message on it was scribbled in pencil and was, indeed, in shorthand, as she saw with a small shock of recognition.

Could we meet? I'll wait in the Green, on the bench at the pond. I need to talk to you. You will know me from the agency. Please come. Lisa.

Phoebe read it three times, then beckoned to the waitress. "Who was it that gave you this?" she asked.

"A girl, miss," the waitress said, a little nervously.

"What sort of girl?"

"Just a girl, miss. A young woman."

"Where was she? Was she here, in the café?"

"No, she was passing by. I think she saw you, through the window, and came down and called me over to the door and gave the paper to me and pointed you out and asked would I give it to you."

"What did she look like?"

The girl frowned, wrinkling her nose. "I don't know, miss. Ordinary."

"What age?"

"The same as you, I'd say."

"Was that all she did, give you the message and ask you to pass it on to me?"

"Yes, and then she went off. She seemed in a great hurry, and agitated, like."

"Thank you."

Phoebe read the message again. Yes, there had been a Lisa in her class at the agency. She couldn't recall her second name, if she ever knew it. A quiet girl, unremarkable, brown hair; that was all she remembered. Why the note, why not come to her table and talk to her? And why had she hurried away? It was all very mysterious. Perhaps someone was having a joke at her expense. She thought of Jimmy again. This was the kind of thing he liked to do, being a practical joker, with a schoolboy's sense of humor. But Jimmy was dead.

She looked around the room. Clerks, shoppers, farmers' wives up from the country. How Jimmy used to turn up his nose when he came in here, Jimmy the newshound, Jimmy the hotshot. All the same, he'd secretly liked the place. He had once said it reminded him of the kitchen at home, down the country, with the tea stewing on the range and his mother making fairy cakes.

She drank a cup of tea and ate half the sandwich. She had lost her appetite; the note from this Lisa person had taken it away. She had an urge to jump up and run over to the Green, to the bench by the pond, and clear up the mystery. Instead she made herself light a cigarette and sat smoking it, trying to see Lisa in her mind, trying to conjure up an image of her.

Ordinary, the waitress had said.

She finished the cigarette, and folded the note and put it into a side pocket in her handbag, paid the bill, and left.

In the street the sunlight blinded her for a second or two. Then she crossed the road, past the jarveys on their jaunting cars, past the heavy, rich smell of their horses, and went in the park by the small gate, plunging into the shade under the trees like a diver, she thought, cleaving smoothly through the surface of a swimming pool, into its dimmer depths. She walked along the cool pathway under the row of lindens. She passed by the little humpbacked bridge.

When she saw the young woman sitting on the bench she remembered her at once. She was pale-complexioned, with dark chestnut hair. She wore no makeup. Her cream-colored linen dress was expensive but not new. She sat very straight, gazing before her as if in a trance, both hands clasped on her handbag on her lap.

"Lisa?"

The young woman started. "Oh!" she said. "It's you. I didn't think you'd come."

Phoebe sat down beside her. "I'm sorry," she said, "I don't remember your second name."

"Smith," the young woman said quickly, and bit her lip. "Lisa Smith. You remember me, from the agency?"

"Yes, of course I remember. I just couldn't recall your name."

The young woman was obviously in a state of terror. She was trembling all over, like a pony that had been galloping in panic for a long time and now had been brought to a stop.

"I couldn't come into the café," she said. "That's why I gave the note to the waitress."

"But — why couldn't you come in?" Phoebe asked.

"I didn't want anyone to see me. There might be someone there that knew me." She put the knuckle of her thumb to her mouth and bit hard on it. "I have to keep moving, I feel if I stay in the open no one will —" She stopped.

"No one will what?"

Lisa looked away, the whites of her eyes flashing. "I don't know," she muttered.

"Well, anyway," Phoebe said, trying to sound brisk and cheerful, "I'm glad to see you again. I don't think we spoke much, when we were on the course, did we?"

"We just said hello, I think," Lisa said. "You were always so busy."

She looked away again, and Phoebe watched her. She really was terrified — but what was it she was terrified of?

"Can I ask," Phoebe said carefully, "can I ask what it is you want to talk to me about?"

Lisa gave her head a rapid shake, not of refusal but in bewilderment. "I don't know. I mean, I don't know how to explain." She opened her handbag and took out a packet of Craven A and a box of matches. She pushed open the packet and offered it to Phoebe. "Would you like one?"

Phoebe shook her head. Lisa's hand was trembling so badly she could hardly hold the flame of the match steady to light the cigarette.

"You seem upset," Phoebe said. "Will you tell me what the matter is?"

"I have to get away," Lisa said in a low, urgent voice. "I have to find somewhere to hide."

"Hide?" Phoebe said, a tingle running down her spine. "Hide from what?"

Lisa gave another quick shake of the head. "I can't tell you." She was even less of a smoker than Phoebe was, and kept taking little pecks at her cigarette and letting the smoke out almost as soon as she had drawn it in. "Something happened," she said. "Something — terrible, and I have to get away." She turned her head suddenly and looked directly at Phoebe. Her lower lip was trembling, and she seemed on the point of tears. Her eyes were a glittering shade of green. "Will you help me? There's no one else I can ask." She looked away then and put a hand to her forehead. "What am I saying? We're practically strangers, we've hardly exchanged a word before in our lives, and here I am, begging you to help me. You must think I'm mad."

Phoebe frowned. What was she supposed to say, what was she supposed to do? It was true, they were strangers, or as good as; certainly she knew nothing about this young woman, who she was or where she came from or why she was in such a desperate state. Yet she felt a tug of sympathy for her, and a sense that she must find a way to help her. Phoebe knew what fear was, knew what it was to be frightened and alone.

"But tell me," Phoebe said, "why you came to me?"

"I didn't! I just looked in the window of the café and saw you there and recognized you. I remembered you from the course. You seemed nice. So I wrote the note and asked the waitress to give it to you." She took another quick, ineffectual drag on her cigarette. "I have no one, no one I can go to. My mother is dead, my father —" She stopped again, and tears welled in her eyes. "There's no one," she whispered, "no one."

Phoebe looked around. On the bench next to them a tramp was asleep, lying full-length on his side with his joined hands cradling his cheek; he looked, Phoebe thought, like the figure of a saint on a tomb. By the pond a small boy was trying to launch a toy sailboat, his nursemaid in her white bonnet standing by, seeming bored and distracted. Ducks quacked, waggling their rear ends. A seagull swooped down, veered, and climbed the air again. The sky was blue, with little white puffs of floating cloud. This was the world, familiar, comforting; terror had no place here, yet here it was, plain in this young woman's face, in her trembling hands, in the wild look of her eyes.

"What do you want to do?" Phoebe asked.

"What?" Lisa stared at her, uncomprehending.

"I mean, do you want to leave the country, is that it?"

"Yes. No. It doesn't matter. No, I don't want to go away. I can't. I just need somewhere to be for a while, somewhere where no one will find me."

"And you can't tell me why."

"No. Not now, anyway." She shook her head yet again. "You probably think I'm some kind of con artist, trying to fool you into helping me so I can rob you. I swear, I'm not."

Phoebe had an urge to put a hand on hers, but didn't.

"I believe you," she said, not knowing what it was exactly she was supposed to believe in.

The young woman caught something in her tone and looked at her more closely. "Have you been in trouble, in your life?"

"Yes," Phoebe said, "I have. A long time ago — at least, it seems a long time."

"What was it? — what happened?"

"It doesn't matter. When you're ready to tell me your story, maybe I'll tell you mine. In the meantime, I think I know a place where you can go."

"A place? Where?"

"At the seaside. Come on, I have to make a phone call."

Lisa, who had relaxed a little, was suddenly tense again. "Come where?"

"Just over to the Shelbourne. There's a public phone there, in the bar — I always use it."

Lisa pressed her lips together tightly. She seemed very young suddenly, like a stubborn child. "I don't want to go in there, into that hotel," she said. "There are people who might see me there, too. That's why I have to get away."

"How do you mean?"

"There are people who will be looking for me. I can't say any more, please don't ask me."

"All right," Phoebe said. "Will you wait here?"

"Will you be long?"

"I'll be as quick as I can. There's a car I need to borrow, which is why I have to make a phone call."

"Then I'll wait," Lisa said. She had thrown away her cigarette and was clutching her handbag again. "I can't tell you how grateful I am. You really must think I'm some crazy person that's latched onto you."

"I don't think you're crazy. But you'll have to tell me, sooner or later, what you're afraid of."

"I will, I will tell you, if I can."

Phoebe stood up. "I want you to promise me that you'll be here when I come back. You have to trust me, as I'm trusting you. If you go, I'll never know what became of you, and that wouldn't be fair. Would it?"

"I promise," Lisa said. "But if I'm not here, I give you my word it won't be because I went off of my own free will."

Phoebe nodded. "I can't think what kind of awful trouble you're in, but I'll do my best to help you."

She turned quickly and walked back the way she had come. As she was about to cross the street, she paused and looked about herself carefully. She didn't know what she was looking for, but she had a crawling sensation across her back that suggested she was being watched. She told herself she was imagining things. But then, things had happened to her in the past, violent, savage things, that she would have thought were beyond imagining.

■ ■ ■ ■

David answered on the third ring. She had called him at the pathology lab. She told him she needed to borrow the Morris Minor. When he asked her what for, she had her answer prepared: "I told Quirke I'd take him to hospital for his checkup." She always referred to her father by his name; she couldn't imagine calling him anything else.

"What hospital?" David asked. He sounded suspicious.

"St. James's. Then I said maybe he and I would go for a spin in the country. Do you mind? Will you need the car?"

"No, I don't need it at the moment. It's in the garage."

"Well then, can I have it?"

He was silent for some seconds. "Since when did you start taking Quirke for spins in the country?"

"He needs to get out. He's been cooped up for weeks in that mausoleum on Ailesbury Road."

Again a silence. "Oh, all right. You'll have to come and get the keys."

"I'll be there shortly."

She hung up, hearing the pennies fall inside the box, then left the hotel and hur-

64

ried back across the street. She hadn't really expected Lisa to be there still, and was surprised to find her sitting as she had left her, stiff with fear, her handbag on her lap.

"I'll have to go to the Holy Family Hospital," Phoebe said. "The car belongs to my — to my boyfriend, and I have to get the key from him."

"Your boyfriend? Is he a doctor?"

Phoebe smiled wryly. "Sort of," she said. "Now I'm going to get us a taxi. You'll come with me."

"I —"

"That wasn't a question. I'm not going to leave you sitting here, frightened out of your life. You'll be better off with me. You can wait outside the hospital, in the taxi, until I've got the car key."

They hurried to the main gate and left the park and crossed to the taxi rank at the top of Grafton Street. There was a single taxi waiting, all its windows rolled fully down. The driver, a fat bald pink man, was asleep, his head resting at an awkward angle on the back of the seat and his mouth open. When Phoebe touched him, he snorted and shook himself, blinking.

The taxi inside smelled of hot leather, cigarette smoke, and of something else, warm and fleshy, that had to be the driver.

65

He talked about the weather, complaining of the heat. "Can't keep my eyes open," he said, "then I'm awake all night, sweating. The wife says she's going to leave me." He chuckled, phlegm rattling in his throat. "You're welcome, says I, off you go."

The two young women in the back seat were not listening. They sat with their heads turned away from each other, watching the scorched streets go past, a hot wind through the open windows shivering their hair and making their eyes sting.

At the hospital Phoebe told the driver to stop and wait outside the front door. She ran inside, and at Reception asked for the key David had left there for her. The young woman at the desk gave her a surly look — David was the most eligible bachelor at the Holy Family, even if he was a Jew — and handed her the key ring.

"Thanks," Phoebe said, and the receptionist, a mousy little thing with a cast in her eye, said sourly, "You're welcome, I'm sure," and turned away.

Lisa was huddled against the upholstery in the back seat of the taxi, her head sunk between her shoulders and her hands gripping each other in her lap.

"All right," Phoebe said, "now we go to your place and pick up some necessities.

How long will you need to be gone for?"

The question only added to Lisa's anxiety. "I don't know," she said. "I hadn't thought."

"Well, you'll just have to pack whatever you think you'll need."

"Need for where?"

"I told you — the seaside. Well, nearly the seaside. There's a cottage, a chalet really, at —" She glanced at the back of the taxi man's head; Lisa's paranoia was catching. "You'll see when we get there," she said. "It'll be fine. Now: where do you live?"

"Rathmines. I have a flat."

"Good. We can pick up the car first."

When he wasn't using it, David kept the Morris Minor in a lock-up garage in a mews lane behind Herbert Place, where she had her flat. Phoebe didn't like to drive, and rarely did, but this was an emergency. When she had paid the taxi fare — Lisa had tried to give her the money for it but she had brushed her aside — she unlocked the galvanized-iron door and with Lisa's help dragged it up and open.

She hoped there was petrol in the tank. David often forgot to fill it, and they had got stranded more than once; he really shouldn't have a car at all.

The engine was cold — yet how could it be, since the day was so hot? — and she had to use the crank handle to get it started. Then it took her a good five minutes to maneuver out of the narrow space and into the lane. Together she and Lisa hauled the heavy door down again, and Phoebe locked it. Having to help with these things seemed to calm Lisa a little, and she even smiled when Phoebe swore after letting the clutch out too quickly, making the little car buck like a startled horse.

Rathmines was quiet, basking in the afternoon's hazy sunlight. Lisa's flat was on the second floor of a tall, shabby, red-brick terrace house. Lisa went into the bedroom to pack, and Phoebe stood in the living room trying not to look about her too closely; she always felt uneasy in places where other people lived and disliked being among their intimate possessions, which always seemed to her somehow vulnerable and sad. Not that Lisa seemed to have many things of her own. The furnishings were the usual cheap stuff that only landlords would dream of buying. A few pictures hung on the walls, bad reproductions in plastic frames, but there were no photographs of relatives or friends. There was no smell, either, except the usual one that rented flats had. Maybe Lisa had just moved in and hadn't yet had time to impress anything of herself on the place. Or maybe her impression was so light that it hadn't registered, and never would.

Now she came out of the bedroom, carrying a small suitcase. It was made of pigskin, Phoebe noticed, and looked expensive. Who was this young woman, so mysterious, so desperate?

"I've just taken clothes, and a toilet bag," Lisa said uncertainly. "What about sheets and things?"

"Don't worry, clothes are all you'll need. We'll stop on the way and get some supplies."

"Supplies?" Lisa said, in almost a squeak. In her agitated state she seemed to be having trouble comprehending the simplest concepts.

"Food," Phoebe said. "Milk, bread, that kind of thing." She smiled. "You'll have to eat, after all."

Lisa, blushing, attempted to smile in return.

They went down to the car, and Lisa put the suitcase on the back seat. The upholstery was hot already from the sun. This time the engine started without having to be cranked.

"Well then," Phoebe said, in a determinedly lighthearted tone, "here we go!"

She was hungry, and wished she had finished that ham sandwich.

4

Sam Corless lived in a two-room flat above a tobacconist's shop on Dorset Street. After his wife's death from cancer three years previously, he had given up the Council house in Finglas where the couple had lived all their married life. He could no longer bear the place and its lingering memories of his time with Helen and their boy, Leon.

Sam had insisted, against Helen's protests, on naming his son after his hero, Leon Trotsky. Sam was a committed, lifelong believer in permanent revolution. As a Trotskyite, he was opposed to the USSR and its late and, by him at least, unlamented dictator, Joseph Stalin. For Sam Corless, a stage in the long march of world communism had come to an abrupt halt when, on August 20, 1940, at a house in Mexico City, Stalin's agent Ramón Mercader had sunk a mountaineer's ice axe into the back of Trotsky's head, mortally wounding the great man. But Sam did not despair. His hero might be dead, but the revolution would go on.

He had heard the news report on the wireless of the burnt-out car and its unknown driver that had been found in the Phoenix Park that morning but had paid it scant heed. The only deaths that counted were political ones. If some young fellow had spent the night on the town and then driven into a tree in a drunken stupor, that was not so much bad luck as gross irresponsibility. The young had a duty to live, to be politically active, to bring about change. Otherwise they were just cogs in the capitalist machine, and a burden on the state. Sam was not a hard-hearted man, but he was hard-headed. In the struggle for freedom and the triumph of the proletariat, there was no room for sentimentality.

Sam earned his living as a bus driver, and today was his day off. He wasn't concerned when in the middle of the afternoon the detective knocked on his door. That kind of knock had been a permanent marker in his life, a repeated reminder that he was being watched, being monitored, that the state had its unblinking eye ever fixed on him. It gave him a secret feeling of pride, of which he was ashamed, or felt he should be, at any rate.

He knew straightaway that the fellow on the doorstep was police, just by the look of him: the shiny blue suit and the cracked black shoes, the dreamy, thin-lipped half-smile, the sharp little piggy eyes. He looked vaguely familiar, but Sam couldn't think where he had seen him before.

What did surprise him was the other one, standing behind the detective. He wasn't police; he was altogether too well-groomed, in his silk shirt and blue silk tie, his linen jacket and handmade brogues. He could have been a banker, or even a judge, on his day off.

"Mr. Corless?" the sharp-eyed one said. "Hackett's the name. Detective Inspector Hackett. And this is Dr. Quirke."

Sam stood with his hand on the door frame and stared at them stonily. Long experience had taught him that when dealing with the forces of the law it was wisest to say as little as possible. He was trying to calculate what this visit might be about. A detective was one thing — in fact, he was certain by now that he had encountered this one before somewhere — but why a doctor? And what kind of a doctor was he? Medical, or some other kind? He had a hospital air about him, but there was something else, too, something of the dark.

"Could we step inside for a minute, do you think?" Hackett said. "We need to have a word."

The landing where they stood smelled of bad air and fried food, and of the communal lavatory down on the ground floor.

"What exactly is it you want a word about?" Sam asked.

"It's a delicate matter," the detective answered gently. He was holding his hat in front of him, turning the brim in his fingers.

Corless deliberated for a moment, then stood back, opening the door wide. The two stepped past him, and he shut the door and led the way into the tiny living room. There was a sofa and an armchair, and a folding table with the leaves down. A big wireless stood on a smaller table by the window. The lino in places was worn through to the floorboards. In one corner stood a sink and a draining board and a black iron gas stove. Everywhere there were books — on shelves, on the table, on top of the wireless, stacked on the floor. In the cramped space the three men stood awkwardly, hearing each other breathe.

"Your son is named Leon, is that right, Mr. Corless?" Hackett said.

Corless was silent for a moment. This wasn't what he had expected. A shimmering chill passed across his shoulder blades.

"That's right," he said. "Why?"

Hackett was still fiddling with his hat.

"I'm afraid there's bad news," he said. "Very bad news."

Corless's mouth went dry, as if it had suddenly filled with dust. He waited. The other one, the doctor, was watching him steadily, out of an odd, deep stillness.

"Your son," the detective said, "was involved in an accident, a car accident, in the Phoenix Park, in the early hours of this morning. I'm sorry to have to tell you, but he's dead."

At once Corless saw waves, the sea with the sun on it, a blinding glare, and a small figure coming towards him, carrying something. What was it? A crab, its legs waving, one claw opened wide and the other vainly snapping. *Look, Da, look what I caught!* The detective was saying something else, but Corless couldn't make out the words. There was a sort of blaring in his ears. He stepped past the detective and strode to the sink and picked up a mug from the draining board and filled it at the tap and drank, and filled it again, and drank again. His thirst seemed unslakable.

The detective was asking him a question.

But why had they sent a detective? Usually they gave this kind of job to some poor rookie on the beat. And why the doctor?

He turned to Hackett, the mug still in his hand. "What? I'm sorry, I didn't hear what you said."

"I was asking, when was the last time you saw him, your son?"

Corless put a hand to his forehead. He was a short, muscular man, with a bus driver's broad chest and tight-packed shoulders. His black hair was oiled and combed in a sideways slick. He wore cheap glasses with transparent frames, the left earpiece held in place with a wad of sticking plaster. He was in his late forties, maybe fifty. Quirke watched him. Quirke in his own life had known this moment and how it felt, knew that sudden, raw, tearing sensation in the chest, knew the dry mouth, the wet palms, the breathlessness. "You should sit down, Mr. Corless," he said. "Here, I'll move these books from the chair."

He put the books on the floor and Corless sat down, very slowly, gingerly, as if he thought the chair might collapse under him.

"Thank you," he said.

Corless felt shaky and infirm. His heart was racing. He saw the sun shining in the

76

window and was amazed. How could the sun be shining? It should be night, it should be night and darkness and deepest winter. It should be the last night of the end of the world. He braced his hands on his knees. He called silently to his dead wife, saying her name in his head, saying it over and over.

The detective was speaking to him again, asking him some new question, or the same one again.

"What?"

"Have you been in touch with your son recently?" Hackett said. "I mean, would the two of you have been — would you have been close, like?"

Corless was barely listening. Hold fast, he told himself, digging his fingers into the bones of his knees, hold fast: others have suffered worse things than this, comrades whose families were destroyed, whose wives were raped, parents murdered, children tortured before their eyes. Hold fast.

"Close?" he said. "There are things we don't see eye to eye on. Politics, that kind of thing. But he's my son." He gritted his teeth. "Was — he was my son."

Hackett was standing by the window, looking out, as if there were something to see, his hat still in his hands. "So your son wasn't political, didn't follow in the — in the family tradition, as you might say."

Corless gave a brief, harsh laugh. "My son," he said, "is a firm believer in the eventual and inevitable triumph of capitalism." His voice seemed to him to be coming not from his own mouth but from some machine close by, as if he weren't speaking at all, as if the words he was hearing were a recording, badly made, a mechanical trotting out of worn-out slogans, assertions, denunciations. He was surprised at himself. Even now, standing on this precipice with a sea of grief stretching before him, he felt the old bitterness stirring, the old, aggrieved sense of general disappointment and disgust with the failed dream of a world transformed. What did any of it matter, now?

The doctor was by the door, still watching him intently. What did he see? A man lost to himself, a man who had given himself to a cause, had bound himself to an iron ideology. What was politics, compared to the death of loved ones? He clenched his hands on his knees again. No! Hold fast. *Hold fast.*

"There's a question," the doctor said, "about the cause of your son's death, Mr. Corless."

Corless tried to concentrate. What was being said here? What trick was being tried?

"What do you mean? What sort of question?"

The doctor said nothing, only went on gazing at him. What the hell was he looking at, what was he looking for? He might have been squinting down the barrel of a microscope, Corless thought, studying some bug trapped between the glass plates, squirming in panic and torment.

The detective turned from the window. "As I said, there was a — a crash, in the Phoenix Park. Your son's car ran into a tree. There was a fire."

Corless stared, his face wrinkling into a grimace of anguish. "Was he burned?" he asked. "Was Leon burned?"

The detective shook his head. "We're fairly certain — Dr. Quirke here is fairly certain — that he was dead, or at least unconscious, before the car caught fire. So there's that, the fact that he didn't suffer. You should hold on to that."

How do you know he didn't suffer? Corless wanted to ask. *How do you know what happened or what didn't? How do you know what my son's death was like?* Death is death; there's always suffering. He closed his eyes for a moment and saw again his wife, who was hardly recognizable any longer, so wasted and frail was she, leaning over the side of the hospital bed and vomiting bile onto the floor. He had held her forehead in his hand, while the nurse came running. *Sam, Sam, I can't bear it any longer.* And now Leon, burnt to nothing in that damned car that he was so proud of. He saw the irony of it: his son, Sam Corless's only son, dying trapped in the quintessential product of the capitalist market.

He opened his eyes and stared at the doctor. "What do you mean, there's a question about the cause of death? How did he die?"

"His car crashed into a tree," Quirke said, "but from the look of it, he wasn't going very fast at the moment of impact. Also, he suffered a blow of some kind to the side of the skull."

There was a beat of silence.

"What are you saying?" Corless demanded. "Did someone knock him out first?"

Quirke held up his hands and shrugged. "I can't say that for certain, no."

"But you *are* saying it, right? You're saying it's a possibility — maybe more than a possibility."

"I'm not sure what I'm saying, Mr. Corless. Mine is an uncertain science."

"And what is your science?"

"I'm a pathologist."

Corless saw the sea again, molten, aflame, the water's purling edge and the child running towards him.

"So, then, Mr. Corless," the detective said from his place by the window, "you say your son wasn't interested in politics at all — that he wasn't active in any way."

"Why are you asking?" Corless asked. "What does it matter?"

Hackett fingered his blue-shadowed chin. "If your son didn't die by accident, or if he didn't mean to die —"

"What?" Corless half rose from the chair, then subsided again. "What are you saying, 'if he didn't mean to'?"

It was Quirke who answered: "The first people on the scene, the ambulance men, the Guards, assumed it was suicide. But that might be what they were meant to think."

Corless had lowered his head and was shaking it slowly from side to side, a wounded bull. "Leon wouldn't kill himself," he said. This was a dream, surely it had to be. "He just wouldn't."

"Are you sure of that?" the detective asked.

He was regarding Corless closely. Corless only looked away. He hadn't shed a tear, he realized, not a single tear. He was glad; when you weep you're not weeping for the

81

dead, you're only weeping for yourself. He felt numb. That would wear off, though; yes, soon enough the numbness would wear off.

Hackett spoke to him again: "The thing is, Mr. Corless, if Dr. Quirke here is right — and his assistant agrees with him, by the way — and your son died under, well, let's say suspicious circumstances, then it's my job to find out what happened, to find out how Leon did die." He paused. "And yourself, Mr. Corless, you must have enemies. You're a prominent man, your views are well known, and they're not popular."

Again there was a silence in the room. They heard the sounds of the traffic in the street below. A horse and cart went past. Someone shouted a snatch of drunken song. This is a new city, Corless thought, one that came into existence a few minutes ago, when they told him Leon was dead. A new city, and I'm a different man in it. All sorts of things were dead along with his son, and other things had come into being, things that he would feel, when he was no longer numb. Nothing would be the same, ever again.

"I don't understand any of this," he said, suddenly plaintive. "I don't know what you're saying to me, what you're asking."

"I'm sorry," Hackett said. "I understand.

We should leave you in peace."

He glanced at Quirke, who nodded.

In peace, Corless thought. In peace.

The two men moved towards the door. Corless didn't get up from where he was sitting. He had the impression that if he tried to stand he would fall back again, and slump into himself, like a half-filled sack.

The sea. The waves. The child with the sunlight behind him, featureless now.

As they came out into the street the heat hit them again, a smoky miasma, and for a second they could hardly breathe. Hackett consulted his watch. "The Holy Hour is past." He nodded in the direction of a marble-fronted public house on the other side of the street. "That place looks cool enough, and we could do with something to sustain us."

They crossed the road, dodging the traffic, and dived through the double swing doors into sanctuary, dim and tranquil. Quirke never ceased to marvel at the palatial grandeur of Dublin pubs. This one, with its big stained-glass window and pink marble counter, had a churchly aspect. They entered the wood-paneled snug and felt as if they were slipping into a vestry. Quirke longed for alcohol — a gin and tonic, say, with joggling ice cubes and a frosted mist down the side of the glass — but settled instead for soda water with a slice of lime; Hackett ordered a bottle of Bass. The barman too had an ecclesiastical air, being tall, emaciated, and of a mournful cast. He served them through a little square hatch, leaning down his monsignor's long, gaunt face and taking their money as if it were a tithe.

"Corless, that poor man," Hackett said. "I've never had time for him and his socialist mumbo jumbo, but you'd have to admire the way he took the news we brought him today."

Quirke selected a cigarette from his silver case and lit up. It struck him again how pungent the smell of drink was when you weren't drinking yourself. Hackett's glass of beer had the reek of bilgewater.

The barman came with the change. "Isn't that powerful weather," he said in tones of mourning.

They drank their drinks, glad of the stillness of midafternoon. They seemed to be the only customers. A wireless was playing somewhere, an incomprehensible buzzing.

"Well," Quirke said, "what do you think?"

"What do I think of what?"

Quirke knew this wasn't a question; they

had their rituals, he and Hackett. "Would Corless have enemies vengeful enough to kill his son? I can't believe it. Nobody takes Sam Corless seriously except the Archbishop and a few Holy Joes like our old friend Mr. Costigan."

Hackett chuckled. "Aye, he's a godsend to the likes of Costigan. What would they do without each other? Laurel and Hardy."

Joseph Costigan, a zealous Catholic of obscure origins and secretive intent, had cropped up in Quirke's life at certain critical moments, to ill effect. Quirke was sure that Costigan, even though he had been a close associate of Quirke's adoptive father, the late Judge Garret Griffin, had some years before sent that pair of thugs to kick the living daylights out of him, when he'd had the temerity to meddle in the murky affairs of the Knights of St. Patrick, the semi-secret society that Costigan seemed to run single-handed. Costigan was forever railing, in the newspapers and on the wireless, against Sam Corless and his tiny and surely harmless Socialist Left Alliance. No doubt he would be gratified to hear of Corless's tragic loss, and would imply, or maybe even say outright, that his son's death was God's judgment and vengeance on the atheistic Samuel Corless.

"What will you do now?" Quirke asked.

"What'll I do?" Hackett considered the question. "I'll wait and see what the forensics boys have to say about the car. If it did have petrol poured over it and set alight, they'll probably be able to say so, unless they make a bags of it, as they're well capable of doing." He drank the last of his beer in one long swig, and put down the glass and wiped his lips with the back of his hand. "And what about you, Doctor?"

"Me? What about me?"

"How are you feeling, really? In yourself, like. Are you mended, do you think?"

"Well now," Quirke said, with a wry smile, "that's a large question. My head is better, certainly, or not as bad as it was, anyway. I've stopped seeing things, or I think I have. I mean, how would I know, if the things I'm seeing are convincing enough to seem real? I have the odd blank, the odd moment of separation from myself. 'Absence seizures' is what they're called, so I'm told. It's always comforting, to have a name to put to a condition."

Hackett was only half listening, nodding to himself. "And how's that girl of yours?" he asked.

For a moment Quirke was confused — did Hackett mean Phoebe or his sometime

86

lover Isabel Galloway? It must be Phoebe, he decided. He hadn't seen Isabel for a long time, and probably wouldn't for another long time. He stubbed out his cigarette and lit another. "Phoebe is very well, so far as I know," he said. "She left the hat shop. She's working for a doctor in Fitzwilliam Square — a psychiatrist."

"Is that so?" Hackett said, leaning his head back and giving Quirke one of his large, slow stares. "A psychiatrist! Well now."

It was impossible to know what he thought of this news. Quirke didn't think Hackett would approve of Dr. Evelyn Blake, but on the other hand, perhaps he would. Quirke had been acquainted with the policeman for years and knew as little about him now as he had the first time they met. He wasn't even sure where he lived. He knew he had a wife, and two grown sons who lived in England, was it, or America?

They rarely spoke of personal matters, he and Hackett, and when they did, each one kept safely to his side of the invisible barrier between them. Their friendship, and Quirke could not think what else to call it, was of a special, and limited, variety. This suited them both. They had been through half a dozen cases together; did this mean they constituted a duo, a team? There was something faintly absurd about the notion, and Quirke dismissed it. He had never been part of a team in his life, and it was too late to start now.

"Did I tell you I'm lodging with Malachy Griffin and his wife?" he said.

"You did," Hackett answered. "You must be very comfortable there."

Yes, Quirke told himself, that's the word — *comfortable.* "I want to go back to work," he said.

He hadn't thought about work for a long time. He supposed it was Sinclair calling him in to look at the body of Leon Corless that had put the thought into his head. Anyway, he would have had to go back, sooner or later. Or had he imagined he was retiring? Quirke was never fully sure of what was going on inside him, and was forever surprising himself when decisions popped up that he had no knowledge of having made. But yes, yes, he would go back to work. Sinclair would be disappointed; Sinclair, he knew, had written him off long ago. That alone was sufficient reason to turn up on Monday morning at the Hospital of the Holy Family and lay claim to his former position, his former authority, to inhabit again his little domain. What else was there for him to do?

He stood up and went to the hatch and leaned down and spoke to the cadaverous barman. "I'll take a gin and tonic, when you're ready," he said. "A double. Oh, and another bottle of Bass for my friend here."

5

Ballytubber was one of those little coastal townlets that have no obvious reason for being where they are or, indeed, for being anywhere. It was situated some ten miles inland from the sea, sleeping peacefully in a fold between sandy hills. No major roads passed through or even near it. It wasn't on the way to anywhere, except to a couple of other, similar towns. In the years immediately after the war it had enjoyed a brief boom as a summer resort, and a few well-off families from Gorey and Arklow, and even one or two from Dublin, had built holiday homes there. It had three pubs, one general grocery store, a rather lovely little Protestant church — that was how its parishioners liked to describe it, with muted, proprietorial satisfaction — but no matching facility for Catholics, a source of resentment and even, on occasion, communal tension. In the civil war, an ambush had taken place there, at the crossroads just north of the town, which had resulted in the shooting to death of a local young man, celebrated in song and story in many an after-hours session in the Ballytubber Arms or one of its sister establishments. Other than that one moment of blood-stained glory, nothing ever happened in Ballytubber, so Ballytubberians said, unsure whether in boast or lament.

Malachy Griffin was one of the Dublin grandees who had built a house in the town. It wasn't really a house but a one-story wooden chalet, with a tarred roof and tongue-and-groove walls and a glassed-in porch that leaked in the winter and spread a smell of damp through the rooms behind it that even the hottest summer weather couldn't eradicate. It had two bedrooms, one with a real double bed, while the other had a sort of large cot, with springs that jangled every time the sleeper in it stirred but that nevertheless had long ago lost their springiness.

When they arrived at the house, Phoebe attempted to show Lisa around, though Lisa was too distracted to pay attention. They went into the larger bedroom, but Lisa insisted she would take the smaller one. Phoebe said that would be ridiculous, since she would be the only occupant of the house, and in the end she reluctantly agreed, and carried her suitcase into the double-bedded room.

They had stopped at Mahon's General Store, on the Wexford Road, to buy provisions, and while Lisa was unpacking, Phoebe stowed the butter, milk, and eggs in the mesh-fronted larder, a pan loaf in the bread bin, the tea in the tea canister. She put away slices of cooked ham wrapped in greaseproof paper, tomatoes, lettuce and spring onions, and a bag of assorted chocolate biscuits. She was sure they had forgotten something essential. She checked the bathroom for soap and other things, laid out clean towels, lit the geyser above the bath. She felt like a little girl again, playing house.

Wine! They should have bought wine, before they left the city. Too late now, for certainly they wouldn't find any in Mahon's. Anyway, she didn't know if Lisa drank. It was only one of the very many things she didn't know about Lisa.

They made tea, and sat at the kitchen table to drink it. An awkward silence fell, neither of them knowing what to say. There were ants in the sugar bowl.

"You're so kind," Lisa broke out at last. "I

mean, here I am, a complete stranger, practically, and yet you lend me your house."

"Well, it's not mine. It belongs to my uncle. I used to live with him and my aunt. In fact, I lived with them until I was nineteen. I thought they were my parents, you see."

"You thought — ?"

Phoebe laughed. "Oh, it's a complicated story. Maybe I'll tell it to you one day."

They were silent again; then Lisa asked timidly, "Does your uncle know I'm here?"

"No. But he wouldn't mind if he did. His name is Griffin, Malachy Griffin." She stopped. Something had flickered in Lisa's eyes; had she recognized the name? "He used to be a doctor — I mean, he's retired. He hardly comes here anymore, except to check on the place now and then. His first wife died some years ago." She paused, and looked aside with a dreamy expression. "We used to have such times here. It seems like a world away, now."

Yet again the silence fell. Lisa sat crouched over her tea. Despite all the activity of traveling, of buying the things at Mahon's, of arriving at the house and unpacking, Lisa's terror had not abated for a moment. When they had come into the house, first

93

she had gone from window to window and peered out, though Phoebe could not think what she might be expecting to see — pursuers lurking in the shrubbery, potential attackers hiding behind tree trunks?

"Listen, Lisa," she said, "I can see how frightened you are. You're going to have to tell me what's going on. What happened? Did someone do something to you? Why do you think you're being followed?"

Lisa was gazing wide-eyed at the tabletop, so that it wasn't clear if she had even been listening. Then she stirred herself, and sighed, and pushed away the half-drunk mug of tea.

"Someone was hurt," she said, picking her way over the words as if they were so many stepping stones, slimed and treacherous. "It was someone I knew."

"When? I mean, when was he hurt?"

"Last night."

"Last *night*?"

"Yes."

"Is he in hospital?"

"No." A long pause. "No, he's not in hospital. He died."

Phoebe's hand flew to her mouth.

"*Died?*" she said in a whisper. "But how?"

"There was a car crash. He was the only one in the car. It ran into a tree and caught

94

fire. That's what they said on the news."

"And this happened just last night?"

"Early this morning. I'd been with him. I ran away."

Lisa was gazing at the table again, as if mesmerized. She's in shock, Phoebe thought. "What do you mean, you ran away?"

"I can't say any more. I shouldn't even have told you this much."

Phoebe remembered that there used to be a bottle of brandy somewhere in the house. She rose from the table and searched through the cupboards, then went out to the living room and searched there. At last she found the bottle, on a shelf behind the wireless set that no longer worked. There was only a drop of brandy left. She went back to the kitchen and got down a wine glass and emptied the bottle into it and set it in front of Lisa. "Drink that," she said.

Lisa frowned. Fear had filled her with helpless bewilderment; she was like a sleep-walker who had been wakened too suddenly. "What is it?" she asked.

"It's brandy. It's only a little — look. Drink it, now."

Phoebe went to the sink and filled a glass of water from the tap. Ballytubber water was the best and sweetest in the county, everyone said so. There used to be a holy well outside the town, on the road to Enniscorthy; sick people and cripples had come to it from all over, in the old days, and maybe they still did. Also in the town there had been a famous bonesetter; people came to him, too, women especially, not just from round here but from Dublin, and even London. There was a world — there were worlds! — beyond the one she knew, the world of the city, where life was supposed to be so broad and sophisticated but in fact was narrower, in its way, than the life of this little town. There were old, secret ways here, stretching back to times before history began. It was a place of ritual, of sacrifice and slaughter.

She tried to picture it in her head, the park in darkness and at the center of the darkness a pool of fire, under a tree, the flames shooting up into the leaves and scorching them, and behind the windscreen a figure slumped over the steering wheel. What was that line in the Bible, about the burning fiery furnace? She couldn't remember. She felt an edge of fear herself, now. Had she been mad to listen to this desperate young woman? What if Lisa had made up all this, what if she was delusional? She could be anything — she could be an escapee from an asylum. Darkness was pressing against the windows, like something that was trying to get in.

Lisa hadn't touched the brandy. She was crying, tears running down her cheeks, though her expression was still blank.

"I'm so frightened," she said, in a strange, crooning tone. "And I'm going to have a baby."

6

Latterly, dinner at the Griffins' had turned into a solemn procedure, less a meal than a sort of ceremonial, hallowed and ponderous. It wasn't clear how it had come to be that way, and no one seemed to know what to do about it. Rose believed it was all the fault of the house, which she had begun to refer to, out of Mal's hearing, as "the barn," or even "the tomb." It was an enormous place, a mansion, with gilded reception rooms and grand, sweeping staircases that might have been designed by M. C. Escher, leading up to silent landings and gaunt, brocaded chambers meant not for sleeping in, it seemed, but for some other kinds of repose, such as lyings in state, enchanted comas, vampiric dozings.

"I do *hate* the place," Rose would sigh, "and yet I get a real kick out of it, too. I'm perverse, I know."

Rose's American origins were obscure.

Her southern drawl suggested levees, and black servants in frock coats and powdered wigs, and acre upon acre of cotton fields, but she had once admitted to Quirke that at some stage in her past life she had worked in a dry cleaner's.

Quirke too enjoyed the house's awfulness, in a masochistic way. Somehow it suited the state he was in, neither sick nor well, not really alive, floating half-submerged in his own self-absorption. The household had its diversions. There was, for instance, a certain mournful comedy to be derived from Mal's proliferating eccentricities. The garden was his latest enthusiasm. The long spell of fine weather, with fresh, sunny days and brief, soft nights, had him as excited as a bumble-bee, and he spent long and happy hours out among his rosebushes and herbaceous borders. Most of the work was done by the gardener, Casey, a gnarled old party with a kerne's glittering eye — he was a terror with the billhook and the shears — but he allowed Mr. Malachy, as he called the master of the house, in a tone of high irony, to pose as the begetter and cultivator in chief of the season's great abundance.

Mal's particular pride were his sweet peas, and every night for the past week the centerpiece of the dinner table had been a cut-glass bowl of these delicate and, to Quirke's eye, indecently gaudy blossoms. Tonight their drowsy perfume was adding a peculiar, extra savor to the grilled trout and salad that Maisie the maid was serving out to the three diners sitting about the big, polished oak table, like life-sized waxworks.

"Thank you, Maisie," Rose said. "You can leave the salad. We'll help ourselves."

"Yes, ma'am," Maisie said.

Maisie had been an inmate — it was the only word — of the Mother of Mercy Laundry, to which she had been sent by her family when her own father had made her pregnant. The laundry was one of many such institutions that had been set up and funded by Mal's father, Judge Griffin, in partnership with Rose's late husband, Josh Crawford, to accommodate, and hide from view, dozens of girls and young women like Maisie. It was Mal, with Quirke's encouragement, who got Maisie out of the laundry and brought her into the house to work as cook, housekeeper, and general maid. Her grand passion was for tobacco, and Rose regularly had to send her off to the bathroom to scrub the nicotine stains from her fingers with a pumice stone.

The meal dragged on. Mal, in a low drone, rhapsodized about his sweet peas, mildly complaining all the while of Casey's supposed shiftlessness. Rose tried to interest Quirke with an account of a book she was reading, but he couldn't concentrate, and the topic soon lapsed. Outside in the garden, a blackbird whistled on and on, sounding as tense and florid as the male lead in an opera. The grilled trout was dry, the white wine tepid.

"That particular one," Mal said, "is called Winston Churchill."

Rose turned to gaze at him in perplexity. "What?"

"That one, there" — pointing with his knife at a blossom in the bowl, richly red as heart's blood — "it's called after Churchill."

"Fascinating," Rose said, and turned her attention back to her plate.

Quirke watched the two of them, his adoptive brother, prim and fussy and prematurely aged, and Rose, handsome, impatient, dissatisfied. He didn't think they were unhappy together, but neither were they happy. Once again he pondered in vain the mystery of their life together.

"I'm going back to work," he said.

Both Mal and Rose stopped chewing and stared at him, their knives and forks suspended in midair.

"You are?" Rose said.

He nodded. "Yes. I think it's time I began to do something with myself again, something useful. I'm starting to atrophy."

Rose smiled skeptically. "I suppose this is because of that young man coming for you today."

"What young man?" Mal asked, looking from one of them to the other.

"His assistant, at the hospital," Rose said.

Mal turned to Quirke. "Sinclair? He was here?"

"Yes," Quirke said. "He wanted me to have a look at something."

"You went into the Holy Family?"

Quirke put down his knife and fork. The fish, the texture of wadded cotton wool, seemed to have lodged in a lump behind his breastbone. "Yes," he said, "I went in. Peculiar feeling. Like one of those dreams you have of being sent back to school even though you're an adult."

Rose snorted. "And that's what made you decide to return to work? How you do love to suffer, Quirke."

Quirke leaned back in his chair. "I'm going back to the flat, too," he said. "I've already stretched your hospitality beyond all bounds. You'll be glad to have the place to yourselves again."

A patch of skin between Rose's eyebrows

had tightened and turned pale, and her smile was steely. "This is all very sudden," she said in a bright, brittle tone. "You might have given some notice, some warning."

Mal was looking at his plate — Rose when she was angry made all eyes drop. But why was she angry? Quirke wondered, regarding her with a quizzical eye. "I'm sorry," he said. "I didn't mean to spring it on you. As a matter of fact, I just decided myself, just this moment."

He wasn't sure what he was apologizing for. His presence here these past months could hardly have been a source of unalloyed joy for the household. He had never quite decided what Rose felt for him, or what he felt for her. That one time they had gone to bed together, years before, surely that couldn't have meant so much to her? Yet now he recalled how that morning she had spoken of him kissing her, or of her kissing him — he couldn't remember which. He had paid little attention, assuming it was one of Rose's teasing jokes — but what if he was wrong? He couldn't imagine himself desiring Rose now, as he had once desired her, briefly. She was merely Mal's wife now, however anachronistic a match it might appear to be.

Rose had gone back to her food and was

eating, or going through the motions of eating, with fast, angry little movements.

"I'm sorry," Quirke said again. "I've been clumsy, as usual. I'm very grateful to you both for putting me up for so long, but now it's time for me to move on."

Rose didn't even look up, as if she hadn't heard, while Mal peered at him out of what these days seemed a permanent haze of puzzlement, the lenses of his wire-framed spectacles gleaming.

"You don't *have* to go," he said. "You know, of course, you're welcome to stay as long as you like."

Quirke folded his napkin and set it down beside his plate and put both of his hands flat on the table and pushed himself to his feet. Mal was still gazing at him, anxious and bewildered. Rose still would not lift her head. He turned stiffly and left the room. He felt as if he had been given some precious thing to hold and admire, instead of which he had let it slip from his grasp and it had smashed to smithereens at his feet.

Why did everything, always, have to be so difficult?

He went up to the big chilly bedroom: suddenly he saw it as nothing less than a jail cell, cunningly disguised, where for a long

104

time, too long, he had been in voluntary confinement. He packed quickly — he had few things — and carried his suitcase downstairs. Half an hour ago he had seen himself as a part of the place, as fixed as an item of furniture; now he couldn't wait to get away. The house was silent. He knew he should go and find Rose and make his peace with her. Instead he crept along the hall and opened the front door as quietly as he could and slipped out into the sunlit evening.

The shadows on the road were sharply slanted. As he walked, an occasional car went past, none of them a taxi. He didn't mind; he was no longer in a hurry. He had a new sense of freedom, even of lightness. He was an escapee.

He came to Merrion Road and turned left, in the direction of the city. A Garda squad car came up behind him and slowed. The Garda in the passenger seat peered out at him suspiciously. He supposed he did look odd, a man in a dark suit and a dark hat, with a suitcase, strolling aimlessly. The car went on. Then a taxi approached, going in the opposite direction. He hailed it, and it did a U-turn. He got into the back seat. The driver was a countryman with a large round head and red ears.

"Upper Mount Street," Quirke said.

Home, he thought. It wasn't a term he often brought to mind, not when he was thinking of himself, anyway.

And still the day refused to end. At ten-thirty the sky was an inverted bowl of bruised blue radiance, except in the west, where the sunset looked like a firefight at sea, a motionless Trafalgar. He stood at the open window of the flat, craning to see, up past the tall houses opposite, a single pale star suspended above the rooftops, a dagger of shimmering light. It was a long time since he had felt so calm, so untroubled. *Serene:* the word came to him unbidden. He felt serene. Why had he stayed so long at the Griffins'? Why in the first place had he let them take him into their arid lives, in that cold house?

The flat smelled slightly musty, but it didn't matter. Yes, he was home.

He wondered what to do, how to pass this endless night. It was such a luxurious sensation, having again no one to please or even think about except himself. He couldn't go to bed; he wouldn't be able to sleep — who could sleep in these white nights? In the old days he would have gone round to the 47 on Haddington Road, or up to the Shelbourne, where he would have been bound to find someone to drink with him. But he couldn't go back to that old life. If he started drinking now, he'd never stop. He had fallen off the wagon too many times and had the bruises to show for it, the permanent lacerations.

He took his hat and went down to the street.

The whores were out, half a dozen of them, the elderly one with the walking stick who had been in business for as long as he had lived here, and a couple of youngish ones, too, dressed in black and stark as crows, who must be new on the game since he hadn't encountered them before. He often wondered about their lives, where they came from, how they had ended up on the streets. He might have talked to them, asked them about themselves, but he could never work up the courage. He had been brought up in a male world, a world first of priests and Christian Brothers, then of medical students, then doctors, like himself. He had known women too, of course, but it had always been a special kind of knowing, one that stopped just below the surface or, in most cases, just above it. Would things have been different for him if there had been a mother to take care of him, to teach him things, to let him in on the secrets that only mothers were privy to? He would never know. But he supposed he was exaggerating the preciousness of all the things he had not known.

It was a sweet, secret luxury, to feel sorry for himself now and then, to lament his losses and his woes.

Sometimes it seemed to him that all his life he had been standing with his back to a high wall, on the other side of which an endless circus show was going on. Now and then there would come to him on the breeze the sound of a drumroll, or a snatch of brassy music, a gasp of wonderment or a surge of raucous laughter from the crowd. Why could he not scale the wall, haul himself up the side of it, even if his hands bled, his fingernails splintered, and jump down and run to the flap of the big top and peer in? Just to see what the performance looked like, even if he didn't go inside, even if he were only to have that one, hindered glimpse of the dingy, sequined magic — that would be something.

He walked along Merrion Square. The greenery behind the railings was giving off its nocturnal scents. He met no one. The whores didn't come down this far, for some reason, but stayed around Mount Street and the canal, Fitzwilliam Square, Hatch Street.

He was aware of a pleasantly melancholy sensation around his heart, as soft and pervasive as the fragrance of the trees and the plants. He was alive. It seemed an amazing fact, the unlikeliness of it, this mysterious and seemingly aimless project that was his life.

He turned up Merrion Street. There was lamplight in a few of the windows of Government Buildings. He thought of the poor drudges in there, ordered by their ministers to stay on and finish that report, draw up this schedule, frame those parliamentary questions. He wondered if Leon Corless had sat up at one of those windows, late into the night, doing — doing what?

For a while, before he started on his medical studies, Quirke had thought of going for the Civil Service. He had done well in his final school examinations, came out among the top fifty in the country; a career awaited him as a bureaucrat, a mandarin. Strange to think that he might have been behind one of those windows himself now, hunched over his desk, his fountain pen scratching away, covering sheet after sheet of foolscap, as the long day faded into the half-night of midsummer. Strange to think.

At the corner of Merrion Row a lone car was stopped at the traffic light. He drew level with it, and saw that it was Phoebe behind the wheel. The light changed to green just then and the car moved off. He sprinted after it, and caught up, and rapped with his knuckles on the roof. Phoebe braked, and looked up at him in alarm. He opened the passenger door and leaned in. "It's just me!" he said, laughing.

"Quirke! You gave me a fright — I thought it was a tramp or something. What are you doing, wandering the streets at this hour?"

A car came up behind them, and the driver sounded his horn.

"I'm sorry," Quirke said, still with his hand on the door. "I just saw you and I — I thought I'd — I just thought I'd say hello."

Behind them the horn honked again, a longer blast.

"Get in, for goodness' sake!" Phoebe said.

Quirke sat beside her, feeling foolish, and foolishly happy. "Sorry," he said again.

"What's the matter?" Phoebe said, and drove forward and turned onto Baggot Street.

"Nothing's the matter. I —" He stopped. What could he say? How to explain something so ordinary as happiness? "I was out for a walk," he said.

"You're very far from Ailesbury Road."

"Well, that's the thing, you see," he said.

110

"I'm not at Ailesbury Road anymore. I'm back in the flat."

She glanced at him sidelong. "I'm glad to hear it."

"Are you?"

"Of course. I thought you were mad to go and stay there in the first place."

"Why?"

"Oh, Quirke, don't you know anything?"

"Funny, Rose said something the same to me just this morning." He laughed. "Anyway, the answer, of course, is yes — I don't know anything about anything."

They looked at each other, a little helplessly, smiling. It seemed to Quirke somehow an emblematic moment, as if this was how it was always meant to have been between them, meeting by chance, at dusk, and not knowing what to say to each other, and not minding. For it didn't matter; they could speak or be silent, it was all the same. He felt it again, that happiness, a twinge in his breast, a kind of precious pain.

She drove them to Herbert Place. They climbed the dimly lit stairs to her flat on the first floor. Large shapes of shadow hung in the living room, and at the window a parallelogram of yellowish radiance from the streetlamp outside was laid out on the floor like an illustration in a geometry book, one corner of it bent at an angle where it was intersected by a chair leg.

Phoebe dropped her handbag and her keys on the table and went to the window. "I often don't turn on the light," she said, "and just leave the curtains open. Do you mind?"

"I don't mind."

"I like to be in the dark and see the night outside, so glossy and quiet. I imagine there's a huge animal out there, pressed against the house, sleeping."

"The midnight cat," Quirke said.

"What?"

"That's what your mother used to call it — the midnight cat. She liked the dark, too, said she preferred it to daytime. It appealed to her feline side."

He thought of Delia, long dead, of how she used to curl up against him, purring; her feline side. He was glad it was dark; he didn't want Phoebe to see his face, how he looked. He didn't often think of his dead wife, nowadays.

"Will I make us some coffee?" Phoebe asked.

When she turned to him, away from the window, her face became a blank mask, featureless.

"If you want to," he said. "I mean, if

you're going to have some yourself."

"Oh, Quirke," she said, "can't you ever just say yes or no, and leave it at that?"

He followed her into the kitchen. Here she had to turn the light on. He watched her at the sink, filling the kettle. How pale she seemed; tired, too. He wondered where she had been, in the car, Sinclair's car. She didn't like to drive, he knew, especially not at night.

"Are you all right?" he asked.

She didn't look at him. "Yes. Why?"

"I don't know. You seem — I don't know."

"You worry about everyone," she said. "Except about yourself, of course."

"People are always telling me that."

"Don't you think they might be right?"

"Maybe. I doubt it. Sometimes it seems to me I'm all I ever think of, all I'm capable of thinking of. I'm much more selfish than anyone realizes."

"Everyone feels that way, Quirke. We're trapped inside ourselves."

She put the kettle on the stove and lit the flame under it. There was the flabby smell of burning gas. Someday, he thought, someday, for no reason, I'll remember all this, the darkness in the window, the gas flame sputtering, the red-and-white checked tablecloth, the cups, the smell of the ground

113

coffee, and Phoebe in her black dress with the white lace collar, my nunlike daughter.

"What's the matter, Phoebe?" he said.

This time she did look at him, the merest glance. "Oh, it's nothing," she said. "Or maybe it is. I don't know. Let's wait and have our coffee."

The kettle came to the boil, and she poured the steaming water into the percolator and put the percolator on the ring and turned down the gas. Soon the coffee began to burble into the glass lid. She got down cups, saucers, spoons. She poured the coffee. He watched her. Sometimes he thought he would have made a better physician than a pathologist. He had an eye for the way people moved, their tics, their tensions. But would he have been able to deal with the living? As it was, even the dead were almost too much for him.

They returned to the living room, carrying their cups. It took some moments for their eyes to adjust to the darkness. Quirke barked his shin on something. Phoebe asked if she should switch on the light, but he said no. He guessed that she didn't want him to see her face, either. They both preferred the anonymity of darkness.

He groped his way to the table and sat down on a cane-backed chair, while Phoebe went and perched on the arm of the sofa, the light from the streetlamp falling across her knees.

"I met someone today," she said. "Someone I used to know, in the agency where I was doing that shorthand course. It was the strangest thing. I was in the Country Shop, having lunch, when the waitress brought me a note, just a scribble, asking me to come across to the Green."

She paused and watched Quirke light a cigarette. The match when he struck it made a suddenly expanding sphere of yellow light in which for a moment his face loomed like a caricature, the nose grotesquely hooked and the eye sockets empty.

"Who was it from, this note?" he asked.

"A girl called Lisa, Lisa Smith. I hardly knew her during the course, except to nod to or say hello. She'd seen me through the window of the café and wrote the note and gave it to the waitress to give to me. I went over to the Green, as she'd asked, and sure enough there she was, waiting for me, by the pond." She paused. "Give me one of your cigarettes, will you? I've run out."

He rose and went to her, offering his cigarette case. "Did I know you were smoking again?" he asked.

"I don't know. Did you?"

"Probably. I forget everything, all the time. My brain is addled."

She laughed. "That's what Nana Griffin used to say."

"Did she? Well, it's apt. These days I feel as old as everyone's granny."

"Oh, Quirke!"

He went back and sat by the table again. He was using his saucer as an ashtray, though he knew Phoebe would chide him for it. "Go on," he said, "tell me about this girl — what did you say her name was?"

"Lisa Smith. That's what she said it was, anyway."

"I thought you said you knew her?"

"I told you, she was in the same course as I was, that's all. I don't think I ever even knew her name. She was just one of the class." She thought for a moment. " 'Lisa Smith' doesn't sound right, somehow. Lisa, yes, but not Smith. It sounds made up."

"What did she want from you?"

"She wanted help. She's in trouble of some kind. She's pregnant, for a start."

"And not married?"

"No."

"Then yes, she is in trouble."

Phoebe waved a hand dismissively, the glowing tip of her cigarette making a brief arabesque in the darkness. "I don't mean

116

that, I mean real trouble. Her boyfriend was killed."

In Quirke's left ear, or just above it, where his brain was injured, something seemed to click, like a light switch being flipped on. One day, he thought, that may be the very last sound I'll hear, and the light won't be going on.

"Killed?" he said. "How?"

"He was in some kind of accident. A car crash, a fire, I don't know. She started to tell me, and then stopped and wouldn't say any more."

"When did this happen?"

"Sometime last night, or early this morning."

He stood up, making a clatter. "In the Phoenix Park?"

She tried to see him in the darkness. "How did you know?"

He went to the mantelpiece and groped for the small lamp that he knew was there, and switched it on. It shed a cone of weak light downwards.

"His name was Leon Corless," he said. "His car crashed into a tree and went on fire. David did the postmortem on him this morning. He called me in, wanted my advice."

She was watching him intently now, the

cigarette, forgotten in her fingers, sending up a wavering trail of smoke. "Why did he need your advice? What was wrong?"

Quirke began pacing the floor, watching his feet. It was a thing he did.

"There was something on the side of the skull, a contusion. It looked wrong — don't ask me why. You get a sixth sense for these things." He stopped close to her, and looked into her face. Down in the street a car with a faulty exhaust went past, hiccuping and whining. "Tell me what the girl said."

She shrugged. "It was all confused," she said. "I didn't even know whether to believe her or not, it sounded so far-fetched and melodramatic. Yet she was so frightened — I can't stop thinking of the look she gave me as I was leaving, the fear in her eyes." She paused, remembering, then shook her head, as if to shake away the image of Lisa sitting in the kitchen, shriveled into herself, seeming so small and frail and defenseless. "She said she was in the car with him, he was driving her home from somewhere, a party or something. They had a fight, I suppose about her being pregnant, and she made him stop and she got out. She didn't expect him to drive off, but he did. Then another car went past; she thinks it was following him. She was trying to find a taxi when she saw the glow of the burning car, in the park. She went up to where the car was. She recognized it. She could see — what did you say his name was?"

"Leon. Leon Corless."

"She could see him slumped against the wheel, and the flames all round him."

"What did she do?"

"Nothing. She was frightened, and ran off. I suppose she was in a panic by then. She went home to her flat — I think she must have walked all the way to Rathmines — and slept for a while. Or tried to sleep. I don't know where she was going when she saw me in the restaurant. I think she was just wandering around in a daze, not knowing what to do."

Quirke took another cigarette from his case on the table and lit it. A wedge of ice seemed to have lodged itself between his ribs, on the inside. He wanted a drink; he needed a drink; but he must not, must not, *must* not have a drink.

"So what did you do," he said, "when you met her in the Green?"

"I borrowed the car from David and drove her down to Wicklow."

"To Wicklow?"

"To the house in Ballytubber. She needed somewhere to hide, she said, somewhere

where no one would find her."

"Like who?"

"What?"

"Who would want to find her, who was she hiding from?"

"I don't know. I asked her but she wouldn't tell me. She was too frightened."

He walked to the window and stood looking out. Even yet there was a streak of silver radiance in the western sky, and a long smooth plume of cloud the color of smoke.

"Who was he?" Phoebe asked. "Leon Corless, I mean."

Quirke shrugged. "A civil servant. His only claim to fame is that his father is Sam Corless."

"Who's Sam Corless?"

"The Communist. Socialist Left Alliance, or whatever it's called."

"Oh, him. Yes. Was he — the son — was he in politics, too?"

"No. He had no interest in that kind of thing, so his father says."

They were silent, lost in their thoughts. Quirke was recalling Sam Corless sitting in his cluttered little room above the tobacconist's, hands clamped on his knees, haggard and lost. He had always had a certain admiration for Corless, for his fearlessness, his effrontery, for the jeering speeches he made, excoriating state and church, laughing at the golf club plotters, the dinner dance conspirators, all the whited sepulchres, the Judge Garret Griffins and the Josh Crawfords and the Joe Costigans of this mean and mendacious little city.

"The girl, Lisa," Quirke said. "She's pregnant, you say. Was Leon Corless the father?"

"Yes, I think so."

"Christ," he muttered, "what sort of a mess is this." He turned from the window and paced the floor again. "Got any drink?"

"What?"

"Drink. Whiskey, wine. Anything."

"No," she said, "there's no drink. And even if there was, I wouldn't let you have it."

He laughed harshly. She was right, she was right, but oh, how his very nerves were crying out for just one small sip. But of course it wouldn't be that, it wouldn't be one small sip; it never was.

"So you left her in Ballytubber," he said. "How will she manage there, on her own?"

"I don't know. I'll go down and see her tomorrow, find out how she's getting on."

"Does David know about her?"

"No. I told him I was taking you to the hospital for a checkup, and then for a drive

121

somewhere."

He laughed again, more quietly. He was wondering what Sinclair would have made of the notion of him and Phoebe off on a jaunt together. They were hardly that kind of father and daughter. But then, they were hardly any kind of father and daughter, really.

"I'm going home," he said. "It's late — you should sleep. Have you to work tomorrow?"

"Tomorrow is Saturday."

"So it is."

He took up his hat.

"Have you really moved out of Ailesbury Road?" Phoebe asked. "Are you really back in the flat?"

"Yes, I am."

"When did you leave?"

"Tonight, just before I met you. Also, I'm going back to work." He smiled at her in the lamplight. "My sojourn in the desert is over."

"Good," she said. "I was worried about you. What did Rose have to say?"

"About what — about my moving out? Not much. I imagine she's relieved, though she seemed offended. As for Mal, God knows what he thinks. I'm not sure it had sunk in that I was living with them in the first place. You know Mal."

She walked down with him to the front door. They stood together on the top step, looking out into the night. All was still except for the sound of water tumbling over one of the locks in the canal. Quirke had again that sense of pervasive, mild melancholy. He wanted to touch his daughter, to make some gesture that would communicate all he felt for her, whatever that was. But of course he couldn't do it. Faintly, as if from afar, the circus music sounded in his head. Would he ever get over that wall, would he ever see the clowns, the strong man, the sequined bareback rider circling the ring, the trapeze artists swooping through beams of powdered light? He felt a sweet pang of self-pity, and despised himself for it.

"Good night," he said. "Sleep well."

"Good night, Quirke."

She watched him descend the steps and walk off into the night. After shutting the door, she went up to the flat and into the living room and switched off the lamp on the mantelpiece and sat down in the armchair by the window. She wasn't sleepy. She thought of Lisa, alone down there in that little town. She thought of Quirke, too, walking by himself in the dark streets.

For a full minute she sat without stirring.

Then she stood up quickly and took her handbag and the car keys from the table. As she was going down the stairs she heard the bell in St. Stephen's tolling midnight.

The same bell was sounding a later hour when Quirke's telephone rang, making him spring awake. He was sprawled on the sofa in his flat, still dressed, an open book lying face-down on his lap. He must have dozed off. He got up groggily and crossed to the still-shrilling phone and picked up the receiver.

"She's gone," Phoebe said, her voice small and distant and fearful.

"What?" Quirke didn't understand. "Where are you?"

"In Ballytubber."

"How did you get there?"

"I drove down, after you left. I was worried, I couldn't stop thinking of Lisa here on her own. But now she's gone, Quirke."

"Gone where?"

"I don't *know.*" Her voice was a distant wail. "I don't know. Only the house is empty, and she's gone."

7

It had been some time after one o'clock when she arrived, for the second time that night, at the house in Ballytubber. She turned off the engine and doused the headlights and sat in the dark for five minutes or more, telling herself she should turn around and go back to Dublin. What had she been thinking of, coming back here like this? Apart from anything else, if she knocked on the door now it would terrify Lisa, for who would be calling at such a late hour to a house that had been standing empty for so long? And what explanation could she give for turning up again, no more than a couple of hours after she had left? Yet she couldn't deny the instinct that had made her come back. Something was wrong, she knew it was.

In the end she steeled herself and got out of the car. No light showed in the house. Instead of knocking on the front door, she went around by the side, to the window of the bedroom with the double bed, and tapped on the glass and spoke Lisa's name. There was not a stir inside, and no reply came. She tapped again, more sharply this time. She went back to the front door and knocked, even though she knew by now that it was futile to persist. Lisa was not here; she had gone, somehow. Phoebe knelt by the gatepost and, working from memory, removed a stone from the base, and found the spare key that was always kept there.

She dreaded opening the door, onto the dark hall.

The smell of damp and must, so familiar from childhood, was a faint comfort. She shut the door behind her. She thought of switching on the light, but decided against it. She felt her way along the wall, and went first into the living room, on the right. A splash of moonlight showed her that the room was empty. Next she crossed the hall and tapped on the bedroom door. Nothing. She opened the door and switched on the light. Lisa was not there, as she had known she wouldn't be, and neither was her suitcase nor the things she had unpacked. The bed, she could see, had not been slept in. She went into the kitchen. Not a trace remained of their having been here earlier, the two of them, when they had sat at the table drinking tea. The cups they had used had been washed and dried and put away. The brandy bottle was nowhere to be found, not on the table, not in the sink, not even in the black plastic bin under the sink.

It was the bareness of the place that she found most frightening. It was as if some supernatural agency had swooped through the house, leaving behind this eerie desertedness.

She turned off the lights, and went out and locked the front door behind herself and put the key back into its hiding place and reinserted the loose stone to hide it. Her hands were shaking. As she was opening the car door she was sure there was someone behind her, in the darkness, about to seize hold of her and clamp a hand over her mouth to silence her cries. But no one was there. Hastily she got behind the wheel and pulled on the starter switch, praying the engine would start and that she wouldn't have to get out in the dark and use the crank handle. She was in luck, and the engine turned over at the first go. She drove off so quickly that gravel flew from under the tires; she heard it spraying the road behind her.

The telephone booth, on the corner by the Protestant church, smelled of fish and chips and urine. A weak bulb glowed in it, but she wished there were no light at all — she felt terrifyingly vulnerable, huddled there in plain sight, with the phone pressed to her ear, the very picture, she was sure, of panic and fear.

She could hear from the blurriness of his voice that Quirke had been asleep. At first he couldn't understand what she was saying. Then he told her to get back into the car, lock the doors, and return at once to the city. It was not often in her life that she had found herself close to tears of relief and gratitude just to be told what to do, and by Quirke, at that.

There was a full moon and she could almost have driven with the headlights off. The countryside to her right and left, bathed in the moon's ghostly glimmer, turned slowly in the car windows like two giant fans endlessly opening. There were few other vehicles on the road. A Land Rover drawing a horse box overtook her, going much too fast, and disappeared over the brow of a hill, though for some miles she could still see the beams of the headlights raking through the darkness far ahead. A fox ran out of a hedge almost under the front wheels and she had to brake so hard the engine almost cut out. She drove on, tense and trembling.

It was a few minutes before three o'clock when she got to Upper Mount Street and stopped outside Quirke's flat. She couldn't understand it — she had thought a whole night must have passed since she had set off for Wicklow and heard the bell in St. Stephen's tolling midnight.

There was a light in Quirke's flat, and when she rang the bell he came at once to the window and threw the key down to her, wrapped in a handkerchief. He met her on the stairs when she was halfway up. In the urgency of the moment, it seemed he might take her in his arms. She half wished he would, but he didn't.

"Are you all right?" he asked, looking at her all over, as if expecting to see a broken limb, or blood spilling from a wound.

"Yes, of course I'm all right," she said, sounding more impatient than she had meant to. Her nerves were jangling; she imagined them like the mixed-up and still jerkily moving parts of a broken clock.

"Come on," he said, leading the way back upstairs, "I'll cook you some breakfast."

Once they were in the flat, he made her sit in the armchair by the fireplace. It was chilly, at this hour, and he lit the gas fire and turned it low. He went out to the kitchen and made tea, and carried it in on a tray and set it on a low table beside her chair. "There doesn't seem to be anything much to eat," he said. "Would you like — I don't know — an egg, maybe? Or I could open a tin of soup."

Despite herself, she laughed. "I'm fine, Quirke," she said. "I'm not hungry, I don't want anything."

He squatted on his heels to pour the tea. She was reminded again of childhood games, Quirke now her pretend father and she his pretend little girl. It surprised her, how calmly she could think of all they had not had together, of all they could have had, if he had not given her away at birth to Mal and his wife, Sarah, to be their pretend baby. So many lies, so much subterfuge, such grievous betrayals. Why was she not angry? Why was she not in a permanent fury at this man who had behaved so disgracefully towards her, who had robbed her of the childhood she should have had by rights?

He poured tea for himself, too, but she could see he had no intention of drinking it, that he was just being polite. That, it struck her, was what Quirke thought life consisted of: going through the motions, observing the forms, doing the right thing.

130

"Tell me what happened when you got to Ballytubber," he said. "By the way, why *did* you go back, when you'd just been there?"

"I don't know myself," she said. He had put too much sugar in her tea. "I suppose I must have had — I don't know what to call it. A premonition? A bad feeling, anyway. And I was right. The house was empty, Quirke. I mean, not only was Lisa not there, but every trace of her was wiped away. I began to wonder if I'd imagined the whole thing, if I'd never gone down there with her, if I'd never met her in the first place, if all of it was just a figment of my imagination."

Quirke picked up his teacup and put it down again. "Surely there must have been some sign of her having been there," he said.

"There wasn't. The place was bare."

Quirke rose and went to the mantelpiece and took a cigarette from the silver box there and lit it. He wore corduroy trousers and a bulky old sweater the color of wet wheat. Also he had slippers on; she didn't think she had ever seen Quirke in slippers before. The outfit somehow made him seem not homely but, on the contrary, peculiarly sinister, like one of those suave villains in a spy picture, an enemy agent masquerading as a country squire.

"Remind me of her name again," he said.

131

"Lisa Smith."

"Yes, yes, that's right, Lisa Smith. What else do you know about her, aside from her name, which you don't even think is genuine?"

"Nothing," Phoebe said. "Except what I told you, that she's pregnant."

They were silent for a while; then Quirke spoke. "Look," he said, "I'm sure she's all right. What could happen to anyone in Ballytubber? Plus there's the fact that no one knows she was there except you."

"I do know where she lives," Phoebe said. "Or where she has a flat, at least. I don't know anything about her family, about her background. She just appeared out of nowhere, and now she's gone back there." She lifted frightened eyes to Quirke's face. "It was so eerie, Quirke," she said. "The house was completely empty, as if no one had been there. Where can she have gone to? She wouldn't have left by herself, I'm sure of it. Someone must have followed us, someone she knew, that she would open the door to. Otherwise it doesn't make sense." She paused, staring at the flames of the gas fire. "She was so terrified, I could feel it, the way you can feel a child has a raging temperature even without feeling its forehead."

She saw that Quirke was gazing at a framed photograph on the mantelpiece. It was of himself and Delia, Phoebe's mother, arm in arm with Mal and Sarah, Delia's sister. They were dead, both of those sisters. Delia had died giving birth to Phoebe, and Sarah had been struck down by a brain tumor — how long ago was it now? She couldn't remember.

She put the teacup and saucer back on the tray and stood up. "I'm tired," she said. "I'm going home to rest. I can't think anymore — my mind is a blank."

"We'll talk again in the morning," Quirke said. "Mind you" — he glanced at the window — "it is morning, pretty well. The dawn is coming up."

He walked her down to the car. He was right: there was a thin, grayish glow, dirty as dishwater, in the eastern sky, above the rooftops.

"You've still said nothing to David?" he asked, leaning on the open door of the car as she put her hand on the starter.

"No." She didn't look at him. "What would I say?"

He didn't answer that. "I'm glad you came to me," he said.

Now she did look up, startled. "Are you?"

"Yes. Of course." He did his crooked

smile, which in the dawn light was more like a grimace. "Of course I am."

When she got to Herbert Place she went straight into the bedroom and lay down on the bed. She meant to rest there for only a minute or two, and didn't even undress, sure she wouldn't be able to sleep. Hours later, she started awake with the sun shining on her face. She got up, moving stiffly; she felt as if she had run rather than driven all the way back from Ballytubber.

She made coffee and ate a slice of toast, then drew a lukewarm bath and lay in it for a long time, until the water was cold and she began to shiver. The bathroom was so narrow she had to stand sideways to towel herself dry.

She went back to the kitchen and made more coffee — she knew it would give her palpitations, but she didn't care — and sat at the table by the window in her dressing gown. It was early still, and the street was deserted. Also it was Saturday, and all the offices in the houses round about would be closed. She loved the weekends here, when all day long it was so quiet she could hear the sound of canal water from across the road, and the ducks quacking. The sawmill over at Percy Place sometimes opened on

Saturday mornings, but not until ten or even later, and it was only seven yet.

Strong sunshine was falling down through the window, onto the table; it was going to be another hot day. Already people were growing tired of the fine weather; she had heard them on the buses and in the shops, complaining of the heat. She didn't mind it, and while everyone else had put on summer clothes, she saw no reason to change out of her accustomed black. When she had left the Maison des Chapeaux the owner, Mrs. Cuffe-Wilkes, had given her a big straw hat with a floppy brim as a parting gift. She had put it away on the top shelf of the wardrobe, thinking it much too frivolous for her, but today, she decided, she would wear it, no matter how silly it made her look.

She went to the wardrobe and took down the hat box and lifted out the hat. It was very pretty, an elaborate concoction of pale yellow straw with a red ribbon hanging down at the back. The price tag was still on it; Mrs. Cuffe-Wilkes had been careful to leave it there, to let Phoebe know what an expensive gift it was. Three guineas — a lot of money, all right. She turned the thing in her hands, looking at it from all sides. It was as light as a bird's dried wing. She put it on and surveyed herself, a little shyly, in the mirror.

She frowned. She had been trying not to think about Lisa Smith, but now she had to give in, and everything that had happened in the night came flooding back. The sunshine, the coffee, the silly hat — all of it had conspired to let her doubt the night's events, but now she thought of the hunted, haunted look in Lisa's eyes, and it was all too real again.

She would have to find her. She felt it as a solemn duty. A person had been given into her care, troubled and terrified, whom she had tried to help, and, somehow, she had failed.

The face in the mirror gazed back at her accusingly from under the dramatically swooping straw brim of the hat. She took the hat off and put it back in the box and put the box on the shelf. As she was shutting the door of the wardrobe she caught a fleeting glimpse of herself again in the mirror, looking furtive, this time, and guilty, too.

8

It was early when Sam Corless arrived at the hospital. Hackett had sent Sergeant Jenkins in a squad car to collect him. He had on his bus driver's blue serge trousers and an old tweed jacket with a red flag badge in the lapel. He wore no tie, and his shirt collar was open. He looked as a man would look the day after hearing of the violent death of his son. Hackett was waiting for him at the main entrance. Together they entered the hospital and went down the absurdly grand marble staircase, at the foot of which they were met by David Sinclair in his white coat. Hackett introduced the two men.

"I'm sorry, Mr. Corless," Sinclair said. "I know how hard this is."

How many times, he wondered, had he uttered those selfsame words, in this same place?

Sam Corless said nothing. He appeared

physically sick: his skin was puffy and his eyes were bloodshot. They walked along the airless, green-painted corridor, Sinclair and Sam Corless ahead and Hackett following close behind. Sinclair opened the door to the lab. When they came in, Bolger, the porter, whipped a half-smoked cigarette from his mouth and hid it behind his back.

The charred remains of Leon Corless lay on a trolley under a white nylon sheet. A faulty tap was dribbling into one of the big metal sinks. Sam Corless rubbed his reddened eyes, which were stinging already from the harsh light falling from the lamps in the ceiling. Bolger was eyeing him with undisguised interest, the infamous Sam Corless; right now he certainly didn't look like much of a threat to the institutions of the state.

Sinclair lifted back a corner of the sheet. For a second Corless's broad face seemed to fold in on itself.

"This is your son, yes, Mr. Corless?" Sinclair said.

Corless nodded. "Yes," he said. He seemed to be having difficulty swallowing. Hackett stepped forward and put a hand on his arm, just below the elbow. Sinclair let the corner of the sheet fall back.

There was a café opposite the gates of the hospital. Half a dozen Formica-topped tables, some metal chairs, a high counter with glass-fronted compartments that displayed assorted sandwiches and sticky buns. Behind the counter a girl of seventeen or so, fair-haired and nervous, tended a tea urn and a complicated coffee-making machine with many levers and nozzles.

Hackett and Sam Corless sat at a table by the window. Corless said he didn't want anything, but Hackett went to the counter and ordered a cup of tea for him anyway, and one for himself. He hung his hat on a hat stand in the corner and sat down again. Corless was hunched forward at the table, empty-eyed, his hands clasped before him.

"Are you all right?" Hackett asked.

Corless looked at him as if he couldn't remember who he was. "Yes," he said. "I'm all right."

Taking out a packet of Woodbines and a Zippo lighter polished with age, he offered Hackett a cigarette. Hackett shook his head. "I'll smoke my own," he said, "if you don't mind. Them things are too rough for my poor old bronchials." He picked up the lighter and turned it over in his fingers.

"February 1937," Corless said, "the Battle of Jarama, outside Madrid."

"Oh, yes?" Hackett said. "You were in Spain?"

"I was with the Connolly Column. We were at Pingarrón — Suicide Hill, we called it — up against the Thälmann Battalion. I was lying in a ditch with my friend Charlie McRory beside me. One of the German snipers got Charlie in the throat." He nodded at the lighter. "He gave that to me, before he died. Maybe he wanted me to bring it back and give it to his parents, as a keepsake, or maybe he wanted me to have it. He couldn't speak, with the blood in his throat, so I don't know."

Hackett set the lighter down on the table between them.

"That was a brave fight," he said. Corless glanced at him sharply. "The Battle of Jarama. I read up the history of it. It's a hobby I have."

Corless nodded, with a thin smile. Corless would not be a man who would go in for hobbies, Hackett guessed.

"Aye, it was a brave fight," Corless said, "but we lost it. It was hand to hand at the end." He held up both his hands. "I killed men with these. Kill a man up close and

140

nothing in your life is ever the same again. A lot of good comrades died in those few days, Bill Beattie and Bill Henry — the two Bills — and Liam Tumilson and Charlie Donnelly, others, too. I was lucky to get out of it alive. I had a wife at home, and a child." He stopped, and had to clench his mouth to keep his lip from trembling.

"Was Leon your only son?" Hackett asked quietly.

Corless cleared his throat. "Yes, my only boy. His mother died three years ago. So that leaves just me. Maybe it would have been better if it was me that sniper got, on the heights of Pingarrón."

He sipped his tea and smoked the last of his cigarette. There was sunlight in the window beside them, the smoke rolling through it in gray-blue coils.

"Tell me," Corless said, "do I know you? Your face is familiar."

Hackett did his froggy grin, his thin mouth stretching wide. "I arrested you one time, years ago."

"Oh, yes?" Corless said, with no surprise and not much interest; he had been arrested more often than he remembered. "For what?"

"You were mounting a one-man protest outside the Department of External Affairs.

141

I can't remember what the government had done to displease you. I was a sergeant then, in uniform. You threw an egg at the Minister's car. That was a step too far, and I had to take you in."

Corless grinned too. "I got off, though," he said. "I remember now."

"That's right. The judge let you go with a caution. You shook my hand on the way out of the court. I appreciated that."

"I hold it against no man for doing his job."

"Even a capitalist lackey wielding a truncheon?"

"I saw no truncheon."

They smoked in silence for a while, idly looking out the window at the passersby in the street. Hackett wondered what it would be like to lose a son. His two boys, men now, were in America, doing well for themselves. What if a telegram were to arrive with news that one of them had been found in a wrecked car, burnt to a shell of parchment wrapped around a few scorched bones? He pictured himself standing in the hall, with the telegram shaking in his hand, and May behind him crying her eyes out. Would he have to go over to America to identify the body? No, the surviving brother would do that, probably. They would fly the body back home, for burial in the graveyard at Lissenard, where all his people were buried, and where in time Hackett's own bones would be laid to rest.

Corless was lighting another Woodbine but had to stop first for a long bout of coughing. When he had got his breath back, he lit up and inhaled deeply. Nothing like a lungful of smoke to treat a cough like that, Hackett thought grimly.

"Can I ask, Mr. Corless," he said, "if you've given any more consideration to what Dr. Quirke said yesterday?"

"Dr. who?"

"The pathologist — he was with me yesterday when we came to your place to break the news."

"Oh, right. Him. What did he say? My memory of the past twenty-four hours is hazy."

"I'm sure it is, Mr. Corless." Hackett brought out a packet of Player's and lit one. "He mentioned the bang on the head that your son got, that seemed to him, well, highly suspicious."

Corless's eyes narrowed. When he shifted in his chair a waft of his smell came across the table. Hackett recognized it: it was the smell, clammy, dense, and hot, given off by every newly bereaved person he had come

143

across in his long career.

"Tell me the truth," Corless said, his voice turned gravelly. "Was my son killed deliberately? — was he murdered?"

It was some moments before Hackett replied. "I will tell you the truth," he said. "The fact is, it's not clear. Initial word is that it's possible there was petrol splashed into the car and set alight, but that's always a tricky judgment. The car had hit a tree, not very hard, it's true, but all the same it's possible the petrol tank burst on impact, which would explain why there were traces of fuel inside the car, on the seats."

"And what about this wound on his head, the one Dr. what's-his-name thinks was suspicious?"

"Aye, there's that. But again, we can't be sure. Your son might have had his head turned that way at the moment of impact, and it could be the mark of the steering wheel after he hit against it. But Dr. Quirke doesn't think that's the case, nor does Dr. Sinclair, his second-in-command."

"And what about you? What do you think?"

Hackett gave an elaborate shrug. "I'm not a medical man, Mr. Corless. I can only deal with hard evidence — with facts."

"What about — I don't know — footprints? Wouldn't there be footprints around if Leon was knocked out and had to be lifted into the car?"

"We've looked into that, of course, but there's nothing conclusive. The car left the road at a sharp angle and ran down a slope. If your son was the victim of a violent attack, it probably happened on the road, so there'd be no marks left behind, or not ones we could distinguish from the usual wear and tear — that road through the park is a busy one. And then again, your son might have been knocked unconscious elsewhere, and driven in his own car up to the park and transferred to the driving seat unconscious. This is all speculation, you understand. If there was firm evidence of foul play, the fire saw to it that it didn't survive. There's only the blow to the head, if it was a blow, and the possibility that petrol was poured into the car before it was let go running down the slope." He rolled the tip of his cigarette on the rim of the ashtray, sharpening the burning ash to a pencil point. "So the question we have to concentrate on is the question of motive. Your son doesn't seem to me the kind of young fellow that would have enemies, or at any rate enemies of a kind that would want to kill him, and have the nerve to do it."

Corless was gazing into his cup, where the tea, cold now, had developed a shiny skin on the surface, like a miniature petrol spill. Hackett was impressed by the man's self-control, more impressed today, indeed, than he had been yesterday when he'd first broken the news to him of his son's death.

Hackett was familiar with the grief of others, for he had seen much of it, too much, in his time. It took many forms. Some people wept, some cried out, a few even tore open their clothes and clawed at their own flesh. One woman, newly widowed after a burglary, had thrown herself violently at Hackett and beat at his face with her fists, and he had been forced to restrain her. Others, a rare few, held on to themselves as if they were holding on for dear life to a thrumming rope or a heavy hawser; Corless was among them. He was a tough man, a stalwart man; Hackett saw that clearly.

Now Corless stirred himself. "So what you're thinking," he said, "is that if someone murdered Leon, it must have been an enemy not of his, but of mine. Am I right?"

Hackett gave him a level look. "Would you say you have that kind of enemy, Mr. Corless?"

Corless leaned back in his chair and lit yet another Woodbine. He had the working-man's furtive way of smoking, cupping the cigarette in his palm with the lighted end turned inwards.

"The thing about enemies," he said, "is that half the time you don't even know you have them. Three months before Trotsky was assassinated, there'd been an armed attack on his house in Coyoacán, outside Mexico City, by Stalin's agents. You'd think that would have made him take care who he trusted, wouldn't you. Then a fellow called Ramón Mercader turned up and wormed his way into the Trotsky household, saying he was a committed revolutionary, and all the rest of it, though in fact he was one of Stalin's agents. One day, while Trotsky was sitting at a table reading some article Mercader had pointed out to him, Mercader whipped an axe out of his raincoat pocket and split open Trotsky's skull." He took a deep drag on his cigarette, shutting one eye against the smoke. "Are there people who hate me enough to kill my son? I don't know. Probably there are. But if you're asking do I know someone in particular who has that kind of a grudge against me, the answer is no. I'm no Trotsky, whatever Archbishop McQuaid and his big battalions may say."

He crushed his half-smoked cigarette into

the ashtray on the table and stood up. "And now," he said, "if you don't mind, I'm going home."

"Will you be all right?"

"All right? I doubt it. I've lost my son. It doesn't leave me much to live for, but I suppose I'll survive."

Hackett went to the counter and paid the bill, then fetched his hat from the hat stand. They went out into the sunlight. Car roofs gleamed; the tarred road shimmered.

"You know," Hackett said, "you lost that battle, over in Spain. But your people won the war — the real one."

Corless didn't look at him, and glanced about the street instead. He was turning the Zippo lighter in his fingers.

"I suppose they did," he said. "But what did it mean, in the end?"

"It meant, Mr. Corless, that you and I, and a lot of others, are free men today."

Corless did his thin smile.

"Free?" he said. "My son, Leon, thought he was free. And look at him now."

He began to turn away, but not before Hackett had put out a hand. Corless looked at it, then at Hackett. "It's not often I'm invited to shake the hand at the end of the long arm of the law," he said.

Hackett grinned. "You did it once before,

148

why not again?"

Self-consciously they shook hands.

"The heights of Pingarrón," Hackett said. "I'll remember that."

9

Quirke could not remember when he had last been in Hackett's office, a cramped, wedge-shaped room high up under the roof of the Garda station in Pearse Street. Nothing had changed in the meantime. The desk was still cluttered with what seemed the same papers that had always been there, the calendar hanging by a nail on the wall was still years out of date, the window behind Hackett's chair was still painted shut. There was even that same brownish smudge high up on the wall where someone had once squashed a bluebottle. Hackett's shiny blue suit, too, seemed the one he had been wearing since Quirke had first known him. Now he had taken off his jacket and hung it on the back of his chair, and was sitting in his shirtsleeves, leaning back with his feet on the desk.

"So anyway," he said, "this girl, this Lisa Smith, has disappeared, right?"

"She spotted Phoebe in a café. According to Phoebe she was terrified, but wouldn't say why. Phoebe brought her down to Malachy Griffin's holiday place in Wicklow, in Ballytubber, and left her there, safe, so she thought. Then I don't know what happened — Phoebe got nervous, had a premonition, I don't know, but she went back down, and when she did, the girl was gone."

"Gone?"

"I told you — vanished."

"And didn't go of her own free will, you think."

"I don't know what to think. Phoebe believes someone came and got her, someone she knew — probably the person she was terrified of, would be my guess."

"Why would she go with someone she was afraid of?"

"I don't know."

Hackett nodded, thinking. "And Lisa Smith was with Leon Corless before he drove up to the Phoenix Park?"

"They were coming home from a party and had a fight, and she made him let her out of the car, and he drove on, going home to Castleknock, I suppose, on the other side of the park. She was waiting for a taxi when the car went on fire — she saw the glow of the flames and went up to look, but then

151

got frightened when she saw what had happened, and ran off."

Hackett joined the fingers and thumbs of both hands at the tips in front of himself and gazed off dreamily at a corner of the ceiling. "And she's in the family way, with Corless's child?"

"Phoebe believes it's Corless's, yes."

Hackett nodded slowly, his lower lip pushed far out. "And tell me, Doctor," he said, "what are we supposed to make out of all this?"

"Well, that's the question, isn't it."

Quirke got out his silver case and his lighter and lit a cigarette. Hackett watched him. "Do you know what," he said, "I'm thinking of giving up the fags."

Quirke stared at him. "Why would you do that?"

"The lungs are in a terrible state. You should hear me in the evening, before I go to bed, wheezing like an old steam train, and then next day I have a cough that shakes the windowpanes. Plus the wife is at me night, noon, and morning to give them up."

"Not easy," Quirke said, blowing smoke towards the ceiling. "Not easy giving anything up."

Hackett took his feet from the desk and

leaned forward, fiddling among the raft of papers in front of him. "No," he said, "no, we like our little indulgences, don't we." They were both thinking of Quirke's drinking, and his repeated sojourns at the Hospital of St. John of the Cross.

"The girl lives where, did you say?" Hackett said. "Rathmines, was it? Have you the address? Maybe we should take a gander at the place. I'll get Jenkins to bring the car round." He stood up and put on his jacket, then stopped. "Or no, I won't — it's Saturday — young Jenkins will be at home with the wife and kiddies. I'll see who else is on."

They went downstairs to the duty office.

"Is Jenkins married?" Quirke asked. "He looks about nineteen."

Hackett chuckled. "He's young, right enough. He must have been a child bride."

Eventually a driver was found. He was a thin-faced fellow with bad teeth and an unruly slick of fair hair raked back along his skull. He looked even younger than Jenkins, and the outsized uniform he was wearing made him seem younger still.

"Who are you?" Hackett said.

"Wallace, sir."

"Is that your first name or your last?"

The young man frowned warily. "That's my second name, sir."

"Right, then, Garda Wallace. I hope you're old enough to have a driving license?"

"I am, sir."

Hackett sighed. "That was a joke," he said. "Come on."

Quirke and the detective sat together in the back seat. It was hot, and the air was laden with dust and the smells of the city.

"The farmers are praying for rain," Hackett said. "No doubt the good Lord will heed them, sooner or later. They have a powerful voice in heaven, the tillers of the soil."

They came to the canal, and soon were passing by Portobello Bridge. Quirke looked across the water and saw Isabel Galloway's little house. He thought of the first night he had spent there. At a late hour, while Isabel slept, he had got up from her bed and leaned by the window, looking out into the moonlit night, and had seen two swans paddling these waters side by side, unreal-seeming creatures, pale enough to be their own ghosts.

He should ring Isabel. He had treated her badly, dropping out of her life without a word. She had said she loved him. Love, Quirke had long ago decided, was a word people used when their own emotions overwhelmed them and they felt helpless. It was like saying someone was a genius, or a saint, as if at a certain point a barrier was crossed and ordinary human standards no longer applied.

"When I came down here first to work," Hackett said, "straight out of the training depot at Templemore, the city seemed to me a mighty place, bigger than anything I could ever have imagined. I'd get dizzy just seeing so many people in the streets, all of them rushing around, going places, bumping into each other and cursing and hurrying on. Where I came from, no one was ever in a hurry — where would they have been hurrying to?" He shifted on the seat. His hat was balanced on his knees, and he drummed his fingers on the brim. Quirke guessed he was craving a cigarette. "It didn't take me long to realize, though, that this place is just another village. Look at this business with young Corless. He dies in the middle of the night, and the very next day your daughter meets his girlfriend."

"Phoebe didn't meet Lisa Smith," Quirke said. "Lisa Smith came to her. And I'm not sure it was such a coincidence as it seems."

Hackett glanced at him sidelong. "How so?"

"They'd been in a training course together. Maybe Lisa Smith knew who Phoebe was, maybe she knew she was my daughter,

155

and that I knew you. Our names have been in the papers, yours and mine."

"By the Lord Harry," Hackett said, laughing, "if that's the case, she certainly chose a complicated way of seeking the help of the law. She could have gone into any Garda barracks and told them who she was and asked for shelter."

"Phoebe said she was frightened, that's why she was looking for a place to hide."

"She didn't stay in hiding for long."

"You think she left Ballytubber of her own free will?"

"I don't know what else to think. Who knew she was down there, except your daughter?"

They were on Rathmines Road now. There was little traffic. Three-quarters of the way up, they turned right onto a narrow side street of tall, red-brick terraced houses and stopped at No. 17. The street on both sides was lined with cars, and Wallace had to go off in search of somewhere to park. Quirke and the Inspector stood on the pavement and looked up at the house. It had a dingy aspect. The windows were grimy, and tattered lace curtains hung crookedly in a few of them.

"An insalubrious establishment, by the look of it," Hackett said.

There was a panel of electric bell pushes beside the door, but either the labels accompanying them were blank or the names were smudged. Hackett shrugged, and pressed the second-floor bell. They waited, but no one came. Next he pressed the bell for the ground floor. They heard it ringing faintly inside. After a moment, at the window nearest to them, the curtain twitched and a pale, pinched face looked out at them and quickly withdrew. Time passed. Hackett pressed the bell again, and kept his finger on it. Eventually the door opened a little way and there appeared in the crack the same pale, anxious face they had seen at the window.

"Good morning," Hackett said, in his special, detective's voice. "We're looking for a Lisa Smith. Do you know is she in?"

The head shook. It seemed to belong to a young man, though it might as easily have been a young woman's. "No Lisa Smith here," it said.

Hackett put his hand against the door and pushed, gently but firmly. The figure inside resisted, then stepped back, and the door swung open. A smell of frying bacon came from somewhere at the rear of the house.

The person in the hall was definitely a young man. He wore a dirty white singlet

and a pair of extremely dirty khaki shorts.
He was barefoot. He had buck teeth and a
bad case of acne. He looked uncertainly at
the two men standing on the doorstep.

"And you are?" Hackett said.

"How do you mean?" the young man
asked suspiciously.

"I mean" — very slowly and deliberately
— "what is your name?"

"Prentice. Why?"

Hackett smiled with his teeth. "Because I
always like to know the name of the person
I'm speaking to. Now: Lisa Smith. You say
she doesn't live here?"

"Are you from the landlord?" the young
man asked suspiciously.

"We are not from the landlord, no. But
you could tell me the landlord's name, and
where I might find him."

Prentice's initial anxiety was abating, and
he had taken on a cocky look. "Who's asking?" he said, with the beginnings of a sneer.

"I'm Detective Inspector Hackett, and
this" — indicating Quirke — "is my associate."

The young man swallowed, his Adam's
apple bobbing. He turned to Quirke.
"What's going on?" he said.

Quirke made no reply. Hackett's smile was
hardening by the moment.

"What's going on," he said, "is what I already told you. We're inquiring after a young lady by the name of Lisa Smith."

Prentice shook his head. "I told you, there's no one lives here by that name."

Hackett sighed. He was a forbearing, slow-moving man, but there were times when he felt his patience sorely tried. This young fellow, in his filthy undershirt and shorts, was not particularly offensive, certainly not as offensive as some of the members of the public it had fallen to the detective to question in his time, yet there was something about him, something of the ferret, or the stoat, that was distinctly unappealing.

"All right," Hackett said, keeping his voice calm and low. "Then tell me the name of the landlord, and where he can be found."

"I only know the fellow who comes for the rent."

"And what's *his* name?"

"Abercrombie."

Quirke and Hackett looked at each other. Hackett turned back to the young man in the doorway. "Abercrombie," he said, in a flat voice. "The rent collector's name is Abercrombie."

"That's right. I don't know his first name."

"Abercrombie," Hackett said again. "Real people haven't got names like Abercrombie.

You wouldn't be pulling my leg, would you?"

"That's his name!" the young man said indignantly. "I swear."

Hackett shrugged. "All right," he said. "And we'd find him where?"

"He has a room over a chip shop down there." He gestured in the direction of Rathmines Road. "It's called Luigi's. It's just around the corner."

"And Mr. Abercrombie lives upstairs, does he?"

The young man tittered. "I'd say it's more that he roosts there than lives. It's some kip."

Hackett was about to say something more, but instead he abruptly snapped shut his traplike mouth and stalked off.

"Is he really a detective?" the young man asked as Quirke was turning away. He did his squeaky little laugh again. "Old Crombie will have a heart attack."

Quirke followed Hackett and caught up with him at the corner. Hackett shook his head. "The youth of today," he said, "God help us."

They turned to the left and spotted the sign for Luigi's a little way down.

"Tell me something," Quirke said as they walked along. "Do you ever take a day off?"

"A day off?" Hackett seemed to consider

this a comical question. "I do indeed. I'm a keen fisherman, did you not know that? I often take the rod and line and drive down to Wicklow, or over to the west, sometimes — powerful fishing over there, in Connemara. And what about yourself? You seem to me to be always on the job."

"What job do you mean?"

Hackett grinned. "The job of being curious. Isn't that what drives the two of us, me and you alike? We're fierce inquisitive men, it seems to me."

Quirke was silent. He was struck by Hackett's words. In his estimation of himself, he was no more curious or inquiring than the next man. Yet perhaps Hackett was right. Why else was he here, on this bright summer morning, traipsing these grimy streets in the detective's flat-footed wake, in search of a girl who so far as he knew didn't want to be found? He was aware of no great thirst in himself for justice and the righting of wrongs. He had no illusions that the world could be set to rights, at least not by him, who could not even set right his own life.

What drove him, he believed, was the absence of a past. When he looked back, when he tried to look back, to his earliest days, there was only a blank space. He didn't know who he was, where he came from, who had fathered him, who his mother had been. He could almost see himself, a child standing alone in the midst of a vast, bare plain, with nothing behind him but darkness and storm. And so he was here, on the trail of another lost creature.

The chip shop was closed; it only opened at nighttime. They stood back to survey the building, if a building it could be called. It was hardly more than a lean-to made of bricks. The shop was a single room with a big window and a high, steel counter at the back. Perched on top of it was another brick box, tiny, with a single window giving onto the street, and led up to by a set of concrete steps at the side. At the top of the steps was a narrow door, the bottom of which was being eaten away by wet rot. Hackett rapped with his knuckles on the wood. They waited. Quirke wondered how much of the detective's life was spent standing at doors, stolid, patient, inexpectant.

They heard footsteps within, and a loud belch. "Who's there?" a voice demanded.

"Open up," Hackett said gruffly.

"Who are you?" The voice was very close to the door now. "What's your business?"

"I'm a detective. Open up."

There was a long silence, then a rattle of chains and bolts, and the door was opened.

Abercrombie was a large, gaunt, bald man with a stoop. He wore a collarless shirt of striped cotton and a pair of ancient black trousers, shiny with dirt, held up by a pair of brown braces. He had small dark eyes and large hairy ears, the lobes of which hung down like dewlaps. The braces were too short, so that the trousers were hoisted up tight at the crotch and the cuffs hardly reached to his ankles, showing off the bottoms of a pair of woolen long johns in obvious need of washing. He was chewing something, very slowly, his lower jaw moving in a circular motion, like the jaw of a cow chewing its cud.

"Mr. Abercrombie?" Hackett said.

The man stopped chewing. "Who are you?"

Hackett introduced himself and Quirke. Abercrombie, who had resumed chewing, looked from one of them to the other without expression.

"Do you think we might step inside for a minute?" Hackett said.

Abercrombie thought about this for some moments, then stood aside to let them enter.

The room smelled of a number of things, mainly dog. There was a table, covered with old newspapers, on which stood the remains of a meal — a smeared plate, a mug, a beer bottle, the heel of a turnover loaf. Under the table was an old tartan rug, and on this lay a small, shapeless dog with brown-and-white fur and tiny, black, feverish eyes. At the sight of the two strangers it set up a high-pitched yapping. "Shut up to hell out of that!" Abercrombie shouted, stamping his foot, and the dog stopped yapping and whimpered instead. Above the table was a large framed print of a pink-lipped, effeminate Christ coyly displaying a dripping, crimson heart bound in a wreath of thorns and shooting out flames at the top. Below it, mounted on a small wooden bracket, was a perpetual Sacred Heart bulb, the glowing element of which was in the shape of a cross.

Abercrombie picked up the bread and tore off a lump and tossed it to the dog. He turned to Hackett. "You're a detective, you say?" He sounded skeptical.

"That's right," Hackett said.

The dog gave the crust a disdainful sniff and went back to staring vengefully at the two intruders.

"Is it about them bikes?" Abercrombie asked.

"No," Hackett said, "it's not about bikes."

"It must be the darkie, then, is it? He told me he was a medical student. You know he skipped off with three months' rent owing?"

Hackett had a way of standing with his feet planted somewhat apart and his chin sunk on his chest, his thin lower lip protruding. It made him look all the more like a squat, blue-skinned frog. "What I'm here about," he said, "is a young woman by the name of Lisa Smith. She's a tenant in number seventeen, around the corner."

"Lisa who?" Abercrombie growled. "Never heard of her."

Hackett glanced at Quirke.

"She does have a flat there," Quirke said.

Abercrombie glowered at him. "Who says?"

"She was there last night, briefly."

"Oh, she was there *briefly,* was she?" Abercrombie said, with large sarcasm. "Well, whether she was or not, she don't live there. There's no one by that name in number seventeen."

Quirke could not decide which was the more unsettling, the dog's venomous regard or Christ's wistful, wounded gaze.

"You collect the rents there, is that right?" Hackett said.

"I do," Abercrombie answered. "I look after the place generally, to make sure the bowsies living there don't tear it apart. They're a crowd of savages, the lot of them. The Trinity students are the worst." He

165

glanced at Quirke for a second with sour amusement, taking in his handmade shoes, his silk shirt, his expensive linen jacket. "The quality never has any respect for other people's property." He turned to Hackett again. "Who is she, this one — what's her name, Smith?"

"She's someone we need to have a word with," Hackett said. "Are you sure you don't know her? Dr. Quirke here will describe her."

Quirke tried to remember what Phoebe had said. Dark hair, green eyes, pale complexion. "She's in her early twenties," he said. "Probably works as a secretary, something like that."

Abercrombie was eyeing him again with lively contempt. "A secretary in her twenties," he said. "That narrows it down, all right, here in Rathmines."

Quirke took out his cigarette case. He saw Hackett's look of longing, and lifted an inquiring eyebrow. Hackett nodded. Quirke gave him a cigarette.

"I'll take one of them," Abercrombie said. "Then it'll be a real powwow."

The dog under the table sneezed, making a curiously prim, muffled sound.

"How many tenants are there in the house?" Hackett asked.

Abercrombie, savoring his cigarette, gazed at the ceiling for a moment, his lips moving as he counted silently. "Sixteen," he said. "Four of them are sharing, and there's a married couple — they say they're married, anyway. The darkie made seventeen, but he did a flit, like I said."

"Are there any females at all, in their early twenties, living there?" Quirke asked.

Abercrombie, glancing aside, shook his head. Quirke was convinced he was lying. But why would he lie? Abercrombie looked at Quirke again, then at Hackett. "What do you want her for, anyway?" he asked.

"It's a serious matter," Hackett said. "Did you hear it on the news, or see it in the paper, about that crash in the Phoenix Park on Thursday night? Lisa Smith was acquainted with the young man who died."

Abercrombie's expression did not change. Quirke and the detective watched him closely. "I told you," Abercrombie said, "there's no one by that name in number seventeen. Now, can I finish my dinner?"

Hackett sighed. He knew this moment well: the frustrating, the infuriating, moment when, convinced he was being lied to, he could do nothing about it except retreat and try to devise some way of catching out the liar another time, by some means other than straightforward questioning.

"Thanks for your time," he said, turning away.

Abercrombie made no move to accompany them to the door, only stood there at a stoop in the middle of his foul-smelling domain and watched them with a sardonic eye as they filed out. The last thing Quirke saw as he shut the door behind them was the sickly, candy-pink glow of the Sacred Heart light and the soft-bearded image above it, following him with its sorrowfully accusing gaze.

They went down the steps to the street, and Hackett looked about. "We forgot about Wallace," he said. "He's probably after driving around half of south County Dublin, looking for us."

They walked back to the corner and turned into the street of red-brick houses. The squad car was double-parked outside No. 17. Wallace, spotting them in the rear-view mirror, hopped out eagerly and began opening doors for them.

"Did you believe him — Abercrombie?" Quirke asked, as they settled themselves again in the back seat.

"No. Did you?"

They turned away from each other, as the car pulled ahead, and each gazed out of his window, wondering why they had been lied to.

"Abercrombie," Hackett said. "If you'd seen that joker in the street, now, would you have imagined he had a name like that?"

Quirke smiled, and didn't bother to reply.

10

That evening Quirke took Phoebe to dinner at the Russell Hotel. It was their favorite place in town, although Phoebe always fretted about the cost. They went through a routine each time they came there to dine. Phoebe would scan the menu and shake her head at the prices and say they were disgraceful, to which Quirke would reply that they were exactly the same as they had been the last time they were here, and that anyway a lady should never read a menu from right to left. If she persisted, he would close the exchange by pretending to take umbrage and saying that it was his money and he would spend it as he wished, and that one of the ways he wished to spend it was on treating his daughter to a decent dinner. And then they would smile at each other, and the evening would have officially begun.

The waiter came and they ordered, grouse

for Quirke and fish for Phoebe.

"You remind me of your mother when you argue with me about money," Quirke said to her. "You narrow your eyes and purse your mouth in just the way she used to do."

"I wish you'd talk about her more," Phoebe said.

"Do you? I don't know what I could tell you. I remember her in a strange way."

"Strange?"

"I'm not sure it's really her I'm remembering. In my memory she has become a kind of — I don't know — a kind of mythical figure." He smiled, a touch sheepishly. "She's my legend, you could say."

"She's very beautiful, in her photographs."

"Yes, she was lovely." He frowned, running his fingers over the tablecloth, feeling its texture. "She had the most wonderful skin, smooth as silk, and always cool, somehow, even in the hottest weather."

The waiter brought the bottle of Chablis that Quirke had ordered, displayed the label and drew out the cork and tipped a drop into Quirke's glass. Quirke tasted, nodded, the wine was poured, the waiter went away. Quirke always savored this little ritual; it was like a children's game that grown-ups were still allowed to play.

Father and daughter clinked glasses.

171

Phoebe had on her black dress with the lace collar. She never wore jewelry.

"This is the first drink I've had all week," Quirke said; it was only a white lie. "I hope you're proud of me."

Their first course arrived. They were both having smoked salmon.

"Did you know the Russell started up as a temperance hotel?" Quirke said. "Sir Somebody Russell opened it in — I can't remember when. He was very hot on the fight against the demon drink."

Phoebe arched an eyebrow. "Well," she said, "I imagine Sir Somebody has been doing a lot of turning in his grave in the meantime."

Quirke pushed his plate away and leaned back in his chair, the wine already spreading its warm tendrils along his veins. "This is about the last place in Dublin that makes real turtle soup," he said, "did you know that?"

He could see she wasn't listening. Her mood had darkened suddenly. She too had pushed her plate away, and sat with her eyes lowered, fiddling with the remains of a bread roll.

"What are we going to do?" she said in a low, urgent voice. "Whatever that man said to you, Lisa does live there. I was in her flat

— her things were there."

He had told her how he and Inspector Hackett had gone to Rathmines, how they had talked to the young man in the dirty undershirt and afterwards to Abercrombie, and how both men had insisted they knew nothing of any Lisa Smith.

"If she does live there," Quirke said, "she must have given you a false name. You said yourself her name didn't sound convincing."

They drank their wine. A waitress came and took away their plates, and the waiter returned and refilled their wine glasses. The dining room had no windows, and the air was close and uncomfortably warm. Quirke loosened his tie and unbuttoned his shirt collar. His thoughts went back to Delia and her pale, cool skin. His brief time with her had been a kind of ecstatic torment. She had been his obsession; he couldn't get enough of her. She knew it, and would withhold herself, just for the pleasure of seeing him squirm, of having him plead. Had she ever loved him? For a brief time, he supposed; otherwise why would she have married him? He had never understood her. What he had said to Phoebe wasn't really true. Delia wasn't a legend; she was an enigma. His sphinx, beautiful, desperately loved, and malign.

Their main courses arrived.

"Will you see if you can get a list of the people who were in that course with you?" Quirke said. "Maybe one of the names will jog your memory."

Phoebe hadn't touched her main course. "I'm convinced something bad has happened to her," she said.

"You don't know that. Maybe she changed her mind about staying at the house. Maybe she was frightened there, more frightened than she already was, and left and went somewhere else — maybe she even came back to Dublin."

"How could she? She had no car — I drove her down, remember."

"She could have got a hackney cab."

Phoebe shook her head. "No, no," she said. "There wasn't a trace of her having been there. She wouldn't have done that herself, would she?"

"Maybe she's obsessively tidy?"

"No," Phoebe said again, more vehemently this time. "Someone had made sure there wasn't a mark left to show she'd been there. She just disappeared, as if —"

A couple had appeared in the doorway, and stopped there a moment to survey the room. The man was in black tie. He was in his late twenties, perhaps, boyish-looking, with thin fair hair and a sharp, clever-seeming face. The woman was older, in her forties, a little on the heavy side, but attractively so, with a broad face and large, dark eyes. Her hair was prematurely streaked with gray, and cut in an untidy line just below her ears. She had, to Quirke's eye, what he could only define as a dignified beauty. Her gaze fell on Phoebe, and she smiled.

"Oh," Phoebe murmured, "it's —"

The woman said something to the young man, and together they approached the table. Phoebe stood up. "Dr. Blake!" she said. "What a surprise!"

"Good evening, Phoebe," the woman said. "How nice to see you."

She had a slight foreign accent. She looked at Quirke. He stood up.

"This is — this is my father," Phoebe said.

"Ah. How do you do, Mr. Griffin."

"It's Quirke, actually," Quirke said. "How do you do."

They shook hands. He hadn't met her before. Her eyes, up close, were extraordinary, two great still pools of darkness. Quirke felt he had never been looked at in this way before; indeed, it was as if he were being looked at for the first time in his life, and he was unnerved.

"This is Paul Viertel," the woman said, indicating the young man. "Paul, this is Phoebe, the person I told you about, who works with me. And this is Mr. — Mr. Quirke."

Paul Viertel had a surprisingly firm handshake, though his fingers were long and slender, like a woman's.

"How do you do, Mr. Quirke," he said. He too had an accent, more pronounced than the woman's. German, Quirke thought, or else Austrian; he wouldn't be able to tell the difference. The young man turned to Phoebe. "Miss — Griffin, yes?"

"Yes," Phoebe said, stammering a little, "Phoebe, Phoebe Griffin."

"I knew your late husband," Quirke said to the woman.

"Yes, you did, of course. I had forgotten."

It was strange, Quirke thought afterwards, how for that moment it seemed as if there were only the two of them in the room, himself and this large, dark-eyed, oddly lovely woman, gazing at him out of what seemed a vast, inner stillness.

The headwaiter appeared, chafing his hands anxiously, and apologized to the newcomers for not having been there to greet them on their arrival. The woman, Dr.

Blake, turned to him, faintly smiling. "It's nothing," she said, and he too, Quirke saw, felt himself singled out, and marked, somehow, fleetingly. Dr. Blake glanced back at the others. "I'm sorry, we have interrupted your meal." She touched a fingertip to Phoebe's elbow. "Please, do sit. Perhaps we shall see you later, before you leave."

As they moved away, Paul Viertel turned back for a second and smiled at Phoebe and gave a small, quick bow.

Seated again, Quirke felt oddly discomposed. It was as if a sudden gust of wind had blown through the room, leaving everything slightly disturbed in its wake, including him.

"I didn't realize you'd never met her before," Phoebe said.

"Yes," Quirke said distractedly. "I only knew her husband from the hospital, and not very well anyway. He was a surgeon, so our paths didn't cross very often. He drank, I think." He picked at what remained of the grouse; the meat was tough and had little taste. He drank his wine. He should have had red, to go with the game. His hand, he noticed, was not quite steady. "Is she — is she easy to work for?" he asked.

Phoebe raised her eyebrows. "Easy? I suppose she is." She smiled. "She's certainly a change from Mrs. Cuffe-Wilkes and her awful hats."

"Are they awful, the hats? I thought you liked them."

"They're just silly, like Mrs. Cuffe-Wilkes. Dr. Blake, on the other hand, is certainly not silly."

"Yes, she seems" — he groped for the word — "she seems formidable." He pushed his plate aside, feeling slightly queasy now at the look of it, the mess of meat and smeared blood and tiny, dark bones. He lit a cigarette. "Who's the young man?"

"I don't know. A relative, don't you think?"

"He sounded foreign."

"Yes. Austrian, probably, like Dr. Blake."

"What did she say his name was?"

"Feertel, something like that." She looked at him closely. "Are you all right?"

"I'm fine. Why?"

"You look — I don't know. Peculiar."

"The food didn't agree with me." He glanced about for the waiter. "I think I'll have a brandy — it always settles my innards."

She made a comically accusing face, letting her shoulders and the corners of her mouth droop. "Oh, Quirke," she said, "you're such a child."

"What do you mean?"

"If you want a brandy, have a brandy. I think you shouldn't, I really think you shouldn't, but if you do, at least don't lie to yourself about it."

Stung, he glared at her, then shrugged, and smiled ruefully.

"All right," he said, "I won't have a brandy."

"You've done so well," she said, smiling, "please don't give in now."

He looked into her face, into her eyes, her mother's eyes, and felt a slow, wavelike spasm in the region of his diaphragm, and something heavy and warm welled up in him, as if he might be about to burst into tears. The feeling lasted no more than a second or two, but he recognized it. It was something that happened to him now and then, at unexpected moments. Anything could provoke it, a soft word spoken kindly, a sudden poignant memory, a woman's voice heard from another room, or just the look of things, a splashy sunset, a view on a winter morning of some known place transfigured in a mist, a gleam of April light on a rained-on road — anything. It was as if, deep inside him, deep beyond his knowing, there was a still, bottomless pool of longing, of sorrow, of tenderness, out of which on

179

these occasions there rose up, unbidden, a bright and irresistible splash, rose, and fell back again, back into those secret and forever hidden depths.

A stranger; he was a stranger to himself.

But oh, how he yearned for a real drink: for many real drinks.

When they had finished and were leaving, the way out led past the table where Dr. Blake and the young man were seated. Dr. Blake looked up at them out of those dark, calm eyes. She had the air, Quirke thought, of some large, locked place, a castle keep, or a sequestered monastery where vigils were held, and nightlong meditations, and silent ceremonials at dawn.

He caught himself up. Where were such fanciful thoughts coming from?

"I hope you enjoyed your dinner?" Dr. Blake said, looking up at him.

"Yes, yes," Quirke answered, "it was fine, it was very good."

At this she only smiled, as if gently dismissing something superfluous. Her large hands were folded on the tablecloth in front of her, one on top of the other, like a pair of slumbering animals. The fair young man smiled too, but at Phoebe. "Good evening," he said to her, in his clipped accent. "I hope we meet again."

They were at the front door of the hotel before Phoebe's blushes finally began to fade.

11

Quirke bought the Sunday papers from the newsstand outside the church on Haddington Road, and strolled down to the canal in the sunshine by way of Percy Place. He walked along the towpath until he came to his favorite bench under the trees, and sat down. A crowd of boys were out already, swimming from the lock at Mount Street Bridge. He lit a cigarette and watched them idly for a while, skinny, dough-pale creatures in sagging togs, loud and cheerful, and foul-mouthed as dockers. The more daring ones preferred to jump feet-first from the parapet of the bridge, holding their noses and flopping into the water like frogs. They were often here at weekends, and he marveled at their resistance to the countless species of microbes that must be swarming in this filthy water, afloat as it was with assorted garbage and the odd dead dog.

He was reading a long report about improving relations between America and Hungary when he heard the sound of footsteps. Looking up, he was surprised to see Rose Griffin approaching along the towpath.

"Well," she said, "don't you look the picture of ease, sitting here among beechen shade and shadows numberless." She sat down beside him. "That's Keats, by the way, in case you didn't recognize it." She wore a pale cream sleeveless dress and gold-painted sandals, and was carrying a small, white leather handbag. "Got a cigarette?"

He held the lighter for her and she leaned down to the flame, touching the tip of one finger to the back of his hand and glancing up at him from under her lashes.

"Is this a coincidence?" he asked.

"Oh, no. I knew this was your haunt on Sunday mornings. Didn't you use to meet Sarah here?"

Sarah was Mal's late wife, whom Quirke had loved, or had thought he did.

"Yes, she used to come round sometimes, after she'd been to Mass."

"That's right — she was very devout, was Sarah. Her God rewarded her well, didn't he, giving her that brain tumor." She smiled at him. "You were awfully fond of Sarah, weren't you. I was always a little jealous. You had all of us running after you, you

183

cruel man."

He laughed. "What was it you said to me once, about us being alike, you and I? Cold heart and a hot soul — that was how you described us."

"Did I? I don't remember. But I guess it's about right. My Lord, look at that boy, how thin he is — don't they feed their kids around here?"

"They come up from Ringsend. The unkillable children of the poor." He glanced at her with a sly grin. "That's Ezra Pound, by the way."

"Touché, then. You always were well-read."

"No, I'm not. I'm a magpie; I pick up bright scraps and store them away, to impress people later."

"And, of course, we're so easily impressed."

They smoked their cigarettes and watched the boys at play. Rose crossed her knees and let one sandal dangle from her long-toed, shapely foot.

"Have you settled back into all your other old haunts?" she asked without looking at him. He could hear that she was still annoyed at him for moving out of the house on Ailesbury Road so abruptly.

"Settling in is not a thing I do very well," he said.

"But you must be glad to be back in that apartment of yours," she said. "So much livelier than our old place." She paused. "Mal misses you, you know. He was shocked, the way you left like that."

"I'm sorry," Quirke said. "I suppose it seemed ungrateful."

"Oh, we don't require gratitude. We were glad to have you there — we were glad to help."

He turned to her and studied her profile. Still she would not look at him, but kept her eyes on the raucous swimmers.

"What's the matter, Rose?" he said. "It's not just me moving out, is it?"

She said nothing for a while. There was something uncanny in the unwavering gaze she kept trained on the boys at the lock.

"Come round to lunch today," she said at last. "We won't try to hold on to you, or shut you into a room. Mal would like to see you. He has things to talk to you about."

"What sort of things?"

"Oh, I'll let him tell you himself."

She dropped the butt of the cigarette on the gravel and trod on it with the heel of her sandal, then stood up. "By the way," she said, "I almost forgot." She unclasped her handbag and opened it. "I was going through some old things and found this."

She handed him a photograph, faded and badly creased at one corner. It showed him and Mal, in tennis whites, each with an arm around the other's shoulder, smiling into the camera. There were trees behind them and, in the distance, a tall white building. It had been taken in Boston, where Mal and he had studied medicine together.

"My God," he said, "that must be, what, nearly twenty-five years ago?"

"Yes, and don't you two boys look happy."

He glanced up at her from where he sat, the newspapers scattered on the dry ground at his feet.

"What time shall I come?" he asked.

"Oh, whenever. We tend not to keep fixed hours anymore, Mal and I. We just take things as they come."

He tried to return the photograph to her, but she shook her head. "You keep it. Put it in your wallet and just keep it."

They gazed at each other for a long moment, then Rose reached out a hand and touched his face. "The years run on," she said, "don't they." Then she turned and walked quickly away, with her head down.

He went out on foot to Ailesbury Road. It

was a walk of half an hour or so. By noon the heat of the day was intense, and he was glad of his straw hat and his light linen jacket. He had felt like a truant when he left Mal and Rose's house, and a pleasurably guilty sensation of freedom still persisted. His time was his own, and he could do entirely as he wished. Not that Mal or Rose had required anything of him while he was staying with them, yet he realized now how oppressed he had felt in the weeks when he was there, at their house. Why had he given in and let them take him over in the first place? Fear, he supposed. He hadn't quite trusted Philbin's diagnosis of his mental confusions and blackouts, and if he was going to die, he didn't want to die alone. But it seemed now that Philbin had been right, and that he wasn't going to die, and despite himself he savored the quickened sense of life his reprieve had given him.

It was Maisie who answered the doorbell.

"Good day to you, Dr. Quirke," she said. "And isn't it a grand fine day?"

"It is, Maisie, it's a beautiful day."

She took his panama hat and led him through the house, along the absurdly ornate hallway.

"How are you getting on, Maisie?" he asked.

"Oh, I'm getting on grand, Doctor," she said. "Dr. Griffin is a lovely man."

The pointed avoidance of Rose's name made Quirke smile to himself; he could guess what Maisie thought of the mistress of the house.

"Here," he said, "I brought you something." He handed her a packet of twenty Player's. "You're not to say I gave them to you, mind. You shouldn't be smoking at all."

Maisie blushed and grinned and slipped the cigarettes into the pocket of her apron.

"You have me spoiled, so you have, Dr. Quirke."

Maisie's child, hers and her own father's, had been born in the Mother of Mercy Laundry and immediately taken away from her and sent she never knew where — to America, probably, for adoption by a Catholic family there. Quirke supposed it had been for the best. How would she have survived in the world, unmarried and with a child to look after, a child that was the product of an act of incest? Yet he wondered what she felt, now, and if she pined still for her lost infant.

Rose was in the conservatory that gave onto the extensive back garden. She was sitting at a wrought-iron table, in front of a miniature palm tree. She had changed into loose linen trousers and a linen shirt. She had a tall glass before her with ice cubes and a sprig of something green standing in it. "I made myself a mint julep," she said, "just for old times' sake. You want to join me, Quirke?"

"Thanks," Quirke said, "but I think not. Maybe something cool, though." He turned to Maisie. "A glass of tonic water would be good. Plenty of ice, please, Maisie."

"Right you are, Doctor," Maisie said. "I won't be a tick."

"Pull up a chair and sit down," Rose said. "You look hot, all right." There was a book lying on the table. "Ezra Pound," she said, giving him a dry glance. She picked up the book and leafed through it. "*Cantos,* he calls this stuff. I guess they're poems. I don't understand them."

"I don't think anyone does," Quirke said. "I suspect they're not meant to be understood. Think of them as music."

Rose shrugged, and tossed the book back onto the table. "Seems a lot of nonsense to me. No wonder they locked him up in a loony bin. And he sure doesn't think much of the Jews."

He picked up the book and leafed through the pages, stopped at one, and read aloud:

"What thou lovest well remains
    the rest is dross
What thou lov'st well shall not be reft from
    thee
What thou lov'st well is thy true heritage."

"Nice," Rose said, with a skeptical look. "You believe that kind of thing, Quirke? You believe anything remains, when we're gone?"

He shrugged. "I don't know. Children, maybe?"

"Hmm. I haven't got any of them, so I wouldn't know."

"Sorry, Rose."

"For what? I'm not. I didn't want them — too selfish."

Quirke lit a cigarette. The air inside these glass walls was warm and sluggish; he could feel it on his lips and on his eyelids, a heavy, moist lacquer.

"Where's Mal?" he asked.

Rose waved a hand vaguely in the direction of the garden beyond the many panes of glass. "Oh, somewhere off among his beloved flowers. Sometime soon, I think, he's going to turn into a plant himself."

Maisie came back with Quirke's drink. When she leaned down to set his glass on the table he caught a whiff of tobacco smoke. He thanked her, and she smirked and bit her lip and went away again. Rose watched her go. "That girl," she said, "was not born to be a domestic servant."

"Is anyone?" Quirke said.

She gave him a hard look. "You're not going to get all political on me, are you, Quirke?" she said. "The rights of the downtrodden masses and all that stuff?"

"No, Rose," Quirke said, smiling, "I wouldn't dare to lecture you."

"Good." She took a sip of her drink and made a face. "Doesn't taste the same here, somehow," she said. "You've got to be sitting by the bayou, listening to the frogs and the crickets and those old hound dogs a-howling."

"Where exactly was it you were born, Rose?" Quirke asked. It was a thing he had never thought to ask her before.

"Oh, here and there. I don't much like to think about those old times. My daddy was a drunk, and my mother — well, the less said about her, the better."

"Do you miss it, America?"

"Do I miss it?" She thought about that for a while. "I guess I do. It's a crazy country, the folks are mad as mules, but it's exciting. I thought I'd had enough of excitement, which is why I came here."

"And now you're bored?"

She laughed, and leaned over and made a playful slap at him. "You're a mischief-maker, you know that, Quirke? You say these things to me in that butter-wouldn't-melt-in-my-mouth voice, but I know what you're up to, I know you're trying to get me to compromise myself with some injudicious remarks about this green and pleasant land of yours."

"That's Blake," Quirke said, "and he was talking about an altogether different land from this one."

"Oh, you're so smart, ain't you," she said, making another playful slap at him. Then she drifted into silence again, and looked out at the garden. "I wish you hadn't left us so abruptly, Quirke," she said. "I liked having you here. So did Mal — Mal especially. He's real fond of you, you know." She looked at him. "Or do you?"

His glance veered quickly away from her. "I don't think I ever understood him," he said. "And I don't think he understood me, either."

"Oh, he understands you, Quirke. He recognizes that sadness in you, that — oh, that nameless longing." She smiled at him, amused and mocking. "He shares some of it himself. Don't you see that?"

Quirke shifted uneasily on the metal chair. He could feel the perspiration on his back, between his shoulder blades. He had taken off his jacket but he was still too hot. "I don't know, Rose," he said. "I'm no good with this sort of thing. I don't understand myself, much less others. Surely you've realized that by now."

"Well, you've told me, often enough. So often, in fact, that I wonder if it's not just a way of assuring yourself that you don't need to make an effort. Making an effort with people is so tedious, wouldn't you say, Quirke?"

She put her head to one side and gazed at him wide-eyed, smiling. Then abruptly she smacked her palms on the table and stood up. "Let's go find Malachy," she said. "I told him you were coming."

They walked out into the day. After the oppressive air of the glassed-in room, the sky seemed higher than usual and of a richer blue, speckled with motionless small white clouds. The grass underfoot, burnished by a light that seemed not sunlight, was more silvery than green. Birds unseen whistled in the bushes all around.

"Nature," Rose said gloomily. "Doesn't it get you down?"

They found Mal standing in the midst of

a clump of exotic-looking shrubs hung with great bundles of purple blossoms. He was wearing his lamp-shade hat, a khaki shirt, and corduroy trousers balding at the knees.

"Oh, hello, Quirke," he said, looking surprised. "Back again?"

"I told you he was coming, honey," Rose said. "For lunch? Remember?"

"Oh, yes, yes, that's right, so you did." He smiled at Quirke apologetically. "I'm so forgetful, these days."

"How are you, Mal?" Quirke said.

"I'm fine, I'm fine. You look well too, if a little hot."

"I decided to walk out from town. This sun is a killer — you should be careful."

Mal smiled again, wistfully, and glanced at his wife. "Yes, I should, I should take care."

"Well," Rose said, "I'm going to leave you two fine gentlemen to your manly conversings, while I go and check on what that girl has fixed on to burn for our lunch."

The two men watched her walk away. "Poor Rose," Mal said, sighing.

Quirke glanced at him sharply. "What's wrong?" he said.

"What?" Mal's gaze had a groping quality, as if his shortsightedness had suddenly grown worse. "Oh, I feel she has so much

194

to — so much to put up with."

"Such as?"

Mal chuckled. "Such as me, for a start!"

He put a pair of secateurs he had been holding into the breast pocket of his shirt and took off his gardening gloves. "Did you get something to drink?" he asked.

"Yes. I'm fine. I hope Rose really did tell you I was coming, did she?"

"Oh, she did, she did. As I said, I forgot. Sorry, does that seem rude, to forget you were expected? Everything these days is just —" He lifted his hands in a helpless gesture and let them fall again. "Come," he said, "let's sit. You're right, the sun is tiring."

They crossed the lawn to where there was a wooden bench, the legs of which were overgrown with ivy. It was shady here, a cool, greenish spot. They sat down. Mal took off his spectacles and began to polish them with the flap of his shirt.

"The garden looks well," Quirke said. "You've done a lot with it."

"Yes, it's not too bad. We have some nice things, despite our Mr. Casey's best efforts to thwart me and kill off everything that can't be eaten. I'm putting in ornamental grasses now. They're much undervalued, grasses." He smiled, ducking his head shyly. "But all this bores you, I know."

"It's just my ignorance," Quirke said. "I can't tell one flower from another."

"Oh, you'd soon learn. It's not so difficult." He paused, looking about at the plants and the bushes with vague satisfaction. "I planted some new roses, too. I don't think they'll blossom this year — it's too late in the season already." He nodded slowly. "It all goes so quickly."

Quirke was watching him. "What is it, Mal?" he said. "What's wrong?"

"Wrong?"

"Rose came in this morning to summon me here. It was for a reason, wasn't it?"

For a long moment Mal said nothing, and seemed almost not to have heard. Then he put his glasses on again and squinted at the sky, as if searching for something up there, in the blue, among those little floating cloudlets. "Fact is, Quirke," he said, "I'm not well."

How strange it was, Quirke thought, the way certain things, the most momentous, seemed to come not as something new and unexpected but as mere confirmations of things already known. "Tell me," he said.

Mal was still looking at the sky. "Cancer," he said. "The pancreas."

"I see." Quirke let go a long, falling breath. "When did you hear?"

"The other day. I had the tests done last week."

"How bad is it?"

Mal smiled. "It's in the pancreas," he said. "What do you think?"

"Does Rose know?"

"Of course. She's been very good. No tears, no histrionics — well, you know Rose."

Not right now, Quirke thought; right now I don't know anything.

"We're too young for this, Mal," he said. "It's too soon."

"Yes, well, it always is, I imagine. When we were student doctors, in Boston all those years ago, I treated an old fellow for something or other, I can't remember what. Something trivial, an ingrown toenail, that kind of thing. He told me he was ninety-seven. 'You know, young man,' he said to me, 'people say, "Oh, I wouldn't want to live to be your age, to be ninety-seven," but all that changes when they get to be ninety-six.' "

They rose from the bench and walked back together towards the house. They were silent; then Quirke, to be saying something, spoke of Leon Corless's death and Phoebe's strange encounter with Lisa Smith. He could see Mal was only half attending. He

197

had an air about him of soft, slightly dazed amazement; he was like a man who after a long and dreamless sleep awakes to find himself in a world he doesn't recognize.

"Is Phoebe all right?" Mal asked.

"She's concerned, that's all."

Mal nodded. "It must be upsetting for her, the young woman disappearing like that. Phoebe is a good girl. She cares about people, always did. Of course, it gets her into trouble."

Quirke hesitated. "Have you told her — ?"

"No, not yet. I've so many things to think about, to consider. I should make a list. But I will tell her."

"I could do it for you, if you like."

"No, thank you, Quirke. I'll do it myself, soon." He paused. "It's all so — so new."

They were approaching the conservatory. They could see Rose inside, an indistinct figure behind the shadowy reflections on the glass. They stopped.

"What's it like, Mal?" Quirke said. "I mean — knowing."

Mal smiled gently. "Quirke, you're the only person I can think of who'd have the nerve to ask such a question."

"I'm sorry, I —"

"Don't apologize. It's what everyone wants to know." He looked up at the sky yet again, thinking. "It's strange," he said. "I haven't got used to it yet. I feel a kind of — a kind of lightness, as if everything has just fallen away. There's only me, now, facing myself. Does that make sense? I feel almost relieved. It's all suddenly simple."

"You have religion. That must help."

"No, no. That's one of the things that have fallen away. Oh, I suppose I still believe, in some fashion. I'm sure something of me will go on, somehow, I'm sure I won't be entirely annihilated. But all the old stories, God and Saint Peter and the pearly gates, all that stuff, that's gone."

They were silent, standing there on the grass. Quirke noticed how the air seemed to have dimmed, though the sun shone as brightly as ever; it was as if a speck of ink had been dropped into a bowl of clear water.

"This poor chap who died," Mal said. "What did you say his name was? Corless?"

"Yes. Leon Corless. Sam Corless's son."

"The politician? Ah. And you think there was foul play involved?"

"Yes, I think so."

"It sounds like a murky business," Mal said. "I presume your friend Inspector Hackett is investigating? And you'll be helping him, of course." He smiled. "I must say, you didn't take long to get back into the swim."

"You know I'm grateful to you and Rose for putting me up for so long — and for putting up *with* me for so long, too."

"Of course, I know that," Mal said. He paused, seeming to cast about for words. "We've had our difficulties, over the years, you and I, Quirke. Some things I did wrong, some very bad things, and I regret them now, bitterly. I hope you understand that."

Quirke looked away. Years ago Mal had tried to shield his father from the consequences of his wrongdoings, wrongdoings that Quirke had been instrumental in exposing, or that he had attempted to expose. It was all still there in Quirke, the outrage, the frustrated anger, the unexpressed recriminations, but what did any of that matter, now? Mal and he had grown up as brothers, with the jumble of emotions that brotherhood entailed. From here on they would have to find a new accommodation with each other; they wouldn't have much time in which to do it.

As they went through the French doors, into the conservatory, Mal stepped to one side and put a hand on Quirke's shoulder to let him go ahead, and for a moment Quirke saw himself stumble, not actually, but inwardly.

"Well, boys?" Rose said with forced gaiety, rising from the table, glass in hand. "Have you been having a heart-to-heart?"

"Let's go and eat our lunch," Mal said. "I'm hungry, all of a sudden."

They ate in the small dining room at the back of the house, overlooking the garden. The wallpaper was gold flock with dark blue stripes, and the domed ceiling was painted with a scene of gods and garlanded maidens and frolicking cherubs that always set Quirke's head spinning when he made the mistake of looking up at it. Maisie served them vichyssoise and, after that, smoked salmon garnished with slices of cucumber, and potato salad on the side. There was a bottle of dry Riesling in a bucket of ice. Mal, Quirke noticed, wasn't drinking. He spoke of his sweet peas and his flowering shrubs, and Rose teased him in a bright, brittle tone, determinedly smiling, and avoiding Quirke's eyes.

After a lull in the conversation, if it could be called a conversation, Mal said to Rose, "Did you know Quirke is off on another of his investigations?"

"Oh, yes?" Rose said, turning to Quirke with that steely smile. She had drunk three glasses of wine in quick succession and there was a giddy glitter in her eye. "Is that why you left us so suddenly — the call of the chase?"

"A young man was killed in a car crash, in the Phoenix Park," Mal said. "The Guards suspect foul play."

"How awful," Rose exclaimed. She turned to Quirke again. "Why, you must be *so* excited. Though I always find it peculiar, that phrase: 'foul play.' Sounds like something you'd have to give a kid a whipping for."

Quirke knew enough to be wary of Rose when she was like this, drinking too fast and putting on her southern drawl.

"Phoebe is involved too, in a sort of way," Mal said.

Rose was still concentrating on Quirke. "Is that so?" she said. "That girl sure is your daughter, Quirke. What has she done to get herself mixed up in the murder of a young man — I take it murder is what we're speaking of here?"

Quirke told her about Lisa Smith, and how Phoebe had taken her to the house in Ballytubber. Rose widened her eyes exaggeratedly. "Well, I declare!" she said. "I do think she might have checked with us before she started offering a stranger the hospitality of our vacation home."

"Maybe you've forgotten, my dear," Mal said quietly, "I've left the Ballytubber place to Phoebe, so it's almost hers."

"Oh, wonderful," Rose said sourly. "Now we're going to discuss wills, are we?"

Mal reached out and laid a hand on hers. She twitched, and seemed about to snatch her hand away, but didn't.

"I'm sorry," Mal said; it might have been a general apology, aimed at no one in particular.

Rose turned her face away from him, twisting her mouth to one side as she did so. Quirke sat very still, as if to move would be to shatter something. Then Rose relaxed her mouth, and nodded, and turned up her hand under Mal's and squeezed his fingers. "I'm sorry too, old darling," she said. "So sorry."

Maisie came to take their plates away, and Mal smiled at her. "Maisie," he said, "sit down with us for a minute." Maisie stared at him, and so did Rose. "No, no," he said, undaunted, "sit down, just for a little while. Take a glass of wine."

By now Maisie looked terrified. "I have things to do in the kitchen, Doctor," she said in a faltering voice.

"Yes," Rose said to Mal, with a warning

glint, "there'll be all sorts of things waiting for her down there."

"Yes, I know," Mal said, still looking at Maisie. "But they can wait for five minutes. Sit, Maisie."

Maisie cast a wildly questioning look at Rose, who only shrugged in resignation, then drew a chair forward and set it a yard short of the table and sat down, her face ablaze. She would not look at Quirke at all now.

"Let's see," Mal said. "Have we got a glass for you?"

"Oh, no, Doctor," Maisie said quickly. "I never touch the drink."

"No? What a pity. But I suppose you're right — better not to start."

There was silence. They could hear Maisie's rapid breathing. Someone would have to speak, and the task fell to Rose. "Tell me, Maisie," she said, "how is your mother? Do you hear from her?"

Maisie shook her head rapidly. "She's not very good at the writing, ma'am. But I do hear from my brothers, like, and they tell me she's grand."

Rose was about to speak again, but Mal interrupted her. "And your father," he said, "do you hear from him?"

Maisie shook her head again, wringing her

red-knuckled hands. "Ah, God, no, Doctor," she said. "Sure, he wouldn't be having anything to do with me at all."

"Where is he now?" Mal asked. "Is he at home?"

"No, Doctor. I believe he's in Wolverhampton. He do be working on the building sites."

"Oh, yes? And what does he do?"

"He's a plasterer, sir."

"That's a skilled trade, isn't it?"

"I believe so, Doctor."

There was a brief pause; then Mal spoke again: "And do you miss them, your family?" he asked.

"I miss my mother, sir, and some of my brothers."

"And would you like to go and see them?"

Maisie's face grew redder still and seemed to swell, and tears swam in her eyes. "Oh, no, Doctor," she said, with a note of terror in her voice. "I'm grand here."

"It's all right, Maisie," Rose said. "What Dr. Griffin means is, maybe you'd like to pay your family a visit."

Maisie pressed her lips tightly together and gave her head another rapid shake. "No," she said, "no, thanks, I'm grand." She suddenly smiled wildly. "Sure, they'd get the fright of their lives if I turned up on the doorstep out of the blue."

Probably the last time any of her family had seen her, Quirke reflected, was the day she was delivered to the Mother of Mercy Laundry, pregnant with her father's child. He looked hard at Mal, trying to warn him to stop tormenting the poor creature, however unwittingly, and let her go back to her lair in the kitchen. It was clear she thought that for some reason beyond her understanding she was being threatened with the sack.

Mal sat and gazed at her with a vague, distracted smile. Rose turned to her and said firmly, "Maisie, dear, I think maybe it's time we took our coffee. You can run along now."

Maisie fairly sprang to her feet and, casting a last, fearful glance at Mal, hurried from the room.

Rose sighed, and turned to her husband. "Oh, my dear," she said, "you just frightened that poor thing half to death."

He looked at her, blinking. "Why would she be frightened?" he said, genuinely puzzled.

"She thought you were letting her go — don't you see?"

"No," Mal said, laughing a little. "She can't have thought that. I just wanted to talk to her, to ask her about her people, if she missed them." He looked out of the window at the sunlit garden. "There were always so many people that I never spoke to, never even thought about. Nurses, porters, other doctors — my patients, too — them most of all."

"You were always good with patients," Quirke said. "You were known for it."

Mal shook his head slowly. "It was all a performance," he said, "nothing more."

"We're all performers, Mal," Quirke said. "The trick is to make it convincing. What else can we do?"

Mal got up from his chair and went and stood at the window with his hands in his pockets and his back to the table.

"Such growth, this year," he murmured, as if to himself. "So much life."

Quirke and Rose looked at each other, expressionless. Rose said, "Give me a cigarette, will you?"

They returned for their coffee to the conservatory. The sunlight had lost its noonday intensity and the day was a little cooler now, though the air was as heavy and moist as ever. They sat around the little wrought-iron table and Maisie, who seemed to have calmed down after her earlier fright, came and served them, avoiding all eyes. When she had gone, Rose turned to Quirke and said, "Let's hear more about this business Phoebe has got herself involved in."

Quirke told her of Leon Corless, and of his own and Sinclair's suspicions about the circumstances in which the young man had met his death.

"And the girl," Rose said, "the one Phoebe brought down to Ballytubber?"

"Corless's girlfriend. She's pregnant by him, it seems."

Rose leaned back in the chair and sipped her coffee. She seemed not tipsy anymore, as she had been at the lunch table, and her mood was almost languid now. "My," she said, "I thought that kind of thing only happened where I come from, girls getting in a family way and boys ending up in a burning automobile crashed against some big old cottonwood tree. I guess if you had Negroes here you'd be lynching them, too, just like we do."

Quirke was lighting a cigarette. "I'm going to ask a favor of you again, of both of you. I'm going to try to persuade Phoebe to come and stay here for a while." He smiled wryly. "She can have my old room."

Rose glanced at Mal, then turned back to Quirke. "We'd sure be pleased to have her here with us," she said, "but is there a reason?"

"You think she might need protecting?" Mal asked.

Quirke avoided his eye. If Phoebe was in danger, it wouldn't be the first time, as Mal well knew. In the past she had suffered at the hands of people Mal and his father had been associated with. Mal hadn't been to blame for the harm that had been done to her, but he hadn't been entirely innocent, either. This was all old business now, but that didn't mean it was forgotten, or fully forgiven.

"The girl, Lisa Smith, disappeared, without a trace," Quirke said. "That's enough to make me concerned for Phoebe, too."

"Maybe she didn't 'disappear,' " Rose said. "Maybe she just changed her mind and went off. It's what girls do, you know."

"She was frightened," Quirke said. "According to Phoebe, she was terrified. There must have been some threat, one she believed in."

"Oh, girls imagine things," Rose said scoffingly. "Especially when they've just found out they're pregnant and lacking a husband."

"No," Quirke said. "There's something wrong here, something badly wrong."

"And of course," Rose said with a teasing smile, "you're going to find out what it is. You and that little man, the detective, what's his name?"

"Hackett."

"That's it. You and Detective Hackett. What a pair you make. Wyatt Earp and Doc Holliday."

Quirke smiled tolerantly. Rose had always liked to tease, but there was a new bitterness in her tone now, an intent to wound. Well, it was understandable. She had attended the dying of one husband, and now she would have to do the same all over again for another.

"You should definitely speak to Phoebe, then," Mal said, "and encourage her to come to us. She'll be welcome."

"She surely will," Rose said. She hadn't taken her eyes off Quirke. "But what makes you think she'll be safer here than anywhere else? At your place, for instance."

"I thought of that," Quirke said calmly. "But there isn't room."

"No. And you wouldn't want to be inconvenienced in any way, would you?"

She smiled at him sweetly, showing the tips of her teeth. Certainly she was trying to start a fight, but he had no intention of fighting with her. He stood up.

"I should go," he said.

"Things to do?" Rose said, looking up at him, still with that brightly provoking smile. He made no reply, and she turned away, to the garden and the sunshine.

Mal walked with Quirke through the house, to the front door.

"You mustn't take any notice of her," Mal said quietly. "She's doing her best to cope."

"Maybe it would be a bad idea, your taking Phoebe in," Quirke said. "You both have a lot to manage, now, you and Rose."

"No, no. It would be good to have her here." He paused. "Do you really think she's in danger?"

"I don't know," Quirke said. "But I'm afraid she might be." He supposed Mal imagined he had suggested Phoebe should take shelter here as a diversion, to take Mal's thoughts off his own mortal plight, if only for a little while. And maybe it was true, maybe he had. "She's very fond of you, Mal," he said.

"Yes, I know that."

They were at the front door, and Maisie appeared, with Quirke's straw hat. She thrust it into his hand and scuttled away. "Mal," Quirke said, "I think you frightened the daylights out of poor Maisie."

"Oh, Lord, did I, really?" Mal said ruefully. "Everything I do these days seems wrong. I seem to have lost the knack of being normal. I'm sure it's temporary. Nothing stays strange for very long. I imagine death will be just as ordinary and dull as everything else." He laughed softly. "I certainly hope so."

They were standing on the doorstep, under the great slanted shadow of the roof. The sunlight beyond seemed cold and without intensity, a heartless glare.

"I'm sorry, Mal," Quirke said. "I don't know what to say to you."

Mal gazed out at the Sunday-deserted street. "You don't need to say anything. What is there to say? You asked me what it felt like. It's like discovering that all along you've been walking on a tightrope, and suddenly the end of the rope is in sight. You want to get off, but you can't, and you can't stop or retrace your steps, you just have to go on, until you can't go on any farther. Simple as that." He turned to Quirke, earnest yet smiling. "It's no great thing, believe me. That's what I have to tell you. It's no great thing." He stepped back, into the doorway. "Good-bye, Quirke. We'll see you soon. Bring Phoebe — we'll look after her, we'll take care of her."

Quirke said nothing, only nodded, and

turned and went down the steps. When he reached the gate he looked back. Mal was still there, in the doorway, under that wedge of shadow.

12

David Sinclair was plainly dismayed, and angered, even, by his boss's abrupt return to work. He was probably cursing himself, Quirke thought, for having driven out personally that day to summon him to the hospital to look at the mark of the blow on Leon Corless's skull. And maybe Sinclair was right: maybe he wouldn't have come out of convalescence, or whatever to call it, if it hadn't been interrupted. At Mal and Rose's house, he had slipped into a state of torpor that might have continued for months, for years, perhaps, until all his professional expertise had withered away. But now he was back, busy and determined and, as far as Sinclair was concerned, as much of a meddler as ever.

Sinclair had liked being boss round here, Quirke knew; now he was an assistant once more. Quirke smiled to himself.

Most of his first morning back he spent in

his office, going over the records of all procedures that had been carried out in his absence. This intensified Sinclair's sense of grievance. He was outraged to be checked up on like this, though he couldn't risk challenging his boss directly. Quirke guessed what Sinclair was feeling, but didn't care. He was the head of the pathology department, and Sinclair would have to be made to recognize it and accept it; the time had not yet come for the younger man to step into Quirke's place, and that was the end of the matter.

There was a postmortem to be done, on a teenage girl who had managed to poison herself with a dose of domestic bleach; if Quirke ever left off poring over the files, they could get it finished before lunch. Sinclair had already found that the girl had been pregnant. Another illegitimate one; another death.

Quirke had spoken to Phoebe the previous evening, and put to her his plan for her to go and stay with Mal and Rose until Lisa Smith was found and the mystery of her disappearance was cleared up. First Phoebe had dismissed the idea, and then, when Quirke pressed her, had become annoyed, or pretended to. He was being ridiculous, she told him, and besides, even if she was in danger, which she didn't for a moment think she was, she certainly wasn't prepared to uproot herself, albeit temporarily, and move to Ailesbury Road. "You couldn't stay there," she said, "so why do you think it would be different for me?" To that he had no answer. But he could see she wasn't quite as cool and unconcerned as she was pretending to be. Lisa Smith had come to her in terror and then had disappeared without a trace. If, as Phoebe believed, she had been taken away by force, then the ones who had done the taking knew it was Phoebe who had helped her to hide in the first place.

He could find no fault with Sinclair's reports, and he shut the last of the folders and set it aside. Then he lit a cigarette and pushed back his swivel chair and put his feet on the desk. He was like a dog reestablishing his territory; he knew it, and he felt a twinge of shame, but he wasn't going to stop.

Had he been hoping to find some sign of negligence in Sinclair's record keeping, a slipshod conclusion here, a corner cut there, an obviously flawed judgment left to stand? If so, he had been disappointed. Sinclair was a good pathologist, diligent and thorough. What Quirke objected to was the younger man's impenetrable sense of himself and his own worth. Quirke had never known anyone so self-possessed, and he was — he had to admit it — jealous. Or no, not jealous; envious, yes, but not jealous — he had to give himself that. There was a difference, in Quirke's definition of the terms. To be jealous meant you not only wanted something someone else had, you also wanted that someone else to be deprived of it; to be envious was to recognize another's gift and only want to have it too, for yourself. Pondering this distinction was a way of soothing himself.

He swiveled in his chair and squinted at the little window high up under the ceiling. It wasn't really a window, only a shallow panel of glass, no more than six inches deep and reinforced with iron mesh, set on a level with the pavement outside, and of little use as a means of letting in light. He liked to see women in high heels walking past. He thought of Phoebe's new boss, the widowed Dr. Evelyn Blake. He couldn't imagine her wearing high heels. Strange, the way she had looked at him, so calm and seemingly incurious and yet — what was the word? Appraising, yes, that was it. She had an appraising gaze. It had pleased him, in an obscure way, to be thus scrutinized.

He stubbed out his cigarette and stood up.

Sinclair was sitting on a metal chair in the dissecting room, reading a newspaper. He looked up when Quirke, in his white coat, came out of his office.

"Right," Quirke said brusquely, "let's get this done."

The volume of bleach the girl had drunk, though it had done significant damage to the esophagus, shouldn't have been enough to kill her. "When they want to die," Quirke said grimly, "and want it badly enough, they die." It was one of his dictums, regularly expressed; Sinclair said nothing.

When they were done, Quirke left his assistant to tidy up the corpse and took off his surgical gloves and went and sat on the metal chair by the sink where Sinclair had been sitting, and lit another cigarette. He looked about the bare, low-ceilinged room. It was as if he hadn't been away at all, as if the past couple of months had never happened.

"There's another one coming in after lunch," Sinclair said, drawing the sheet over the dead girl. "It's routine. I can do it, if you want to go off."

"Go off where?" Quirke asked, a touch suspiciously.

Sinclair carefully smoothed the wrinkles out of the sheet and stood back to admire his handiwork. That was another annoying thing about him: his obsessive tidiness.

"It's your first day back," he said. "I thought you might want to knock off early."

"Thanks," Quirke said, and Sinclair glanced at him quickly over his shoulder. "Sorry, Sinclair. My temper's not the best. I had a row with Phoebe last evening. Well, not a row. We had words, as they say."

"Yes," Sinclair said without emphasis, "she told me."

"I only suggested she go and stay at Dr. Griffin's house for her own good. A young man is dead, and a girl is missing."

Sinclair murmured something under his breath, and Quirke had to ask him to repeat it. "I said, I'll look after her."

"Good," Quirke said. "I'm glad to hear it." He didn't sound glad.

"I'm as concerned for Phoebe's safety as you are," Sinclair said, obviously controlling himself.

"Right. I'm sure you are. What will you do — sleep in the Morris Minor outside her flat?"

He frowned. Had he meant to say that? Often nowadays he heard things coming out of his mouth that he hadn't expected, and hardly recognized as the result of anything that had been in his head. Was that due to the lesion on his brain, or was he just ordinarily turning into a curmudgeon, bad-tempered and irresponsible and unable to govern his tongue?

"As a matter of fact," Sinclair said, "I asked her to move in with me, for a while."

Quirke did not look at him. "Oh, yes?" he said in an ominously neutral tone.

"She said no, of course."

"Well, she's an independent girl."

"Young woman, you mean."

Now it was Quirke's turn to control himself. He made himself say nothing. He lit a cigarette. His heart was beating very fast. He looked at the glowing tip of ash. Count to three. Then count to three again.

Sinclair was leaning over the sink at the other end of the room, scrubbing his hands. "If you disapprove of me," he said, "you should say so." His tone was mild, and he didn't look up from the sink.

"Disapprove of you in what way?" Quirke said. "As Phoebe's boyfriend — if that's the word? Would it matter, if I did?"

"It depends in what way you think it might matter. Phoebe would care, but maybe not as much as you might imagine."

Sinclair was drying his hands on the roller

220

towel attached to the wall above the sink.

"And what about *you*?" Quirke asked, his voice quivering from the effort of keeping his anger in check. "Would *you* care?"

Sinclair turned, and leaned back against the sink and folded his arms and considered the toe caps of his shoes.

"You and I have to work together," he said. "It would be awkward, if I thought you felt I wasn't good enough for her."

Quirke fairly pounced. "Who said anything about being good enough or not?"

"I think," Sinclair said evenly, "you have something against me. I could make a guess at what it is, but that might be to do you an injustice."

Quirke began to say something but stopped. Was he being accused of disapproving of Sinclair because he was a Jew?

"Then don't — do me an injustice, I mean."

They fell into a tight-lipped silence. Neither of them seemed quite sure what it was that had just happened. Had it been a fight? If so, it seemed to be over, and without a winner. They had never fought before. Maybe it was just one of the consequences of the great heat outside, pressing on the air in this underground chamber of the dead. Atmospheric pressure, resulting in

221

tension that had to be released somehow. Always best to blame the weather.

Quirke went back into his office, and Sinclair left, on his way to the cubbyhole down the corridor he had been allotted as an office, to write up his report, yet another one, succinct, measured, and perfectly typed. Quirke scowled. Maybe he shouldn't have come back to work yet; maybe what Sinclair had seemed to imply was true, that he wasn't ready to take up his old life again. But if not now, when?

The telephone rang. It was Hackett, asking him if he would come and meet him at the café across the road.

They ate ham sandwiches and an awful salad, wilted and watery. The heat was a torment. The sun shining in through the window had made the plastic top of the table so hot they could hardly touch it. Hackett ordered a glass of red lemonade; Quirke smelled the sugary fragrance of it and felt his stomach heave. He had a sudden, clear image of Hackett as a boy, plump, crop-headed, with pink ears and bare knees, out on the bog after a morning's turf cutting with his father, sitting on a grassy tussock and munching his way through a sandwich, with a lemonade bottle full of milk at his feet, stoppered with a twist of greaseproof paper. It wasn't Hackett he was seeing, of course, but himself, and there was no father there, only Brother Clifford, who had sewn a ha'penny into the tip of his leather strap to give it added weight and an extra sting.

He drifted slowly back from the past. Hackett was speaking to him, showing him what seemed to be a list of names. He tried to concentrate. His head was pounding; were they getting worse, these head pains he was suffering from lately?

"Your daughter got it this morning," Hackett said. "It's the names of the girls who were in that shorthand course with her. Here, have a look."

The sheet of paper had been in Hackett's pocket and was crumpled, and one corner had got torn off. He put it on the table and smoothed it flat with the side of his fist. Quirke felt an odd little tug of tenderness at the sight of his daughter's handwriting. When had he last seen it? He couldn't remember. Years ago, when she was still at school. It hadn't changed; it was still back-hand, with big loops under the *y*'s and tiny circles for dots over the *i*'s. He began to read out the names, murmuring them under his breath: "Siobhan Armstrong, Annette

Bellamy, Denise Bergin, Elizabeth Costigan, Doris Cranitch, Philomena Davis." His eye skipped down the list. "Siobhan Latimer, Lisa Murtell, Elspeth Noyek, Aileen Quirke, Julianne Richardson, Alida Vernon, Estella Yorke."

"I see there's one of your own there," Hackett said. "Miss Aileen Quirke. Any relation, would you say?" He chuckled. "Isn't it a poem, the whole thing? You can see the lot of them, bent over their notebooks, scribbling away like the good girls they are."

"The only Lisa is this one," Quirke said, pointing. "Lisa Murtell."

"Aye. And no Smiths, at all."

"There's a Costigan, I notice."

"What's she called?" Hackett said, twisting his neck to read the name. "Elizabeth. Maybe he has a daughter, the same Joe Costigan."

They looked at each other for a moment, then both shrugged at the same time. Quirke pushed the list aside. "It's not much help, is it," he said. A thought struck him. "Where did you see Phoebe," he asked, "that she gave you this?"

"She telephoned me, to say she'd got it from the agency, and could she bring it down to me. I sent Jenkins in the squad car up to her place of work. Fitzwilliam Square

224

— very nice. She must like it, there."

Quirke was surprised at how annoyed he was that Phoebe had called Hackett and not him. Well, he acknowledged, he deserved the snub. She had her sly way of reminding him, every so often, of the nearly twenty years during which he had pretended, to her and to everyone else, that she was not his daughter.

"So what's next?" Quirke asked.

Hackett took a drink of his lemonade, while Quirke looked away. It was the color of the stuff that was most repulsive.

"I've sent a couple of my boys up to the house in Rathmines, with a search warrant."

"What will they be looking for?"

"Your daughter insists she was in Lisa Smith's flat in that house, and I believe her, whatever the bold Mr. Abercrombie may say." He fingered an uneaten crust from his sandwich. "I'm also due to have a word with young Corless's boss down in Government Buildings. I thought" — he gave a soft little cough — "I thought you might come along, if you have an hour to spare."

Quirke always forgot how nervous Hackett was when it came to dealing with what he referred to, with a mixture of deference and scorn, as "the gentry." For the detective, this class included all professionals,

225

such as lawyers and doctors and the higher orders of the church, and any kind of government official.

"Yes, all right," Quirke said, "I'll come with you."

They paid for their sandwiches and crossed the road to the hospital car park, where young Garda Wallace, he of the bad teeth and drooping cowlick, was waiting for them in a squad car. It was hot in the back seat, and they opened their windows on either side, though the muggy air that came in from outside afforded little relief.

"Tell me again which department it is that Corless worked in?" Quirke asked.

"Health. Crawley is the Minister. Creepy Crawley they call him. Or the Monsignor — he's renowned for his piety. Has twelve children, three of them priests and one a nun. He has his place reserved for him in heaven, that's for sure."

"Is that who we're going to see?" Quirke asked.

"Not at all — he's altogether too grand to be talking to the Guards. It's a fellow called O'Connor, or Ó Conchubhair, as he sometimes styles himself, when he's feeling extra patriotic, I suppose." He chuckled. "He's the Secretary of the department, which I

226

imagine doesn't mean he does the typing."

In Merrion Street they were let in through a side gate and directed to park next to an imposing, carved oak door. Inside, a girl behind a hatch told them to go up two flights and they'd be met. On the second floor another girl showed them into a big high room with plaster carvings on the ceiling. Two high windows looked out onto Merrion Street. Between the windows there was an enormous desk, behind which sat a small fat man in a three-piece blue suit. His head was as round as a melon, and he was entirely bald save for a few long, greasy strands of colorless hair coaxed round from somewhere at the back and plastered laterally across his pinkish-gray skull. He wore a dark blue bow tie with dark red polka dots. A gold watch chain was looped across the front of his buttoned waistcoat. He could have been any age between thirty-five and fifty. He stood up, assuming a wintry smile, and said, *"Dea-lá a thabhairt duit, uaisle."*

"Dea-tráthnóna, a dhuine uasail," Hackett replied, in his flattest Midlands accent. "Detective Inspector Hackett. And this is Dr. Quirke."

The little man gave Quirke a small, plump hand to shake. "Turlough O'Connor," he said. His smooth brow developed a furrow.

"I think I know you, do I, Dr. Quirke?"

"I'm at the Hospital of the Holy Family," Quirke said. "Pathology department. But you might have met me at the home of Judge Garret Griffin."

Something moved in the depths of O'Connor's pale eyes, something sharp and cold. "The very place," he said. "You'd be Garret's son, then."

"Adopted," Quirke said stonily.

"Yes, yes, of course." A spot of pink appeared high on each of the man's cheekbones, and he coughed softly. "And how is Garret's other — how is Dr. Malachy, how is he keeping, these days?"

"He's retired."

"Is he, now. Well, well." He coughed again. "Please, sit down, gentlemen — bring over those chairs and make yourselves comfortable. Now: what can I do for you?"

"It's about one of your staff. Leon Corless."

O'Connor nodded, closing his smooth, bulbous eyelids for a moment and then opening them again, wider than before. "Ah, yes," he said. "Poor Leon — a shocking thing. Do you know what happened? I read about it in the paper. What can he have been doing out so late?"

Hackett took out a packet of Player's,

pushed open the flap, and flicked the cigarettes expertly into a stack, like a miniature set of organ pipes, and offered them across the desk. O'Connor waved his chubby hands in front of him. "Thank you, no, I'm not a smoker."

Nor a drinker, either, Quirke saw, from the Pioneer pin fixed in his lapel, just below the *fáinne,* the little gold ring proclaiming him an advocate for the Irish language. Quirke couldn't but marvel at the polished completeness of the man: the blue suit with lapel pins, the bow tie, the watch chain, the mincing manner. Maybe there was a school for civil servants, like a drama school for actors.

"We believe," Hackett said, vigorously shaking a match to extinguish it, "that Leon Corless had been to a party and was on his way home across the Phoenix Park to Castleknock, where he lives, or lived, in digs at the house of a relative, an aunt by marriage. His car ran into a tree and caught fire."

O'Connor nodded; his head seemed set directly on to his trunk, without the interposition of a neck. "Yes, that's what the paper said. Although there was no mention of a party." He clicked his tongue, partly in sympathy and partly to deplore. "These

229

late-night parties are becoming more and more the thing nowadays, among the young. I suppose he had been drinking?"

"There was alcohol in his blood, yes," Quirke said, "but not so much that he would drive into a tree."

O'Connor seemed not to have heard. "It's very bad," he said, "very bad. From what I knew of him, I wouldn't have thought there was wildness in him. Of course, his family background, his father . . ." He let his voice trail off.

There was a brief silence; then Hackett shifted on his chair and said, "Can you tell us, Mr. O'Connor, what sort of work did Leon Corless do here in the department?"

Again O'Connor softly closed his lids and again dilated them; it was a tic, it seemed, and slightly unnerving. "Well now, I can tell you he was a very promising young fellow, very promising indeed. He came in as a junior ex— he did very well in his exams, remarkably well — and it wasn't long before his potential was spotted. He had a wonderful head for detail, not only a good memory but also a great capacity for organizing material. So I put him on statistics. It's a new field we're moving into, and Leon seemed just the type for it. And so it proved. He had a fine career ahead of him, Inspector, a fine career, tragically cut short."

Quirke watched him; it was indeed, he felt, like watching a great actor in a minor role, but playing it with all his smooth, accustomed genius. This building teemed with people like him, the drivers of the nation, playing earnestly at being in charge, the reins of state firmly in their pudgy little hands. By instinct he despised and loathed the type. It was people like O'Connor who, with the flick of a pen, had condemned him to a childhood of cruelty and terror.

"And tell us," Hackett said, "what was the nature of his work, exactly?"

O'Connor blandly smiled and folded his hands neatly before him on the desk. "Well, I don't think I can tell you *exactly*. I wouldn't want to blind you with — ha ha — statistics."

Hackett's look was as affable as ever. "Maybe, then, you'd give us a general idea," he said. "Would that be possible, do you think?"

O'Connor stared at him in silence for a moment, measuring him, trying to calculate how much authority he might have at his disposal, how much of a threat he might represent. They were both employees of the state, after all, and as such they were natural enemies.

Steepling his fingers, O'Connor frowned down at his desk. "I can tell you," he said, "that Leon was working in — what shall I say? — in a sensitive area. As you know, the Archbishop's Palace keeps a vigilant eye on matters to do with health, and particularly" — he lifted his eyes and fixed on Quirke — "when it comes to mother-and-child issues."

There was a moment of silence. Hackett stirred again in his chair.

"But would you be able to say," he asked, with a patient smile, "in general, what duties he was engaged in? I'm not sure what 'statistics' means."

O'Connor glanced to the side, pursing his lips. "As I say, Inspector, this is a sensitive area."

Hackett waited, and when nothing more was forthcoming, he said, "Yes, Mr. O'Connor, and what we're looking into is sensitive also, possibly involving a crime."

O'Connor turned his head quickly and stared at him. It was, Quirke thought, the first time he had shown a genuine reaction to anything that had been said to him so far.

"A crime," he said, in a hushed voice. "What kind of crime?"

"From investigations carried out by Dr. Quirke and his team, there is the possibility that there was foul play involved in the death of Leon Corless."

"You mean" — O'Connor was verging on breathlessness — "you mean his death wasn't accidental?"

"It doesn't appear that way, no."

O'Connor turned to Quirke with an expression of growing alarm.

"There was a contusion on the side of the skull," Quirke said, "that didn't seem to us to be the consequence of the car crash. It seems as if he was knocked unconscious before the car ran into the tree."

"Are you saying this might be a case of murder?"

"That's the possibility we're considering," Hackett said.

There was another silence, this time of longer duration. O'Connor put his hands flat on the desk before him and glanced agitatedly this way and that; he suddenly seemed a man clinging to a raft in a tempestuous sea.

"But that's — that's impossible," he muttered, more to himself than to the other two. "Leon Corless murdered? It can't be. He was just a young fellow doing his job."

"And his job," Hackett said, "was keeping statistics on — on what, exactly?"

O'Connor, wild-eyed and breathing heavily, seemed to have forgotten about the two men before him, but now he came back from whatever panic-stricken plain his thoughts had been ranging over.

"I don't think," he said, "that I should say anything more, at this juncture. I shall have to — I shall have to take advice — I shall have to consult the Minister." He looked at Hackett. "You understand, Inspector, any hint of — of scandal or of crime, why —" He stopped, and gazed before himself, horrified.

"But we can take it, can we, Mr. O'Connor," Quirke said, "that Leon Corless was engaged in compiling statistics to do with, let's say, childbearing, birth rates, infant mortality, even" — he let a beat pass — "adoption?"

O'Connor waved his little hands again in front of himself, crossing them back and forth rapidly. "I've said all I have to say, for the present. I shall speak to the Minister. Perhaps" — he turned to Hackett — "perhaps you should ask to see the Minister yourself. Mr. Crawley has the authority that I lack, in this matter." He stood up; he looked slightly sick. "I'll bid you good day, gentlemen. Miss O'Malley will show you out."

Quirke and Hackett glanced at each other

doubtfully. They knew they had no choice but to leave, that the interview, such as it had been, was over, for now, at least. They stood up slowly from their chairs, their hats in their hands. O'Connor bustled with them to the door. The young woman who had met them when they arrived on the second floor was waiting in the corridor.

"Ah, Deirdre," O'Connor said, "please show these gentlemen the way out." He turned to the two men behind him. "Inspector, Dr. Quirke, good day to you. And Dr. Quirke, please tell Dr. Griffin I was asking for him."

He smiled unhappily, shook hands with both of them hurriedly, and scuttled back into his office and shut the door.

The young woman, who had dark hair and wore a vaguely Celtic-looking dress with an embroidered bodice, smiled at the two men. There was a mischievous light in her eyes. "This way, gentlemen," she said. "It's just down the stairs here, the way you came up. At the bottom of the stairs you'll see the door in front of you." She was biting her lip, trying not to smirk. No doubt, Quirke thought, it wasn't every day she saw her boss so flustered, and obviously she had enjoyed the spectacle.

They descended the stairs, their heels

ringing on the marble steps.

"All these buildings," Hackett remarked, "they remind me of hospitals. I suppose you wouldn't have the same impression, since you work in a real hospital."

They reached the ground floor. The girl behind the hatch smiled at them; she looked like a framed snapshot of herself.

Outside, the heat was pounding down. Wallace had got out of the car and was standing in the shade, having a smoke. When he saw them approaching, he dropped the cigarette hastily and trod on it. He opened the back door and Hackett climbed in, while Quirke went round to the other side. The upholstery of the seats was hot to the touch.

Wallace got behind the wheel and started the engine. Hackett leaned forward and tapped Garda Wallace on the shoulder. "Open them air vents, will you?" he said. "We're suffocating back here." They nosed their way out through the narrow gate and onto Merrion Street.

"Well," Quirke said, "what did you make of that?"

Hackett didn't answer at first. Quirke noticed again his way of sitting in a car, upright, with his back straight and his hands on his knees, like a child being taken for a treat.

"I'll tell you what I think," he said at length. "I think we're getting into a sticky place with the powers that be."

"Again?" Quirke said drily, with a faint smile.

Hackett got out at Pearse Street and told Wallace to drive Quirke on to the hospital. Hackett said he would telephone as soon as he got a report from the two detectives he had sent with a search warrant to the house in Rathmines. Then he strolled into the station with his hat on the back of his head, and Wallace swung the big car away from the curb, into the afternoon traffic.

Quirke, in the back seat, watched the simmering streets roll past. A double-decker bus had broken down on O'Connell Bridge, and even though Wallace put the siren on, it still took them a good ten minutes to negotiate their way through the jam of cars and lorries and horse-drawn drays. It was low tide, and the river was a soupy trickle between two banks of shining blue mud. The stench from the water made Quirke cover his nose and breathe through his mouth, but it did little to block out the noxious fumes. At last they were free of the snarl-up, and sped along O'Connell Street and on to Parnell Square.

"What's he like to work for, the Inspector?" Quirke asked.

The Guard's eyes sought his in the rearview mirror. "Oh, he's a fair man," he said, "if you don't cross him."

"And what happens if you do cross him?"

The young man chuckled. "You don't, that's the thing."

"Right," Quirke said. "Right."

When he got to the hospital, he was told that Sinclair had used some of his time in lieu and gone off for the afternoon. He started to become angry, but checked himself. Why shouldn't Sinclair take an afternoon off? It was useless — and worse than useless, it was childishly vindictive — to look so eagerly for grievances to hold against his assistant.

He went into his office, hung his hat on the stand, and sat down at the desk. There was paperwork to do, but he couldn't face it. He felt that tickle along his spine that was, he knew, the harbinger of boredom. In the ordinary run of things, being bored was one of Quirke's keenest fears. He opened the bottom drawer of his desk, where in former times he kept a naggin of whiskey, for emergencies, which used to occur with remarkable regularity. The drawer was empty. Had he thrown away the last bottle? He couldn't remember. He was sorry it wasn't there; he liked to have a tot of booze on hand, just for the comfort of it, even if he had no intention of drinking it.

He had been reduced to reading an article, in an old copy of the *Lancet,* on new research into the classification of blood groups when Hackett rang. His men had poked Abercrombie out of his lair and made him let them into the house in Rathmines. They had gone through all the flats and found no trace of Lisa Smith. One of the flats was vacant and had been for a long time, according to Abercrombie. They had searched it anyway, but found nothing. Hackett had called Phoebe at Dr. Blake's office and given her his men's description of the empty flat, and she had said it sounded like the one that Lisa Smith had brought her to. If it was the same flat, someone had scrubbed it of all traces of the missing girl, in the same way that they had cleared out the house in Ballytubber.

"What do you think, Doctor?" Hackett asked.

Quirke thought that the affair of Lisa Smith was looking blacker with each hour that passed. He felt something tighten in the pit of his stomach, like a hand forming itself into a fist.

13

Late in the afternoon Quirke took a taxi to Fitzwilliam Square. He had thought he would meet Phoebe after work and take her for a drink; that, at least, was what he told himself. It was just short of five-thirty when he got there, and he decided to wait, loitering by the railings, under the trees that to him always smelled, mysteriously, of cat piss. The latening sun on the fronts of the houses made them seem assembled out of ingots of baked gold. He still had a headache, and he fingered gingerly the place on the side of his skull under which the lesion in his brain was located. It was, he realized, exactly the same area where Leon Corless had been struck on the head. Coincidence. Quirke didn't like coincidences; they seemed to him flaws in the fabric of the world, and, as far as he was concerned, none of them was ever happy.

At a few minutes after half past, when

Phoebe appeared, Dr. Blake was with her. The two women came down the steps from the house, not speaking, but certainly together. His heart had set up a dull, slow thumping. Dr. Blake wore a white sleeveless dress with a design of crimson flowers strewn diagonally across it. The effect, at this distance, was dramatic and unsettling; the flowers looked like an untidy splash of blood.

He hung back in the gloom under the trees. Should he cross the road and speak to them, and if not, why not? They were obviously going somewhere together, down to the Shelbourne, maybe. Against the rich gold of the evening sunlight, and in contrast to the encrimsoned woman beside her, Phoebe in her neat black dress with the white collar looked more nunlike than ever.

Just when he had decided to let them go on ungreeted, Phoebe spotted him, and came towards him across the road. She peered at him, and laughed.

"What are you doing," she said, "lurking there in the shadows? You look like somebody up to no good."

"I was passing by," he lied. Dr. Blake was waiting on the other side of the street. "I thought I'd stop and say hello, but I see you and the good doctor are off somewhere."

"We're not. She was just walking home with me. Her car is in a garage behind Herbert Place, being repaired."

He hesitated; he didn't know what to say, didn't know what he wanted to do. His heart was still going at that ridiculous, rumbling pace.

"You heard what Hackett's people had to say about the house in Rathmines?" he said.

"Yes, he called me. They found no trace of Lisa Smith. I can't understand it."

He went with her back across the road.

"Hello, Dr. Blake," he said.

She said nothing, only gazed at him with that peculiar, penetrating light in her huge dark eyes.

"I was telling him," Phoebe said, "that your car is in the garage."

"Yes," the woman said, "it was, it seems, very ill but now is cured."

She didn't smile, yet managed to show her amusement, not only at the predicament of her motorcar, but also, somehow, at the world's absurdity in general.

"Shall we walk down together?" Phoebe said.

They set off along the square. Quirke found himself in the middle, with the women on either side of him. He felt pleasantly hemmed in. Phoebe talked, while he

243

and Dr. Blake were silent. He thought it must be his imagination, but he seemed to sense a faint tingle in the space separating him from this strange, unruffled, heavy-footed woman in her white-and-blood-red dress. But then, when did he ever walk beside a woman and not feel the air vibrating? He noticed that she carried no handbag; it seemed to him he had never come across a woman without a handbag before. Without something to hold on her arm she walked like a man, heavily, with her fists at her sides.

Phoebe soon ran out of topics of conversation, and they went on in silence. They turned along Baggot Street and presently came to the canal, and descended the steps to the towpath. Here they had to walk in single file, Phoebe leading, then Dr. Blake, and lastly Quirke. A moorhen and her chicks sailed beside them along the glassy water, each tiny creature sending out behind it a tiny fan-shaped wake. The sedge was green; Quirke had never noticed green sedge before. The soft fragrance of cut planks wafted to them from the sawmill on the other bank. A man with his dog passed them by. The man saluted each woman in turn, and glanced at Quirke with a jocular eye. What did he see, what was it he thought he saw? A girl-woman in a thin black dress, a large grave lady with pensive eyes, and, drawing up the rear, a sheepish fellow with a shifty look to him.

"Watch out," Phoebe called back, "there's a dead bird here, don't step on it."

It was a fledgling, a featherless sack with a scrawny neck and beak agape. Harsh world, Quirke thought, in which the weakest die.

Ahead, Phoebe stopped, turned. "Well," she said, "this is me. Good-bye, Dr. Blake, I'll see you tomorrow."

She held Quirke briefly by the arm and kissed him on the cheek — when was the last time she had kissed him? — and smiled a thin, complicit smile into his face, then turned again and walked up to the gap in the railings and, casting one last, playful glance at her father, was gone.

"Will you go also?" Dr. Blake asked, brushing a leaf from the shoulder of her dress.

"I might walk with you," Quirke said, "to the garage."

"Certainly."

She set off along the path, and he followed after her.

What age was she? he wondered. Younger than he was, but not by much. Her arms, he saw, thanks to the sleeveless dress, were firm and shapely. The upper parts of women's arms, so plumply vulnerable, he always found affecting, the elbows too, those little wizened whorls.

"What was wrong with your car?" he asked, to be asking something.

"I have no idea," she said, without turning her head or slowing her step. "I know nothing about cars. Indeed, there are many things I know nothing of." This seemed to amuse her. "And you, Dr. Quirke, are you — what do you say? — mechanically minded?"

"No, I'm afraid not."

It was strange, speaking to the back of her head like this.

"Like me, then. That's good."

Why, he wondered, was it good?

She was wearing gilded sandals, like the ones Rose Griffin had worn yesterday. The skin over her Achilles tendons was wrinkled and a little chafed, like her elbows. He imagined holding her foot in his hand; he imagined holding both of them — her feet, in his hands. He thought: How strange life is, sometimes!

They came to Huband Bridge and crossed the road to the Pepper Canister Church and turned left into Herbert Lane. He knew, with a dreamlike certainty, what their destination was to be. He had kept a car here once, an Alvis, a beautiful machine, in a rented lock-up garage that David Sinclair had somehow inherited and now kept his Morris Minor in. It was up the lane a little way from Perry Otway's repair shop, and sure enough, here was Perry himself, Perry of the soiled blond hair and rolling gait, in his putty-colored boilersuit, coming out of his workshop, wiping his hands on an oily rag.

"Dr. Quirke!" he exclaimed, in his plummy accent. "And Dr. Blake, too! My, my, it's a small world."

Dr. Blake's car was a Volkswagen; it lurked in the narrow recess of the workshop, shiny black and somehow menacing, like a giant scarab. Perry explained at some length what the trouble had been and how he had fixed it. Dr. Blake listened gravely, her head bent forward a little, her eyes fixed on Perry's broad, bland face. Quirke noticed her upper lip, babyish, heavy, shaped like a child's stylized drawing of a seagull, with a plump little bleb of almost transparent flesh in the middle of it.

Perry, his surgical report done with, handed over the key, holding it daintily between the tips of an oily finger and thumb and dropping it into Dr. Blake's palm.

"You will send me a bill," she said, "yes?"

Perry, wiping his hands with the rag again, turned to Quirke. "Ah, that motor of yours," he said, shaking his head, "she was a beauty." He turned back to the woman, who was edging her way between the flank of the car and the greasy workshop wall. "An Alvis, it was," he said to her. "And not just any old Alvis — a TC 108 Super Graber Coupe. Magnificent beast!"

Quirke wished Perry would shut up. Quirke had crashed the Alvis and let it topple over the side of a cliff into the sea. It was not a happy memory.

Dr. Blake had managed to get the door open and slide in behind the wheel at last. She started the engine, and the two men stood aside to allow her room to maneuver out of the narrow space in which it seemed the little car had been wedged. She rolled down the window and said to Quirke, "Can I bring you somewhere?"

"No, no," he said, "thank you. I live round the corner here."

"Ah. I see."

Still she sat there, her hands on the wheel, looking up at him. He noted again the way she had of concentrating her gaze, on an object or a person, so that it seemed as if everything else around had fallen away, into a fog of insignificance. Quirke felt himself almost blushing; he was not accustomed to being looked at like that, with such calm intensity.

"Nevertheless," she said, "let me give you a lift. Get in."

He walked around to the passenger side, and she leaned across and unlocked the door for him. Perry, ignored now, waved the filthy rag in farewell, and disappeared into the garage's oily gloom.

They drove along the lane, turned right and right again, onto Herbert Street.

"I'm round the corner, as I say," Quirke said.

"I know, yes. But I think I don't want to go home yet. Will you come with me for a drink, perhaps?"

"Yes," Quirke said.

Yes.

She parked on Merrion Street and they walked up to Doheny & Nesbitt. They drank a whiskey and soda each. Afterwards he couldn't remember what they had talked about. This was strange, for they had talked for a long time, intensely, about many things. He wondered uneasily if she might have managed somehow to hypnotize him in some mild way — wasn't that what

psychiatrists did to their patients sometimes? — to ensure that he would forget all
that had been said. A mad notion, of course.
Why would she want him to forget?

There were to be things about that evening
he would not forget, things he would never
forget, but they weren't things to be expressed in words.

After their drink she drove him to Upper
Mount Street, to his flat, but when they
reached the house they sat outside in the
car for a long time and had another conversation, and this one too he couldn't recall
afterwards. Late sunlight in the street was
like a gold river flowing around them.

They couldn't part, they didn't know how,
and Dr. Blake — Evelyn — suggested they
go for a walk. They left the car and went
past the Pepper Canister again, in the opposite direction this time, and across to the
canal, and sat on the metal bench by the
bridge where Quirke liked to spend his
Sunday mornings. He told her about the
boys who came here on the weekends to
swim, diving from the lock and even from
the bridge itself. He told her how Rose
Griffin had come and invited him to lunch,
and how he had talked to Mal in the garden
and Mal had told him he was dying. After
that they went back to his flat.

■ ■ ■ ■

Dense light of evening in the big window above the bed, and a small round cloud seemingly motionless in the western sky. "So funny," Evelyn said, lying beside him, propped on an elbow, "so funny, the way we had to walk."

"What?" he said. "Where?"

"By the canal, with Phoebe. Her, me, you, like Indians on the trail of something."

"On the trail of ourselves."

"Yes, yes," she said, smiling. "That's it, we were tracking ourselves. I could feel you looking at me, from behind. Did I look nice?"

"Very nice."

"My big bottom."

"Your wonderful big bottom."

Undressing her had been a delightful operation, like peeling a large smooth pale egg. She watched him as he did it, fiddling with zips, buttons, clasps. She laughed and said he looked like a little boy, eager and clumsy. When they kissed she kept her eyes open, and so did he.

"Are we not too old for this?" she said.

"Yes," he said, smiling, "much too old."

When she lay down on her back her

251

breasts splayed out over her rib cage, wobbling. There were stretch marks on her belly. "I had a son," she said. "He died." He leaned his head down and traced the marks with the tip of his tongue; they were pearly and smooth and slightly brittle, like dried snail trails.

"How lovely you are," he said.

"Oh, no."

"You are."

"All right, then."

She paid attention to everything he did, as if she had never made love before and were memorizing how it was done. She wrapped herself around him, her arms, her legs. "I want to swallow you," she whispered, "I want to swallow you, all of you, into me."

She was Austrian. "Salzburg," she said, and made a face. "A Nazi town, always, and still. I will not go back there." Her maiden name was Nussbaum. "Nut tree," she said. "Isn't that nice?" Her family — parents, two sisters, and a brother — had died in the camps. She put a finger to his lips. "Ssh," she said. "Not to be spoken of. Not speakable."

He asked her about the young man who had been at dinner with her in the Russell. "Paul," she said. "Paul Viertel. The son of my sister, the oldest one."

"Was she — ?"

"Yes, yes. Theresienstadt. Tuberculosis, and so one of the lucky ones, you could say."

She made him close his eyes so she could kiss the lids. "Like kissing a moth," she said.

They sat up, with the sheet over their knees, and shared a cigarette, passing it back and forth between them. "I can taste you on the paper," she said. "My taste, too, from your lips. Both of us." She laughed. "I had a boyfriend, when I was young, thirteen, fourteen. Very innocent. He had to go away, with his family. We wrote each other letters. I used to try to lift up the — what do you call it? the flap? — I used to try to lift it up and lick where he had licked." She sighed, smiling. "He was such a nice boy. Not a Jew. He said it didn't matter that I was, but it did, I think, in the end. Best, perhaps, that he went away."

They got up, and put on some clothes, and sat at the kitchen table. The light in the sky was fading fast now. The gloaming, he told her, was another name for twilight. "Gloaming," she said. "I will remember that."

She was wearing his dressing gown. She hadn't pulled it fully closed and he could see the slopes of her breasts; they gleamed, and in the cleft between them they were the

253

color of a knife blade. When he was speaking, she had a way of lowering her head with her chin tucked in and gazing at him from under her gray-streaked fringe. Her plump upper lip was plumper still from his kisses.

He asked her what Paul did, Paul Viertel, her dead sister's son. She told him he was studying to be a doctor. "A proper one," she said, smiling, "not like you, not a body snatcher."

He laughed. "Is that what I am?"

"Or do I mean a sawbones? I don't know."

They spoke of Phoebe. "Your daughter is unhappy," she said.

"Is she? Are you sure? What is she unhappy about?"

"Many things. Herself. You."

"Me?"

"Yes, you. She loves you very much."

"She does?"

"You don't believe it because you can't see it."

He made a mock bow. *"Jawohl, Herr Doktor,"* he said.

"Frau Doktor, please! Do I seem so mannish to you?"

Each time a car went past in the street, its headlights turned the dusk a little darker.

"Unhappiness is not so bad," Evelyn said. "Once a woman came to Freud who was very sick, very sick in the head, you know, and asked him if he could cure her. 'I cannot cure you,' Freud said, 'but I can perhaps make you be ordinarily unhappy.' That was so wise, don't you think? Ordinarily unhappy, like everyone else."

He asked her about her husband. "Oh, Richard," she said, "he was *more* than unhappy."

"I didn't really know him," Quirke said. "What was his trouble?"

"Everything. Including me, I think. He had, one might say, a talent for unhappiness, poor man. And of course, he drank — you knew that?"

Quirke nodded. "Where did you meet?"

Smiling, she shook her head slowly. "You must understand," she said, "there are things I will not speak of. Not because they are so terrible, like what happened to my family, or so private, like Robert's uncurable sorrow, or our son who died."

"Why, then?"

She looked up at the window and the darkening blue air outside.

"It seems to me," she said, "that each one of us has a store of things that are — I don't know what the word is. I am like a ship carrying a precious cargo through a great storm. All the sailors are telling the captain he must throw the cargo overboard or the ship will sink and all of them will be lost to the sea. But no, the captain tells them, no, if I do as you say, the loss will be greater than the risk of death — not the loss to the merchants who own the cargo, and who can always get more, but to ourselves. We shall arrive in harbor and be less than we were when we set out." She laid a hand on his. "Do you see?"

He was frowning. "No," he said, "I don't understand. Isn't that the point of what you do, isn't it your job to get people to talk about things, especially things that are painful, or private?"

"Ah yes," she said, "and that is why I am a doctor, and not a patient."

They went into the bedroom to finish dressing. With their clothes on, they found they were suddenly shy of each other. He walked her down the stairs to the street. That single star, stiletto-shaped, glimmered low in the sky above the roofstops.

"Look at this," Evelyn said, gesturing disgustedly at the Volkswagen. "My little Hitler car. I should be ashamed."

She unlocked the car door. He felt a sudden rush of panic. "Will you see me again?" he said, touching her on the elbow.

She was getting into the car, and paused

now and glanced back at him over her shoulder. "Why, of course," she said. "Why would I not?"

"Yes, but —" He didn't know what he wanted to say. "I mean — I mean like this. Will you see me again like this?"

She sat behind the wheel.

"I don't know," she said. She was facing the windscreen, frowning, and didn't look up at him. "I think so. It was very nice, between us."

He leaned down and put his head in through the low doorway and kissed her awkwardly. She caught him by his shirt collar and held him captive, crouching, half in and half out of the car, barely keeping his balance.

"My dear," she said, "look at you, so silly. You think perhaps we can be unhappy together, ordinarily unhappy?"

"Like everyone else?"

"Yes. Like everyone else."

She let go of him, and he stood back and swung the door shut. She didn't roll down the window, but pressed the ignition, and switched on the headlights, and drove away.

Half an hour later, his telephone rang. It was Evelyn. He carried the phone to the window with the receiver to his ear and stood looking out at that star glistening tremulously above the roofs. He wondered what it was called. Sirius, was it, the Dog Star? Were these the dog days? He didn't know.

"I just wanted to say good night," Evelyn said.

"I'm glad you called."

"Are you?"

All her questions, he noticed, no matter how inconsequential they might seem, were real questions, demanding real answers.

"Yes," he said. "I am. I was thinking about you."

"Good." She was silent for a time. "It's so strange," she said, "I have something of you inside me still. Just now I put my finger there and tasted it."

"Did you? What does it taste like?"

"Bread."

"That's good."

"Bread and pearls."

"Pearls don't taste of anything."

"How do you know? Anyway, it sounds nice, yes?"

"Yes, it does."

"Listen to me," she said. "Will you tell Phoebe about tonight, about us?"

"I don't know. I hadn't thought."

"Then I shall."

"You'll tell her?"

"Yes. Why not? She'll be glad, I think. She worries about you, that you are lonely."

He felt a tiny stab of misgiving. Did she too think of him as lonely, was that why she had let him take her clothes off and make love to her?

"I can hear you thinking," Evelyn said. "You mustn't think sad thoughts. You are loved — this is true, what I'm telling you. Even if you and I were never to see each other again, you would have been loved, by me. And always you have your daughter." She paused. "Be kind to yourself, my dear. Try to be."

He was silent.

"Are you there?"

"Yes, I'm here," he said. "I don't know what to say to you."

"Say nothing, then. Keep your cargo, throw none of it overboard."

"You know what I'm thinking anyway."

She gave a low laugh. "Of course I do. I am the witch doctor, of course. I have a patient who tells me that after every session with me he feels empty, as if I have put a spell on him and drained his blood."

"Is that good or bad? It sounds bad."

"It is neither. It is just a part of the process."

"Part of the cure?"

"There is no cure. I told you this. Only the process."

"I think I'm in love with you, Evelyn."

"Yes, yes, I know you do." She spoke softly, as if to soothe a child.

"You know I love you, or you know I only think I love you, which?"

"Both, maybe. But I am tired now, and I must go to sleep. I will not wash my hands or brush my teeth. I want to wake up in the night and smell and taste you." She sighed. "I am being ridiculous."

"We both are. It doesn't matter."

"No," she said, "it doesn't."

14

Hackett's office was stifling — he told himself he must get that bloody window unstuck so he could open it and let in a bit of air. Instead he thought he might venture out for a stroll. It was another unendurably hot day, the sky cloudless and the city lying torpid, like a huge, stranded turtle, under the sun's relentless glare. He had thought of buying himself a straw hat, like the rakish one Quirke was sporting these days, but he didn't think he would have the nerve to wear it. And anyway, May would be bound to laugh at him. His wife had a good heart, and loved him, in her way, as he loved her, but she had a merciless eye for his foibles and his foolishnesses and would let none of them pass unremarked. So he took up his old felt trilby and shut the office door behind himself and went down to the street.

He walked up to College Green and along Westmoreland Street. Bewley's was belching clouds of smoke from the big vat of roasting coffee just inside the open front door. The clock over the offices of the *Irish Times* told him it was eleven twenty-five exactly, but even as he looked at it, the minute hand moved on with a jerk and a tiny quiver. He kept his eyes averted from the shop windows because he didn't care to catch sight of his own reflection. May had been on him recently to take up a diet and reduce his potbelly, but he knew he wouldn't; it was too late for him to try shifting so much fat. He sighed. Life was tricky, that was for sure.

By the time he was halfway along O'Connell Street his shirt was wet under the armpits, the band of his hat seemed to have become welded to his forehead, and he had to keep mopping the back of his neck with a handkerchief that was already sodden and limp. So he crossed the road and jumped onto a bus for Dorset Street just as it was moving off. He didn't bother to look for a seat, but stayed standing on the platform, holding on to the rail, trading complaints with the conductor about the heat wave that was showing no sign of ending.

When he got to Dorset Street he stood outside the tobacconist's shop and peered up at Sam Corless's window. There was nothing to be seen, of course, except grimed glass and a frayed cretonne curtain. Maybe he shouldn't have come up here, he thought, maybe he should leave the poor man to his grieving. Nevertheless he rang the bell, and after a minute or two Corless came down and opened the door. He was gray and haggard, and seemed to have lost weight even in the short time since his son's death — his face was so gaunt his spectacles, still with the lump of sticking plaster around the earpiece, looked far too big for him, like an ill-fitting prosthesis.

"Good day to you, Mr. Corless," Hackett said. "The name is —"

"I remember you," Corless said. "I'd hardly forget, would I." His voice, feathery and hollow, seemed to be coming out of an echoing underground cistern. "What do you want?"

"Well, I was just out for a stroll and I thought I'd pay a call and see how you were getting on. If I'm an annoyance to you, say so."

Corless managed a sort of grin. "Why would I be annoyed," he said, "by a visit from the police?" He stood back, holding open the door. "Come in, you may as well."

Hackett followed the stooped and plodding figure up the narrow stairs. In the flat the air was thicker than ever, and there was a dull, brownish smell, the smell of things left long unwashed.

"Sit down," Corless said. "Throw them books on the floor. Will you have a drink? I've no beer. There's only whiskey."

"A drop of whiskey would be grand," Hackett said, looking for somewhere to put his hat down. "They say spirits have a cooling effect, despite what you might think."

Corless rummaged about under the sink and came up with a bottle of Powers, three-quarters empty. "I should be fairly cool myself, then," he said. "I've drunk enough of the bloody stuff these past couple of days. This is the second bottle, unless it's the third. I've lost count."

He set two small glasses on the draining board and filled them to the brim.

"Your good health," Hackett said, lifting the glass to eye level.

Corless, leaning against the sink, did not return the toast. He drank, taking half of the measure in one swallow.

Dance music was playing somewhere, not loud. Corless pointed to the floor. "That bastard below has the wireless going non-stop all day long," he said. "It always seems to be the same stuff. I think he must be

264

practicing to be a ballroom dancer. And then comedians, and the audience in fits. Furlong is his name. Doesn't smoke, himself. Imagine that, a tobacconist who doesn't smoke."

They listened to the music for a while. Glenn Miller, Joe Loss, one of those — Hackett knew nothing about dance bands, never having been much of a dancer.

"The funeral was yesterday, I saw," he said. "I'd like to have gone, but I couldn't. How was it?"

Corless gave a sardonic laugh. "Oh, smashing," he said. "A great crowd attended, and a fine time was had by all. Talk about dancing — it was round-the-house-and-mind-the-dresser till the small hours of the morning." He made a sour face and drank off the rest of the whiskey in his glass. "There was me, and my dead wife's sister, and some old fellow I didn't know from Adam, who'd strayed into the wrong funeral, if I'm not mistaken. The wife's sister had to go home and make her husband's dinner."

"Sorry," Hackett said gruffly. "I should have gone."

"It's no matter. Burying the dead is best done quickly. I don't hold with keening and wailing."

He refilled his glass and offered the bottle wordlessly to Hackett, who shook his head.

"All the same, a sad occasion, a funeral," Hackett said. "It's the finality of it. I buried my mother not long ago. It was only when I saw the coffin down in the hole that it dawned on me at last that she was gone."

Corless, still leaning against the sink, shrugged his shoulders impatiently. "I have the suspicion," he said, "that you didn't come here to console me. Have you found out anything?"

Hackett rose from the chair and held out his glass. "Maybe I will take a sup more," he said.

Corless poured the whiskey. His hand was unsteady. Hackett returned to his chair. The dance band on the wireless below was playing "Chattanooga Choo Choo"; even Hackett recognized that one.

"Tell me, Mr. Corless," he said, "did your son ever talk to you about his work?"

"Didn't you ask me that already, the other day?"

"I don't think so, but of course, the old memory is not what it was." He took a careful drink from his glass. "Anyway, I'll ask it again now: did he?"

"I told you, Leon and I didn't talk very often. He disapproved of me, didn't like my politics. The feeling was mutual."

"But you must have seen him, the odd time?"

"Oh, we saw each other for a pint, now and then." He noticed Hackett's look, and sighed. "You're thinking I wasn't much of a father. Maybe I wasn't. But I loved him, all the same. I just wasn't much good at showing it. He understood. He was the same himself. As my old mother used to say, we're not the kissing kind."

"Did you ever meet his girlfriend?"

Corless stared. "Did he have a girlfriend? That's news to me."

"A girl called Lisa."

"Lisa who?"

"Smith, she calls herself," Hackett said, "though we're not entirely sure that's really her name. It seems she was there, the night your son died."

"Was where? Where was she?"

Hackett got out his cigarettes. "Will you smoke a Player's?"

"No, thanks, I'll stick to the Woodbines."

The both lit up. At the first intake of smoke Corless coughed so hard he had to put the whiskey down on the draining board so as not to spill it. "Jesus Christ," he said, gasping, "one of these days I'll bring up a lung." He stood with his head lowered, taking deep breaths, then picked up his glass again and drank. The cigarette was still burning in his fingers.

"It seems," Hackett said, "this girl, this young woman, Lisa, had been to a party of some kind with your son. They were coming home late and they had a row, and she made Leon stop, and she got out of the car to take a taxi. Next thing she saw was the car in flames, apparently."

Corless stood motionless, watching him. "And then what did she do?"

"She got into a panic, I think, and went home."

"She went home? She didn't try to help Leon, she didn't call an ambulance, or the Guards?"

"I don't think there was anything to be done, by that stage," Hackett said, looking down at his hat where he had put it on top of the pile of books on the floor beside his chair. "Not anything that would have helped your son, anyway."

Corless's mouth was set in a thin, bitter line. "Who is she, anyway?" he asked.

"Well, that's what we don't know, you see."

"What *do* you know?"

Hackett sipped his whiskey.

"It's a queer sort of a situation," he said.

"You remember Dr. Quirke, that was here with me the other day, the pathologist? It seems the girl, Lisa, knew his daughter from a course they were in together, and came to her and asked for her help, saying she was frightened and needed somewhere to hide."

"What was she frightened of?"

"She wouldn't say. Anyhow, Dr. Quirke's daughter brought Lisa to a house down in Wicklow, a holiday house that the family had, and left her there. Later on, Phoebe, Dr. Quirke's girl, got worried, and went back down to the house, only to find that she was gone, that Lisa was gone, without leaving a trace behind her. We also searched in Lisa's flat, up in Rathmines, or what we think was her flat, anyway, but there was nothing there, either. She just — well, she just vanished."

Corless's eyes were fixed on Hackett. "So you're taking this as another sign that Leon didn't die by accident?"

"We don't know how to take it, Mr. Corless, and that's the truth. It has us baffled, I don't mind confessing."

Corless lit a new cigarette from the butt of the old one and dropped the butt into the sink, where it made a tiny hiss.

"You asked me, when you came in," he said, "if Leon ever talked to me about his

269

work. What was that about?"

"I went to see Leon's boss, a chap called O'Connor, up in the department. Do you know him?"

"I know of him. Patriot, church stalwart, Knights of St. Patrick, that kind of thing."

"That's the man. He said Leon was doing work, keeping some kind of statistics, in the mother-and-child area. Know anything about that?"

"How many times do I have to tell you, Leon didn't talk to me about his work."

"Was he secretive, would you say?"

"It wasn't that. He knew I wouldn't be interested. I don't care a damn what this rotten gang, our so-called government, gets up to."

"But your son," Hackett said softly, "was a government employee."

"You don't have to tell me that!" Corless snapped. "As I said to you about your own" — he smiled thinly — "profession, I never hold it against a man how he earns his living." He looked aside, blinking. "I never told him how proud of him I was. It's another thing not to forgive myself for."

"Right. Right." Hackett had finished his whiskey, and now he balanced the empty glass on his knee. He pursed his lips and considered his hat again. "It's only," he said, "that when I began to ask about Leon's work, Mr. O'Connor seemed to get very agitated, and talked about things being delicate, and mentioned the Archbishop's Palace." He glanced at Corless and smiled. "I find that when I hear the Archbishop spoken of by a person of position and power such as Mr. O'Connor, my ears begin to tingle, in an interested sort of way."

Corless closed his eyes and massaged the skin at the bridge of his nose with a thumb and two fingers. "It's a funny thing," he said, "but I can't concentrate these days. Even when I'm not thinking about Leon, my mind still seems to be somewhere else all the time. It's like being in that state when you wake up after being knocked out."

"I'm sorry," Hackett said. "I should take myself off and leave you alone."

Corless waved a hand. "No, no," he said, "don't mind me, I'm just — I'm just —"

"You're exhausted, Mr. Corless," Hackett said. "That's all it is. Sorrow is a wearying thing."

Corless poured himself another drink. This time he didn't bother to offer Hackett a refill.

"Tell me," he said, "tell me what it is you're talking about. Tell me what you think is going on here. All my life I've had to guard against imagining that there are conspiracies all around me. It's an occupational hazard for an old revolutionary." He chuckled dully. "Look at Stalin. But from what you say, or at least from the tone you say it in, it seems to me you have the idea that there's a great big mess under our feet here, and that Leon's death is part of that mess. Am I right?"

Hackett took his time before answering.

"I don't know," he said. "That's to say, I know that there must be a whole lot more here than meets the eye, only I can't tell you what it is. There's not only the death of your son, there's this young one, Lisa, and the way she disappeared. There's Mr. O'Connor nearly wetting himself when I asked him a few simple questions about Leon's work in the department." He picked up his hat. "Every web, Mr. Corless, has a spider sitting at the center of it. That's my experience, anyway."

He stood up. His sweat-soaked cotton shirt was cold now, and he shivered. The feeling made him think of childhood, of being on the beach on gray summer days, his teeth chattering, with a wet towel wrapped around him and clamped under his armpits. Nothing ever gets lost, he thought, it's all in there, somewhere, ready to spring out at the least hint of an invitation. He could imagine what poor Corless was having to put up with these days, the past pouring out, an unstoppable torrent.

"I'll go now, Mr. Corless," he said. "Thank you indeed for the whiskey. It was a great tonic, though I imagine I'll have to have a little sleep later on in the afternoon."

Corless walked behind him down the stairs. The air in the street was blue with exhaust smoke and the dust thrown up by wheels and hooves and feet.

"You'll keep me informed," Corless said.

"Oh, I will indeed. What I'm going to do is, I'm going to shake the web. I'm going to give it a good shake, and see what might come running out."

Corless was studying him, his head to one side. "What will you do if you find out for definite that my son was killed?"

They could hear the wireless playing in the shop beside them. This time Hackett couldn't identify the tune.

"I'll look for the killer, and bring him to justice," he said. "What else would I do?"

Corless laughed shortly.

"Oh, right," he said. "What else would you do."

Hackett walked away. When he reached the corner and glanced back, Corless was still standing in the doorway, watching him. Hackett waved, he wasn't sure why, and turned down North Frederick Street. Outside Findlater's Church, a one-legged beggar leaned against the wall, playing a mouth organ.

Should he have told Corless that Lisa Smith was expecting his grandson? He judged the man had enough momentous things to deal with already.

Shake the web, yes; shake the web.

15

Phoebe was surprised when Dr. Blake asked if she could accompany her to lunch. Mr. Jolly had just left at the end of his session, looking secretive and conspiratorial. He paused as he passed by Phoebe's desk and leaned down and whispered excitedly, "Oh, I've been a naughty boy — a very naughty boy!" She supposed he was harmless, although Mrs. Jolly, if there was one, probably wouldn't agree. She was clearing up her desk when Dr. Blake came out and said to her, "Oh, Phoebe, are you going to that place you told me about, that nice café in that nice cool basement? Perhaps I will come with you. You'll permit, yes?"

They walked along Fitzwilliam Square in the sun.

"We have a key to the gate here, haven't we?" Dr. Blake said.

"Yes. I think they're only supposed to be for residents, but there is one in the office."

"Good. We should bring a picnic lunch one day and have it in there, in the square. It would be so nice. This fine weather will not last, and then we will be sorry."

Phoebe glanced at her sidelong. She seemed to be smiling to herself. She was in a strange mood today. Maybe it was the effect of her hour with Mr. Jolly, for she was somewhat as he had been, as if she had a secret and was brimming over with it.

Phoebe wondered more and more keenly what exactly it was that went on behind the consulting room's reinforced door. Surely it would be boring, sitting for hour after hour, listening to people pouring out their troubles, their obsessions, their manias. She supposed it must be part of a psychiatrist's training to sit very still and just listen. In her deepest heart she believed that most of Dr. Blake's patients had nothing wrong with them at all, apart from their ordinary eccentricities — everyone was eccentric, there was no such thing as absolute normality — and that all they were suffering from, if it could be called suffering, was a kind of inverted pride, the arrogance of the self-obsessed.

In the Country Shop they sat at Phoebe's favorite table by the window. Dr. Blake read the menu with the same calmness and deep concentration she brought to everything she did. "Yes," she said, "I shall have a salad with some cold chicken. That will be good."

The waitress came, and they ordered. Phoebe had her usual ham sandwich. Then Dr. Blake leaned forward at the table with her fingers entwined in front of her.

"There is something I wish to talk to you about, Phoebe," she said. "It is something that might affect our professional relationship, and so we should speak of it, and then" — she moved her hands to the right — "put it aside. Yes?"

Phoebe felt a chill along her spine. Had she done something wrong, was her work not satisfactory? She couldn't bear the thought of having to give up her office, her desk, her routine that already, in the short time she had been in the job, had become so important for her. She would even miss her encounters with Mr. Jolly, and the thumb sucker, and all the other patients, except maybe the mother with the uncontrollable son.

Dr. Blake was looking at her expectantly, waiting for an answer. But what had the question been?

"I hope," Phoebe said, "I hope there isn't anything wrong?"

"No, no," Dr. Blake said quickly. "There

is nothing wrong at all. But last evening, after we left you, I went with your father for a drink. We sat in that nice pub, the one on Baggot Street."

"Doheny and Nesbitt's?"

"Yes, yes, that one. We drank whiskey with soda, very nice. Then I drove him to his flat and we sat outside in my car for a long time, talking about all sorts of things, his life, his upbringing, or" — she smiled — "his sad lack of upbringing, and after that we went for a little walk. We sat on a bench by the canal, and he told me — well, he told me about someone he knows who is gravely ill. This has upset him very much, but of course, you know your father — he is aware of so very little of what goes on inside him." She paused while the waitress set out glasses and a jug of water. "So then, after our talk by the canal, we returned to your father's flat, and there we went to bed together."

Phoebe blinked. At once, as if the thing itself had popped up in front of her, she saw in her mind the photograph Quirke kept on his mantelpiece, of himself and Mal, and Sarah and Delia, together long ago, in Boston.

"I see," she said, falteringly, and then, "I'm sorry, I don't know what to say."

Dr. Blake smiled. "Are you shocked? I

hope not. There was nothing shocking about it, you know. He is a very sweet man, your father, very gentle, very kind, even. Oh, I know he thinks he is a terrible person, but that's not so at all. Surely you know this?"

"Yes, I suppose I do," Phoebe said. "But —"

"But? Yes?"

Phoebe groped for words. She felt so help-less. She was trying to picture Quirke in bed with this large, plain woman, with her baby's fat upper lip and her cropped, gray-ing hair, her huge, calm, dark eyes. But it was impossible.

"Will you — will you see him again?" she said. "I mean, are you — ?"

"Will we be together for some time, is that what you want to ask? That I cannot answer. Certainly, yes, I will see him, it would be strange if I did not, and no doubt I will go to his flat again, and he may come to my house, too." She paused. "I think I made him a little happy, last night. Oh, it was not just sex, you know, that's not important, despite what everyone says, even Dr. Freud." She smiled what for her was a mischievous smile.

"What, then?" Phoebe asked. By now she was genuinely curious — indeed, by now she was in a fever of curiosity.

"Well," Dr. Blake said, "of that I am not sure. That is, I am not sure why I would have been able to make him happy, and why he would allow himself to be happy with me." She looked aside, frowning. "That will be for me to consider. Yes, I shall have to think about that."

My God, Phoebe thought, will Quirke become a case study, to be mulled over, analyzed, maybe even written up one day? The possibility was either appalling or comic; perhaps it was both.

The waitress brought their food. Phoebe didn't know how she was going to manage to eat it, in this world turned upside down.

"I hope," Dr. Blake said, "what I have told you will not affect how we are together in the office. Mmm, this chicken is very good. What is this sauce on the salad, though?"

"It comes out of a bottle," Phoebe said.

"Ah. It does not taste of very much except — what is it? Vinegar?"

"Dr. Blake," Phoebe said suddenly, "has Mr. Jolly really got a wife?"

The doctor did not lift her eyes from her plate.

"Why do you ask this?"

"Well, he talks to me about her all the time. He always comes early for his session, a half hour, forty-five minutes, and just sits there, talking, while you're with another patient."

Dr. Blake smiled at her plate. "Perhaps you should charge him a fee." She looked up. "What does one drink here? That man has a glass of milk, look. And he is eating stew. There are many things in this country that are still a mystery to me."

Phoebe toyed miserably with her sandwich. "I'm sorry," she said in a small voice, "I shouldn't have asked about Mr. Jolly."

"Why not? It is natural to be curious."

"But it's unprofessional. And that's what I want to be, I want to be professional. I want" — she couldn't stop herself — "I want to be like you."

"Do you? This is interesting. Why, do you think?"

"Because you're — because you're admirable."

"Am I? In what way?"

"I don't know. I want to be calm, like you."

"Calm," the doctor said, seeming to turn the word over and examine it from all sides. "I suppose that is a good quality. But not very — what shall I say? — not very positive."

"Oh, but it is!" Phoebe said quickly. "You've been through so much, you've seen so many terrible things, and yet you look at the world in such a tranquil way."

"Calm. Tranquil. This is a very interesting view you have of me." She ate some more of her food. "This salad sauce really is rather unpleasant," she said. She moved her plate aside and set her elbows on the table. "Yes, Mr. Jolly has a wife, I can tell you that. I can also tell you she is a very aggressive woman."

"Aggressive? But he tells me that he beats her, all the time."

Dr. Blake produced an an old little hiccuping sound; it took Phoebe a moment to recognize it as laughter.

"Ah, Mr. Jolly! He is so well named. Such a funny man — funny, and quite sick. Now, I would like a coffee. Is the coffee good here? I suppose not."

Phoebe saw the manageress making her way between the tables, carrying a bulky parcel wrapped neatly in brown paper and tied with string. She stopped at their table. She was a small, bossy woman with a bad perm that made her hair look like a tightly packed mass of steel shavings. "Are you Miss Griffin?" she asked coldly, consulting the label on the parcel. "Miss Phoebe Griffin? This was left in for you. It's laundry, I believe."

"Laundry?" Phoebe said weakly, baffled.

"Yes. This is a restaurant, you know, not a collection depot." She pronounced it *DEEP-oh*. "Kindly direct deliveries to your home in future."

She dropped the parcel on the table with a thud and turned on her heel and marched away.

"Thank you," Phoebe said weakly to her departing back, and was ignored.

The two women gazed at the parcel.

"I don't know what this is," Phoebe said. "I never asked for laundry to be delivered here."

"How very strange," Dr. Blake said. "You really know nothing about it? Jung has some interesting things to say on this kind of phenomenon. Otherwise, of course, he is a charlatan."

They ordered coffee, which, when it came, Dr. Blake, without rancor, pronounced undrinkable. "I'd like to smoke a cigarette," she said. "Do you permit?"

"Yes, of course. Have one of mine."

"Thank you. What are they called? Let me see the packet. Gold Flake! What a beautiful name. Are they very exclusive?"

"No, no, they're just — ordinary."

"Gold Flake. This I must remember."

I know what it's like, Phoebe suddenly thought, being here with her: it's like *Alice in Wonderland.* It's all completely logical, and completely mad.

"What is funny?" Dr. Blake asked.

"Oh, nothing. I was just thinking about you and my father, and how — how wonderful it is."

"You think so? I am glad." She had a peculiar way of holding her cigarette, between her middle fingers and resting on her thumb, as if it were a chopstick. And she didn't inhale, but drew the smoke barely past her lips and quickly expelled it again. "My father gave me my first cigarette to smoke when I was ten years old," she said. "My mother argued with him, but he said, no, children must be allowed to experience everything as soon as they are ready — sooner, indeed."

Phoebe wondered, somewhat uneasily, what Herr Nussbaum's notion of "everything" might have encompassed.

After a few puffs, the doctor stubbed out the cigarette. "Now we shall go back to work, I think," she said. "Who have we this afternoon?"

"Mr. Doherty is first. You know, I always suspect he's a priest."

"Do you? Why?"

"I don't know."

"Does he give off — what do you call it?

— the odor of sanctity?"

"No. It's the white socks, I think."

Dr. Blake did her hiccupy laugh again, and stood up. "Let me pay for this," she said. "You hardly ate any of your food. Was it not good? Perhaps what I told you about your father and me, perhaps that took away your appetite. So difficult, when one is young, to believe that older people also make love. Inconceivable, I should say. Ha! What a word to use. You see? Language is never innocent." She had produced a tiny leather purse from the pocket of her dress and was counting out coins. "What do you call this one?"

"A half crown."

"Yes, that's right. How many years have I been living here and I still do not understand the money. My husband tried to teach me, but he would always get so angry. Now I go into a shop and I say, 'How much is that?' and the answer is 'One pound, nineteen, and eleven pence ha'penny.' I am baffled. So always I hand over notes, and my purse fills up with coins. You should see, at home, I have jars filled with florins and sixpences — what is this one?"

"That's a threepenny bit."

"Ah," Dr. Blake said, with a look of mock despair, "I shall never learn."

Phoebe's eyes wandered uneasily to the paper parcel at her elbow. It was a large, solid cube, expertly packed. She thought of pretending to forget it and leaving it behind, but she knew the manageress would come running after her with it and make her take it. She picked it up. It did feel like laundry. She turned it over in her hands. Certainly that was her name on the label: "Miss Phoebe Griffin, c/o The Country Shop, Stephen's Green." She couldn't understand it.

"It is a package from Dr. Jung, perhaps," Dr. Blake said. "If it were from Freud, of course, it would be dirty laundry." She beamed, pleased with her joke. "Come now," she said, leading the way towards the door, "let us go and deal with the holy man in the white socks."

When they got back to the office, Phoebe put the parcel under her desk, at her feet, and tried to forget about it. She could have taken it into the lavatory on the ground floor and opened it there, but she felt an almost superstitious unwillingness to know what was in it. Was someone playing a prank at her expense? That was the kind of thing her friend Jimmy Minor would have done, sending her a package of rags wrapped up in brown paper and tied neatly with string, just for a joke, but Jimmy was gone, and she knew no one else who had his peculiar sense of humor. Could it be a gift from Quirke, a new dress or something? But why would he send it to her at the Country Shop? Quirke certainly didn't go in for jokes or surprises.

Mr. Doherty arrived then, with that expression of bland blamelessness she believed he put on specially for her, though he still looked furtive. She noticed he was wearing gray socks today, and wondered if it meant his mental condition, whatever it might be, was improving.

She was conscious of the parcel at her feet, so innocent-looking, yet to her it was like a time bomb, ticking away.

At the end of his hour Mr. Doherty sidled out of the consulting room, smiled at her with his thin pale lips — his eyes were otherwise occupied, gazing at horrors, so it seemed — and hurried away. Next in should be Mrs. Francis and her feral son, but they were late, as usual.

Of all the people who passed through the office, Mrs. Francis seemed to Phoebe the saddest, which was ironic, since she wasn't the patient. In other circumstances she would probably have been a nice woman, easygoing and kind, but Derek, the son, who was obviously ruining her life, had made her into a wild-eyed harridan. The little boy — little devil, more like — would sit on one of the straight-backed chairs with his legs dangling and stare at Phoebe with relentless, heavy-lidded intensity, smiling to himself. His mother talked to him nonstop, asking him bright little questions — was his tummy all right now? would he like to have a look at this nice magazine with the colored pictures in it? — but he ignored her with a contempt so vast and comprehensive that Phoebe, despite herself, had to admire him for it. She supposed there must be something genuinely the matter with him, for surely Dr. Blake wouldn't be seeing him twice a week if there weren't, yet she couldn't get it out of her head that what he really needed was a good smack. But then, she supposed, that was why she was sitting out here at the reception desk while it was Dr. Blake who was in the consulting room.

After a while she stopped worrying about the parcel. Indeed, she had almost forgotten about it when at half past five she put the cover on her typewriter and locked away the appointments book and the folder she kept the patients' accounts in and was preparing to go home. As she stood up from the desk, however, her foot touched it; she sighed and picked it up.

It occurred to her how dissimilar things were from people. People would take on a different aspect depending on how you thought about them — seeming fearsome if you were afraid of them or harmless if you weren't — but objects were always obstinately themselves. Or no, not obstinately; that was the wrong word. Indifferently, that was what she meant. She recalled what her father had said to her once, long ago, in the days before she knew he was her father. The thing to remember, Phoebe, he had said, is that the world is indifferent to us and what we do. He'd been a little drunk, of course — he was almost always a little drunk, then — but she had never forgotten him saying it.

The parcel was an awkward shape to hold, and she felt conspicuous with it under her arm. She tried carrying it by the string, but it soon bit into her skin and cut off the blood supply to the tips of her fingers. In the end she hailed a taxi. The taxi driver was annoyed at her because the journey was so short and the fare was only one and sixpence. She ignored his accusing glare in the rearview mirror, and looked out the window at the sunlit shopfronts of Baggot Street going by. The parcel was on the seat beside her. She knew it was foolish, but she couldn't get rid of the feeling that it was staring at her, just like Derek Francis, the feral boy.

In the flat she put the parcel on the table and deliberately left it there while she went to the kitchen and poured herself a glass of wine. She hardly ever drank by herself. The wine, a bottle of Liebfraumilch, had been open for some time in the fridge, and tasted peculiar, but she drank it anyway. Then at last she took up the dressmaker's scissors she kept in the drawer beside the cooker and advanced determinedly on the parcel and severed the string.

There were articles of table linens — napkins, an embroidered tablecloth — along with sheets and pillowcases, all ironed and neatly folded. She lifted them up one by one and shook them out. They gave off a strong smell of starch. There were no identifying tags or initials, only the usual pink laundry slips held in place with tiny safety pins. Then, when she was halfway through the pile, a sheet of paper slithered out. It was a laundry list, headed "Mother of Mercy Laundry Ltd." What was written out on it was not a list, however, but a hastily scrawled message, addressed, like the parcel itself, to her.

16

Edward Gallagher, known to all as Ned, was Secretary-General at the Department of the Taoiseach, and hence the Prime Minister's right-hand man. In fact, he was much more than that. He was the most powerful civil servant in Leinster House. He knew everything that went on, not only in his own department but in all the others as well, even the least significant and underfunded of them. Able men in their time had set themselves against him and tried to wrest power from him, to their great cost. When it came to strategic maneuvering, there was no one to match big Ned Gallagher. He had, in his chosen profession, the weight and durability of a boulder. There was a saying among his colleagues, that prime ministers might come and go, but Ned Gallagher went on forever.

He had been a civil servant for more than thirty years, starting out in a junior clerkship in the Department of Agriculture and steadily climbing the greasy pole of preferment with little apparent effort. Buggins' turn might apply to other, less brilliant men, but there was a sense of inevitability to Ned Gallagher's rise to the dizzy heights that was a source of awe to those who witnessed it, especially those young enough to have heard of it only by way of departmental legend. There wasn't a colleague who didn't respect him — nor a politician in the House, no matter how brutish or wily, who wasn't afraid of him.

Yet Ned Gallagher was, outwardly at least, the most affable of men. He was large, well over six feet tall, broad-shouldered and athletic still, though he would be fifty-five on his next birthday, with a great rectangular head of sandy hair, periwinkle-blue eyes, and a wide, artless, and irresistible smile. He had never lost his Kerry accent and spoke perfect Irish with a musical lilt. He had a fine, semidetached house in Drumcondra, conveniently close to the Archbishop's Palace. It was to the palace that he would call in, discreetly, after work every Thursday evening, for a chat with His Grace about the past week's happenings along the subtly winding corridors of power. Often these chats developed into strategy discussions on how best to safeguard the welfare of Holy Mother Church and promote her influence in all areas of life, public and private.

Ned was married to a former nurse. They had three children, two girls, one of them a Carmelite nun, and a son who had followed in his father's footsteps and gone for the Civil Service, and who, at the age of only twenty-three, was already on his way up. His name was Fergus but his colleagues had nicknamed him Neidín; he was the apple of his father's eye, and while Ned senior was a charmer, Neidín was regarded universally as a bastard: ruthless and utterly unscrupulous, a young man not to be crossed.

Inspector Hackett had known Ned Gallagher for a long time; they went, as the saying had it, way back. Few people, if any, remembered or knew exactly how the two men had become acquainted, and this suited them both, especially Ned. Ned did not care to remind himself of the circumstances of his first encounter with the policeman. It had occurred on a long-ago November night, dismal and rainy, when a young Guard on the beat had caught Ned in the company of a traveling salesman in the underground public lavatory at the top of Burgh Quay. The traveler, his trousers round his ankles, was leaning back with both hands braced on the rim of one of the sinks, while Ned was on his knees in front of him.

It had been a moment of absolute madness, of course, for which Ned, in despair and terror, roundly cursed himself. Why couldn't they have locked themselves in one of the stalls, for God's sake? The answer, of course, was the dark joy to be had from taking the worst of all possible risks. At the time, in the heat of that mad moment, it had seemed worth it. But it had taken only a second, with the hand of the law on his shoulder, for Ned to realize the catastrophe he was facing, a catastrophe that seemed to him all the more terrible because it was entirely of his own making, and could so easily have been avoided.

Ned had always been lucky, however, and that night his luck held. The Guard who had chanced on the two men about their shocking business had recognized Ned — his photograph had been in the paper that very week, over a story about a visit to Ireland by an American congressman — and, worried, had used his walkie-talkie to call the home number of Sergeant Hackett, whose sage advice he urgently sought. "Bring the bugger into the station," Hackett had said, "but take him down to the cells and don't let anyone see him."

Hackett came into Pearse Street, interviewed Ned briefly, and let him go with a caution. Hackett knew the world and its ways, and despite the anathemas of church and state alike, he held it against no man for giving in to the carnal impulse, no matter what form that impulse took. What he had never told anyone was that his youngest brother, his favorite among his siblings, was that way inclined. As far as Hackett was concerned, it was for the good Lord, and not the law and its officers, to judge us for our grubby misdemeanors.

Besides, they were all living in a land of glass houses, where public stone throwing was inadvisable. The church, the arbiter in all matters of faith and morals, had her weaknesses when it came to the sins of the flesh. Indeed, Hackett had heard certain rumors, uttered only in secret and in the softest of whispers, about the Archbishop himself, rumors that, if true, would have scandalized the faithful and rocked the church to its foundations.

Hackett had run across Ned Gallagher on a number of occasions since that momentous night in the swirling fog on Burgh Quay, but in decidedly different circumstances. Ned had learned his lesson, and these days conducted his secret life with circumspection and the greatest discretion. So when the Inspector telephoned Ned's office and asked his secretary to have her boss call him, not ten minutes elapsed before Ned was on the phone, sounding ebullient as ever, though not without a catch of concern in his voice. They chatted briefly, but Hackett could almost hear Ned urging him, anxious in his impatience, to get to the point.

"There's a small matter I'd like to consult you on," Hackett said. "Would you have a minute, this afternoon, or maybe this evening?"

"Oh, certainly, certainly," Gallagher said. "Sure, why wouldn't I have time to talk to the law, ha ha?"

He was perceptibly startled, however, when he heard where Hackett proposed they should meet.

"The Hangman, you say?" he said, as if he had never heard of the place. "Remind me, now, where is that?"

"It's up there at Kingsbridge Station, on the other side of the river. I'm sure you know it." Hackett smiled into the receiver. "If it wouldn't be too much out of your way. Would five o'clock suit you? It'll be nice and quiet at that time of the evening."

"Oh, fine, so," Gallagher said. Hackett could hear the reluctance, and the growing worry, in his voice.

O'Driscoll's public house, popularly known as the Hangman, was on a cobbled street away from the river, wedged between a mattress warehouse and a garage that had long ago closed down. It was a disreputable establishment, frequented by various species of criminal life. It was also known, in certain circles, as the haunt of men with special predilections, and Hackett had no doubt whatsoever that Ned Gallagher, despite his show of vagueness on the phone, knew the place, and knew it intimately.

The Inspector was the first to arrive. He sat in the dimness of the public bar, at a small table in the corner, with a bottle of Bass and a greasy copy of the *Evening Mail* that someone had left behind. He had lately given up drinking Guinness, thinking it too heavy on the stomach, but he was still finding it hard to get used to bottled beer, although, perversely, he liked its sudsy consistency. He lit a cigarette; tobacco smoke always dulled the edge of even the most unpleasant tastes, he found.

The only customers, apart from himself, were a couple of heavyset types, railway porters, probably, sitting hunched at the bar with their backs turned to him. The barman, a skinny fellow with sloping shoulders and an impossibly long neck, was leaning on the bar with his arms folded, listening to what sounded like a horse-racing commentary on the wireless. In here there was no sense of the intense light and pulsing heat of outdoors — the summer day was showing no signs of waning yet. Hackett read a report on efforts being made by the Dublin dioceses to hold another Eucharistic Congress to match the great success of 1932; His Grace Archbishop McQuaid himself, it was said, was considering traveling to Rome to make a personal approach to the Vatican. Hackett took a drink of the insipid beer and turned to the sports pages.

When Ned Gallagher arrived, he stopped in the doorway and scanned the room quickly. He wore a dark blue, three-piece pinstriped suit. He was visibly relieved to see only Hackett there, in his gloomy corner, and the two rough fellows at the bar; the people who might have recognized him tended to come in much later, near closing time, emboldened by the general tipsiness of the clientele and their consequent approachability. Seeing Ned's anxious look, Hackett felt a slight regret at having summoned him to the Hangman; Hackett wasn't a mischievous man, and he took no real pleasure in the discomfort even of puffed-up hypocrites of the likes of Ned Gallagher.

"Ah, there you are!" Gallagher said, approaching Hackett with a hand extended. "Isn't it great weather we're having?" He pointed to Hackett's glass. "Will you take another of them?"

"No, no," Hackett said, rising. "My round. What'll you have?"

"Just a bottle of orange. I'm off on retreat tomorrow — to Glenstal, you know — so I'd better stick to the soft stuff. It wouldn't do to arrive at the blessed abbey stinking of porter."

Hackett smiled tolerantly and went to the bar. The two fellows sitting there turned their heads and regarded him blankly. There was something about the dead look in their eyes that made him think they probably weren't porters after all. He decided it would be prudent to ignore them. Meanwhile he, in turn, was ignored by the skinny barman. He waited a polite interval, then spoke: "Hand us out a bottle of minerals, there, Mick," he said.

The barman gave him a hostile stare. "My name is not Mick," he growled.

"Is that so?" Hackett said easily. "I'll take that bottle of Orange Crush, all the same, and another bottle of Bass. And maybe you'd bring them over for me, will you?"

He ambled back to the table in the corner.

"Busy as ever, I suppose, Inspector?" Ned Gallagher said.

"Oh, as ever." He glanced in the direction of the two hunched backs at the bar. "For all my efforts, the world refuses to give up its wicked ways. I see your name in the papers, now and then."

Gallagher shifted uneasily in his chair; there was a number of possible ways in which his name might appear in the public prints, some of which didn't bear contemplating.

The barman brought their drinks and banged them down bad-temperedly on the table. "That'll be two and fourpence," he said.

Hackett counted out the coins and handed them over and the barman slouched away. Ned Gallagher tipped the bottle of Orange Crush into his glass and held it aloft. *"Sláinte,"* he said.

Hackett poured the foaming ale; it made a joggling sound as it toppled into the glass. He sipped. The taste really wasn't getting any better. He would stick with Bass until the end of the week, and if it hadn't grown on him by then he'd go back to the Guinness, whatever smart remarks May might make about his waistline.

"Were you at the match on Sunday?" Gallagher said.

"No," Hackett answered. "As it happens, I had to work. You saw in the paper about that young fellow dying in a crash in the Phoenix Park? Leon Corless. One of yours." Gallagher stared at him wildly. "Civil servant, I mean."

"Oh. Right. Yes." He coughed softly into his fist. "Corless, yes. In Agriculture and Fisheries, wasn't he?"

"No," Hackett said. "Health."

He didn't doubt that Gallagher had known perfectly well where Leon Corless worked. By now, lying was second nature to poor Ned.

"Ah, right. I didn't know him —" He broke off, hearing how defensive he had sounded. "I mean, I didn't come across him. Somebody said he was a bright spark."

"So I'm told. Statistics, that was his field, I believe."

"Oh, they all have some new-fangled speciality, the bright boys."

Hackett was lighting a cigarette.

"I went up to the department to have a

word with his boss. Chap called O'Connor."

Gallagher nodded. "Turlough O'Connor," he said. "Yes, a sound man."

"He seemed a bit" — Hackett blew out the match — "nervous, to me."

"Nervous? About what?"

"Hard to say. About whatever it was young Corless was working on, before he died, so it seemed."

Gallagher had gone very still, like an old fox hearing faintly from afar the sound of the huntsman's horn.

"And what class of work was it he was doing?" he asked carefully.

"Mr. O'Connor wouldn't say, exactly. Something in the mother-and-child area, I believe."

Gallagher nodded. His unease was growing by the minute. Civil servants, Hackett reflected, were by nature a cautious species, but none was more cautious than one with a secret of his own to hide.

"I see," Gallagher said. "That would be a sensitive area, now."

"Yes. Turlough O'Connor said much the same thing, when I spoke to him. And when he was saying it he looked almost as worried as you do now, Mr. Gallagher."

Gallagher blinked. "You'd be worried yourself, Inspector, if you knew half the

302

things that a man in my position is privy to."

"I'm sure you're right. But the point is, you see, there's sort of a criminal investigation going on over the death of young Mr. Corless."

"What do you mean, a sort of investigation?"

Hackett scratched his chin, producing a sandpapery sound. "There are suspicious circumstances surrounding his death."

"Such as?"

"Such as the fact, and it seems to be a fact, that he was dead, or at least unconscious, before his car crashed."

"Did he have a heart attack or something?"

"No, he didn't."

"Ah, I see. So someone else is involved, then?"

"That's the way it's looking."

Gallagher thought this over, a muscle working in his big square jaw. "Corless," he said. "Isn't he a son of what's-his-name Corless, the Communist fellow?"

"Samuel Corless. He was, yes."

"Hmm. In that case, God knows what kind of stuff he was mixed up in. The father has a steady flow of red rubles coming in by the month from Moscow, I hear, and he's supposed to be in cahoots with the IRA, too. We get regular reports on him from the Special Branch. Like father, like son, eh?"

"Have you knowledge that young Corless was political, like his father? You said a minute ago he had a reputation as a bright spark. Bright sparks in your line of work tend to steer a steady course, I'm sure."

"There's nothing on him that I know of," Gallagher said.

"Nothing to suggest he might have been mixed up with subversives, for instance?"

"I told you, I don't know." Gallagher was turning sullen, though he was showing signs of being relieved, too, thinking he knew now what it was Hackett was going to ask him to do. "I can run a check on him, in the morning. There's a couple of fellows in the Branch I know well — they'll tell me anything there is to tell."

Hackett was silent for a while, lighting another Player's. "You haven't touched your glass of orange," he said. "Are you sure you wouldn't like something else? Though I'd hate to make a man break his fast who's going on a retreat."

Gallagher shook his head sulkily; no doubt it rankled sorely with him that he had to sit here meekly and take all this guff from a jumped-up peeler.

Hackett leaned forward, lowering his voice. "The thing is, Mr. Gallagher," he said, "I don't think for a moment that Leon Corless was involved in politics, subversive or otherwise. I don't think he even had any interest in such things. He was a scientist, a technician. And himself and his father were hardly on speaking terms."

"How do you know that?"

"Because his father told me so."

Gallagher drew back his head and looked at Hackett with a witheringly skeptical smile. "Ah, now, Inspector, come on. Why would you believe a word out of the mouth of that champion of atheistic communism?"

Hackett was still leaning across the table, looking up sideways at Gallagher, and now he too smiled. It was a gentle smile, tender, almost, and it brought back all of Gallagher's unease and worried resentment.

"I believe Sam Corless is an honest man," Hackett said. "I may be wrong, of course, as I have been, many times, in the past. Be that as it may, I don't think his son was killed, if he was killed, out of political motives. Or at least, not the kind of political motives you seem to be suggesting."

He stopped, and sat back in his chair and drank the dregs of his beer. Gallagher was regarding him with a sort of fascination.

This encounter was, for Gallagher, a novel experience. He was used to being the one sitting at his ease, with some terrified underling squirming and sweating in front of him.

"Look, Inspector," he said, in a wheedling tone he couldn't suppress and that made him angry with himself, "I should be getting home, the missus will be wondering where —"

"Yes, yes," Hackett said, lifting a hand, "I won't keep you more than another minute, for I'm sure my own tea is on the table and going cold even as we speak. What I want is a small favor. Tomorrow when you go into the office —" He stopped, and put on a look of polite concern. "But tell me, what time will you be setting off for Glenstal and your retreat?"

"First thing."

Hackett shook his head sadly. "Ah, that's a pity. For I really do need this little favor done. Do you think, by any chance, you might delay your departure by an hour or two? Because what I want is for you to find out for me what sort of work it was exactly that young Leon Corless was engaged in, at the department, in the area of the mother and the child."

A silence fell, as the two men confronted

each other across the table. Gallagher's brow colored, and a hard gleam came into his eyes. Hackett gazed back at him blandly, with his blandest, gentlest smile.

"What do you think I am," Gallagher said gratingly, unable to restrain himself, "some sort of a clerk, some sort of a messenger boy?"

Hackett reared back in feigned astonishment and shock.

"Oh, Mr. Gallagher, I certainly think no such thing," he said. "If you feel this little task is beneath you, don't give it another thought. We'll finish our drinks and go home to our wives and forget we ever met here this evening. It's just that, with all the matters you're privy to, I thought this wouldn't be such a great thing to ask."

He started to get to his feet. Gallagher, in control again, waved at him to sit down. "All right," he said, with an angry sigh, "all right, I'll put off leaving until lunchtime. There's a later train I can get."

Hackett, subsiding into the chair, smiled at him in happy gratitude. "As I say, I'm sure 'twill take you no longer than a few minutes to do me this little favor. All I want to know is the nature of young Corless's work, and what sort of statistics they were he was gathering. Sure, it's probably of no consequence at all, what he was doing. It's only that I'd like to know, so I can eliminate that particular line of inquiry."

Gallagher was looking at him now with a bitter, tight little smile. "It's true, what they say," he said quietly. "There's never a favor done that won't be called in, sooner or later."

Hackett had his hat in his hand. "Oh, you're in the right of it there, Mr. Gallagher," he said genially. Then he, too, lowered his voice. "The thing to do, though, is not to put yourself in the way of needing a favor, in the first place. Wouldn't you say?"

17

When the doorbell rang, Quirke pulled up the lower half of his front window and put his head out and looked down into the street and was surprised to see Phoebe standing below on the step. He wrapped the front door key in his handkerchief and dropped it down to her. The street was thick with the evening's smoky sunlight. He went back into the kitchen, where he had been eating a lamb chop with bread and sliced tomatoes; it was his standard dinner when he was dining alone, if dining it could be called. He scraped the plate into the bin under the sink and rinsed it at the tap. He rinsed his knife and fork, too, and put them with the plate on the draining board and laid a tea towel over them. Then he stopped, surprised at himself. Why try to hide the fact that he had been having his dinner? After all, Phoebe too lived alone, and must often eat by herself.

He heard her tap at the door and let her in. He always felt shy of her when there were just the two of them together. He frowned at her agitated look.

"What's wrong?" he asked.

"Nothing," she said. "Nothing's wrong." She stepped past him and went into the living room. There was a splash of late sunlight on the floor by the window. She turned to him, holding out a sheet of paper. "I got this today."

"What is it?"

She handed him the page. The first thing his eye fixed on was the Mother of Mercy heading. The message was in shorthand, with Phoebe's translation written out below it.

Dear Phoebe sorry this is the only way I can contact you I'm being kept here against my will please help me Lisa

"I don't understand," he said. "Is this from Lisa Smith? How did you get it?"

"It was in a parcel of laundry."

"What sort of laundry?"

"Just laundry. Not mine. It was delivered to the Country Shop, and they kept it for me."

Quirke sat down at the table and read the

message again. Years ago, he had gone to the Mother of Mercy Laundry in search of a young woman called Christine Falls; later there was the business of getting Maisie out of there; and now here was a plea from another young woman, from the same place.

"I don't understand," he said again.

"Isn't that laundry the one where that girl had a baby that was sent away to America? The place Grandfather Griffin was involved in funding?"

He nodded. "Yes. Your grandfather and his friends in the Knights of St. Patrick used it as a maternity home–cum–detention center for unmarried mothers. But how would Lisa Smith be in there?"

"Someone must have known she was in the house in Ballytubber, and came and took her away. I'm going to go to that Mother of Mercy place and find out what's going on. From what she says, you'd think it was prison she was talking about, not a laundry."

Quirke sighed. "You'll be wasting your time. No one will tell you anything. That place is run on secrecy and fear."

"What do you mean? It's a *laundry,* for God's sake."

"Sit down, Phoebe," he said. She came to the table and sat opposite him. "There are things you don't know about, believe me. The church controls this country, the church and its agents in organizations like the Knights of St. Patrick. You can't imagine the power they hold. They're not ignorant, they're not just bigots. Well, they are bigots, they are ignorant, but they're also very clever and very subtle, and they know exactly what they're doing. They have a philosophy, of sorts. Or ideology, I suppose, is a better word. They're just the same as the Communists they're always warning us about — two sides of the same coin. The child they took from Christine Falls and sent to America was only one of hundreds of babies, maybe thousands, that over the years have been sent abroad in secret and given to Catholic families to bring up as their own." He paused, with a bitter laugh. "Hackett and I tried to put a stop to it. The only result was that I got beaten up, Hackett was taken off the case, and that was the end of it."

Phoebe was gazing at him, baffled and indignant. "So it's still going on?"

"I suppose so."

"But surely it's illegal?"

"It probably is. I don't know."

"But there are adoption laws."

"Laws can always be got round, or just

ignored. This is Ireland, Phoebe. There's nothing the church can't get away with."

She sprang to her feet. "I don't believe that," she said. "The church isn't above the law."

He smiled up at her sadly. "In this country, it is."

"I don't care. I'm going up to that place and I'll demand to see Lisa. You read the note: she needs our help."

She started towards the door, but he reached up and caught her by the wrist. "Wait," he said. "Sit down. Please, Phoebe."

She hesitated, her lips set in a thin, pale line — *How much she looks like her mother when she's angry,* Quirke thought — then reluctantly went back and sat down again, holding herself erect, with her hands on the table.

"Well?" she said coldly.

"I've told you, there's no point in going up there. They'll deny everything. They'll say they never heard of Lisa Smith."

"Then I'll go to the Guards."

"The Guards won't do anything. Places like that laundry are protected — there's an invisible fence around them that you won't break through. Take my word for it. I tried, and I failed. Inspector Hackett failed. That's the way it is." She began to protest, but he held up a hand. "Wait. Listen. There might be a way to get her out, if she is there."

"How?"

"There's one person who can get in, if anyone can." He stood up. "Come on. It's a long shot, but let's try it, at least."

Taxis were scarce at that time of the evening, and they had to walk up to Baggot Street before they spotted one and flagged it down. The sun was setting behind the rooftops, and spiked shadows lay along the road and against the housefronts. Quirke asked Phoebe to recount again, in detail, how the parcel of laundry had got to her, but she could add nothing to what she had already told him: it had been left at the Country Shop with her name on it. "Probably it came with the ordinary delivery from the laundry," she said. "The manageress, when she gave me the parcel, wasn't in a mood to be helpful."

"But why at the Country Shop?"

"Because Lisa Smith doesn't know where I live. She must have put the note in the parcel and addressed it to me at the only place she thought I was likely to be." She looked out at the street and the houses passing by. "How can they keep her there, virtually a prisoner, in this day and age?"

"Because they can, that's all," Quirke said.

The taxi crossed the canal over the hump-backed bridge and drove down into Lower Baggot Street.

"By the way," Phoebe said, "I had lunch today with Dr. Blake."

Quirke set his jaw and stared straight ahead. "Oh, yes?"

"Yes. She's very frank, isn't she."

"Is she?"

She leaned around so that she could look him in the face. "Why, Quirke," she said, "I do believe you're blushing. Are you in love?"

"What a question."

"It's a very simple question, I think." She sat back, smiling to herself, pleased. "I like her a lot. Though I wouldn't have thought she was your type."

"And what's my type?"

"Oh, I don't know. Lean and svelte?" She glanced at him. His left ear, the one she could see, was bright pink. "I mean, Dr. Blake is hardly Isabel Galloway, now, is she."

Still Quirke gazed stolidly before him, past the taxi man's head and out through the windscreen. They were on Merrion Road now. There was the salt smell of the bay, off to their left, unseen behind the houses.

"Listen, Phoebe," Quirke said, "I have something to tell you."

315

"Do I want to hear it? I always get nervous when you look like that."

"It's about Mal." He paused. "He's — he's not well."

Phoebe was quiet for a moment. She turned her face to the window beside her, away from him.

"How not well is not well?"

"It's bad. He's dying."

"Of what?"

"Cancer. Cancer of the pancreas. It's inoperable."

She was surprised not to be surprised. For years, she realized, Mal had been slowly dying; cancer was only a confirmation of the process, the official seal on his fate. Long ago something had stopped in him; a light had gone out. She had seen it when he took early retirement from his position as head of obstetrics at the Holy Family Hospital. His marriage to Rose, which others might have mistaken for an eager grasping at life and all it had to offer, Phoebe knew to be merely a thing he had let himself drift into, absentmindedly.

But it was his father who had passed the death sentence itself on him. All his adult life Mal had supported Judge Griffin and covered up for him, had made excuses, told lies, had forged documents, even, to save the old man from having to pay for his wrongdoings. And all he had got in return was his father's contempt.

She loved Mal. Somehow she hadn't known this simple fact, until now. From her earliest days she had believed that Mal was her father, until Quirke finally worked up the nerve to tell her the truth. Even yet Mal seemed more like a father to her than Quirke did. Mal was finical, distant, disapproving, yet always there, always concerned, always loving, in his undemonstrative way. Soon, though, he would be there no more.

"I'm sorry," Quirke said.

She didn't look at him. "For what?"

"I don't know. For being the bearer of bad news, I suppose."

"I'm glad you told me."

"He asked me not to tell you."

"Does Rose know?"

"Of course."

As if the mention of her name had conjured her, there was Rose now, in her Bentley, pulling in at the gateway of the house. The taxi drew up and Quirke paid the fare. Rose, getting out of her car, turned in surprise as they walked towards her.

"My, my, how nice," she said. "A family visit, no less." She kissed Phoebe lightly on the cheek. "I can see, by your look, that you've heard our sorrowful tidings." She turned to Quirke. "I thought Mal said you weren't to tell her, that he'd do it himself."

"Yes," Quirke said, "he did."

"You never could keep your mouth shut, could you, Quirke."

"Oh, Rose," Phoebe said, "I'm so sorry."

"Yes, well, it's a sorry thing."

They climbed the steps to the front door, Rose and Phoebe ahead, with Quirke following. Phoebe had a sudden, clear image of the three of them — in what, six months, a year from now? — walking up these same steps, wearing black armbands.

"Mal is resting," Rose said. "He tires easily, these days."

Phoebe experienced a sudden flash of anger. Why had Rose interfered in their lives? Why did she marry Mal, the most unlikely husband she could have chosen, and bring him to live in this vast, painted corpse of a house? But her anger subsided as quickly as it had arisen. It wasn't Rose who had sapped the life from Mal. He had suffered too many losses. His father had betrayed him, and then Sarah, his wife, had died, and now he was dying himself. It wasn't fair.

They went into the big gold drawing room. The wallpaper was a deep shade of yellow, and there were gilt chairs, and even the plaster cornice around the four edges of the ceiling was gilded.

"Can I offer anyone a drink?" Rose said. "I'll call Maisie."

She pressed a porcelain button set into the wall beside the fireplace.

"In fact," Quirke said, "it's Maisie we've come to see."

Rose turned to him in surprise. "Maisie?"

"Yes. There's something we want to ask her to do."

There was a tap at the door and Maisie appeared, in her black-and-white maid's uniform.

"Ah, Maisie," Rose said, with a chilly smile. "Dr. Quirke and his daughter have come specially to see you. What do you say to that?"

Maisie's cheeks flushed and her eyes flitted anxiously from Rose to Quirke and back again.

"Come over here," Quirke said, taking her by the arm, "come over to the table and sit down. I want to talk to you."

Maisie looked at Rose again, and Rose shrugged and turned away and took a cigarette from the ormolu box on the mantelpiece and lit it. Quirke led Maisie to the table, and they sat down.

"Tell me," Quirke said, "is there anyone you know at the Mother of Mercy Laundry? Anyone there that you're still in contact with?"

"At that place?" Maisie said incredulously. "Sure, why would I want to keep contact with anyone there?"

"The thing is, Maisie, I — we — we need someone to go into the laundry and — and make inquiries. You see, Phoebe here has a friend who we think is in the laundry, and who wrote to her, asking for her help."

Maisie darted a glance in Phoebe's direction, then turned back to Quirke. "What sort of a friend?"

"It's a girl, a young woman, called Lisa, Lisa Smith."

"And what's she doing in the Mother of Mercy?"

"We don't know. She vanished a few days ago, without a trace. Then, today, Phoebe got a message from her, smuggled out in a batch of laundry."

"Oh, aye," Maisie said, nodding, "that's the way we used to do it, when we wanted to write to someone. The van drivers were in on it. We used to bribe them with cigarettes, or sometimes we'd steal a nice tablecloth, or a blouse or something, for their wives. What did the note say?"

"That she was in the laundry against her will, and asking Phoebe to help her."

Maisie snorted. "I don't know of anyone who'd be in that place that it wasn't against their will. Even the nuns themselves are like prisoners, in there."

"The trouble is, Maisie, we're not sure who Lisa Smith is."

"You don't know — ?" She turned to Phoebe. "But she's your friend, isn't she?"

"Not really," Phoebe said. "I was in a course with her, but I didn't really know her. I'm not even sure that Lisa Smith is her real name."

"So you see," Quirke said to Maisie, "we've got to be sure she's in the laundry — we've got to be sure we're not being misled, that it's not all some kind of hoax." He smiled. "Think, Maisie," he said. "Isn't there someone at the laundry you could find an excuse to visit?"

Maisie lowered her eyes. In all the time she had been here, working for the Griffins, she had never got the hang of them and their ways. It was as if she was in a room with a glass ceiling; above her the others — Dr. Griffin and Mrs. Griffin, and Dr. Quirke, and the girl with him who either was his daughter or wasn't — carried on their incomprehensible business, plain to be seen and yet shut off from her. There was a book she'd read once, in school or somewhere, that had pictures in it of Chinese people, or maybe they were Japanese, emperors and their wives and children, the men with wispy mustaches reaching nearly to the ground and the women with things that looked like knitting needles stuck in their hair. The women had funny little pursed-up mouths, and their faces were painted with some sort of white clayey stuff, and they all, even the children, had their hands tucked deep into the big drooping sleeves of the silk gowns they wore. They wouldn't have been much stranger, those Chinese or Japanese or whatever they were, than this crowd, talking in code and eyeing each other suspiciously all the time. God knows, she thought, what they're up to now. All the same, she had better help them, or say that she'd try, anyway. You'd never know what might be in it for her if she did, or what they might do to her if she didn't.

"There's one of the nuns," she said slowly, "a young one, Sister Agnes, that was always nice to me. She wasn't sly, like the others, who'd pinch your fags and and then run to the Mother Superior and tell her they'd seen you smoking. Sister Agnes had a soft heart. How she wound up in that place, I don't know."

"And is she still there?" Quirke asked. "Is she still at the laundry?"

"So far as I know, she is. Though I haven't been back to the place since I got out of it."

"Would you go back, now?" Quirke asked. "Just once? Just to see Sister Agnes, and talk to her?"

"I suppose I could," Maisie said reluctantly. "I suppose they'd let me in."

"I'm sure they would," Quirke said. "I'll go up with you, and wait outside."

"But what if they won't let me out again?"

"I'll make sure they do. There's no question of them keeping you there, no question of that at all. You have my word."

She gazed at him doubtfully. Could she trust him? Could she trust any of them? She wished Dr. Griffin was here; he was the only one she had time for. Dr. Griffin was a gentleman, and now, God bless the mark, he was sick, and spent half his time in the bed.

She swallowed hard, and nodded. "All right," she said. "Only how will I get in touch with her, with Sister Agnes?"

"I'll phone the laundry," Quirke said, "or Phoebe will, and say you'd like to pay Sister Agnes a visit, that you'd been wondering how she was getting on, since you left. Then, when you see Sister Agnes, ask her if she knows of Lisa Smith."

"And if she says she does know her, what'll I say?"

Now Phoebe spoke up: "Ask her to tell Lisa that Phoebe Griffin said hello. Then she'll know I got her note, that we know she's there, and that help will be on the way."

Maisie sighed unhappily. The thought of setting foot in the Mother of Mercy gave her the shivers. "In what kind of a way are you going to help her?" she asked suspiciously.

"We're going to get her out of that place," Phoebe said. "I'm sure that's why she wrote to me, to come and take her away."

Maisie turned back to Quirke, shaking her head. "There's no getting away from them, if they don't want you to go."

"They let you out," Quirke said.

Maisie's look turned evasive. "That was different. They were glad to see the back of me."

"Why?" Quirke asked.

"Oh, just because."

"Just because what?"

"They said I was a troublemaker. They took my babby from me and gave him away, to some swanky crowd in America, I suppose —" She stopped, glancing quickly at Rose, who still stood at the window with her back to the room. "Some family there, like. Not that they'd ever tell me. They never told anyone where their babbies had gone to. *That's no business of yours,* they'd snap at you, and order you to get on with your work." She paused again, and her look darkened. "Anyway, it was only because Dr. Griffin came up to talk to them that they let me go."

"Well, this time I'll go," Quirke said.

Maisie looked doubtful again.

"I'd be very nervous, going in there," she said. "I'd feel like some sort of a spy."

"You'd be helping someone," Quirke said, "the same way that Dr. Griffin helped you."

There was a long pause. Maisie, looking miserable, heaved another sigh.

"All right then," she said. "I'll do it."

She stood up. Quirke walked with her to the door. As she was going out, she caught him by the sleeve and drew him after her into the hall.

"What is it?" he said.

"Ssh!" Her voice sank to an urgent whisper. "You know them boxes of Player's cigarettes, the navy blue ones with two hundred in them — do you know them?" He nodded. "Will you get me one of them?"

He laughed. "Oh, Maisie," he said, "two hundred Player's! You'll smoke yourself to death. Let me give you money instead."

She shook her head vehemently. "I don't want money. I'll do it for one of them boxes." Her face softened. "I love the look of them — they're real fancy, with the tissue paper inside and the lovely smell of tobacco." She plucked at his sleeve again. "Not a word to Mrs. Griffin, mind! She'd be down on me like a ton of bricks." She winked. "This is between the two of us."

"All right, Maisie," he said, laughing again. "It's a deal."

She grinned, and nodded, and hurried off.

He went back into the drawing room. Phoebe had taken up her handbag and was saying good-bye to Rose. She was on her way to meet David Sinclair. Rose went with her to see her out. Quirke took a cigarette from the box on the mantelpiece and lit it. When he turned, Rose was leaning in the doorway, watching him.

"Tell me what you're up to, Quirke," she said. "Somehow I don't see you as a knight in shining armor, galloping to the aid of a damsel in distress."

"Don't you?"

"Seems to me it's just another one of the games you play, these kids' games you amuse yourself with." She crossed the room to him and took the cigarette from his fingers. "I don't care about this laundry and this girl who's being held there against her will. I don't care about any of that, Quirke. I don't believe in chivalry. The world is full of girls in trouble, always was and always will be."

"You've never been in a place like the Mother of Mercy Laundry," he said.

"You think not? You know, darlin'," she drawled, putting the cigarette to her lips, "there's all kinds of institutions. There's the famous institution of marriage, for instance. I've been in that, twice."

He shrugged, smiling. "I'm sorry, Rose," he said. "I don't know what to say to you. I never do."

"No, I guess you don't." She stepped closer to him and peered searchingly into his face. "There's something different about you," she said, "I can see it. You look —" She stopped. "I know what it is. You're happy." She laughed in wonderment. "I'm right, aren't I? Yes. You know, I don't believe I've ever seen you happy before, except maybe once, long ago, that time you were in bed with me. What's happened? Have you met someone?" He said nothing, holding her gaze. She nodded slowly. "That's it, isn't it. Who is she?"

He turned away from her and walked to the window and stood with his hands in his pockets and his back turned to her.

"It's the shrink, isn't it," she said. "What's her name, Blake? The one Phoebe works for? Have I guessed right? I have, haven't I. I can read you like a book, Quirke, I always could."

Still he would not speak. She came and stood beside him, smoking his cigarette. They were silent, both of them, looking into the garden. Casey the gardener, a gnarled and wiry little man, was rootling among the shrubbery, hacking at something. The shadow of a cloud swished through the street; then there was sunlight again, as strong as before.

"Oh, how smart you are, Quirke," she said.

"What do you mean?"

"I underestimated you. Hell, you've got the whole thing figured out. First you get a head doctor all of your own, then you go up to that laundry and rescue the girl and make up for all the things you never did for your own daughter. Congratulations. It'll be like going to that confession you Catholics have and telling all your sins and having them forgiven. My, my."

He turned to her, his face flushed. "You

really think that's what I'm doing? You really think I'm that selfish?"

"You know you are, honey," she said, smiling. "We all are. But I've got to confess, I'm jealous."

"Are you? I'm sorry."

"Here." She gave him back his cigarette. "Oh, too bad," she said, "I always do get lipstick on them, don't I."

Dusk was gathering in the tops of the trees along O'Connell Street. Phoebe, who had been sitting on the upper deck of the bus, got off before it turned the corner onto Parnell Square, and walked over to the Shakespeare. The pub was crowded with theatergoers who had rushed down from the Gate to snatch a quick drink during the interval. She hoped she wouldn't run into Isabel Galloway, who often acted at the Gate. Isabel had been her friend, once, but her affair with Quirke and its petering out had soured relations between them. Phoebe regretted this, but there was nothing to be done about it.

David had kept a place for her at the bar. She sat up on the stool beside him and asked for a gin and tonic. She noticed that he didn't kiss her, yet otherwise everything seemed as usual. She never knew quite where she was, with David. Somehow his mind always seemed to be elsewhere.

She asked him about his day, but he said he didn't want to talk about it, that it was too boring. This was how it always was, she asking and him refusing; it had become a sort of unfunny comic turn between the two of them. But she supposed he was right: there probably wasn't much to be said, if you had spent the past eight hours dissecting dead bodies. She wondered, not for the first time, why he had become a pathologist in the first place. Quirke, now, could have been born into the job, but David always seemed to her to have been meant for other things, though she couldn't imagine what those other things might be.

She told him about Lisa Smith, and the note in the parcel of laundry. They talked about it for a while, and about Leon Corless's death and Lisa Smith's connection with him.

"Quirke loves to get mixed up in this kind of thing, doesn't he," David said.

"He doesn't go looking for trouble, if that's what you mean. Don't you ever feel the urge to follow up on something you uncovered in a postmortem?"

"I'm a doctor," he said, "not a detective." He fingered his glass, rotating it on its base and frowning. "He shouldn't involve you,

you know."

"Shouldn't he? Why not?"

He turned his head and gave her a long look. "Because it's dangerous. You didn't see Leon Corless's body, or what was left of it. I did. If I were your father, I'd make very sure you didn't go anywhere near people capable of doing that kind of thing."

She began to say something but stopped herself. She didn't want to fight with David. Once, she would have; not now.

They drank in silence for a while. Phoebe liked the way the ice cubes, submerged among the rushing bubbles, creaked and cracked, though the place was so crowded with noisy drinkers that to hear the effect she had to put the glass close to her ear. She had the secret notion that all things, even inanimate objects, had a life of their own, and their own way of expressing themselves. She knew David would laugh at her if she told him this, and so she never had. There were, she reflected, many things she didn't tell him, and she was sure there were many things too that he didn't tell her. They were not, she reflected, your ordinary couple. If, indeed, they were a couple at all.

"Have another drink," he said.

"No, I don't think so."

He was finishing a pint of Guinness.

"Mind if I do?"

"Of course not."

He signaled to the barman by lifting the empty glass and waggling it. The barman nodded, and took down a fresh glass and put it under the spout and pulled slowly on the wooden handle, and the gleaming black liquid gushed out in a thin, frothing stream.

"I had a letter from my friend Yotam today," David said.

"Oh, yes? In Tel Aviv, is it?"

"He lives in Tel Aviv, but he's on a kibbutz at the moment, helping out in the medical center."

"That must be interesting."

"Yes," he said. He was watching the barman pulling the last of the pint and putting the finishing touches to the creamy head. "He certainly makes it sound interesting."

"You haven't been to Israel, have you?"

"No. My father was there. He went out in forty-eight, to fight the Arabs."

"Was he all right? I mean, he didn't get wounded or anything?"

"No. But there were other kinds of scars, of course. It was a dirty war."

The barman brought the pint. David paid for it, and left it sitting on its cork mat, and folded his arms on the bar and watched a slow trail of cream sliding down the outside of the glass.

"He suggested I should come out there," he said, not looking at her.

She was confused. "Your father?"

"No, no." He laughed. "Yotam. He says I'd enjoy it, that the country is buzzing, really alive."

She said nothing for a moment. The last of the ice cubes were melting in the bottom of her glass. The slice of lemon looked abandoned and forlorn. She had known a girl at school who used to eat lemons. She would cut them into four segments and suck the juice out of them. She used to look funny, with the slice in her mouth, like a set of smooth, bright yellow dentures.

"Do you think you'd like to go there," she said at last, "on a visit?"

He rolled his shoulders in a shrug. "Oh, I don't know. Somehow Israel isn't the kind of place you go to for a holiday. Everything is too — too serious, for that. I can't see myself sightseeing in a country that's fighting every day for its very existence."

"Yes," she said, "I know what you mean. I think I do, anyway."

"He tells me — Yotam tells me — there's a job going in Haifa." He laughed shyly. "He says it would suit me perfectly."

"A job as a pathologist?"

"No. As a general physician."

"Could you do that, could you be an ordinary doctor? I mean, a doctor who deals with living people?"

"Yes," he said, "I think I could. I'd probably have to take a course or two, but that wouldn't matter."

They were silent again. A sense of something — embarrassment, perhaps — was seeping up between them like fog, like smoke. The pub was rapidly emptying as the Gate crowd downed the last of their drinks and hurried back to the theater.

"So you're thinking about it, are you?" Phoebe said carefully. "You're thinking about the job in Haifa?"

He turned to look at her. "Yes, I suppose I am. The thing is" — he touched a hand to his forehead; he looked miserable suddenly — "the thing is, I don't think I'm cut out to be a pathologist. A bit late to come to that realization, you'll say, and you'll be right. But you have to look at things squarely, and if they're wrong you have to do something about it, or try to, before it's too late."

Phoebe didn't look at him. "I think I will have another drink," she said, swallowing.

David signaled again to the barman, pointing to her empty glass. Again the barman nodded. It must be strange, Phoebe thought, to be a barman, standing behind the bar all night, serving out drinks and watching people getting tipsy while you had to stay stone-cold sober. That must be why barmen were so slow and taciturn, a bit like policemen; that was their professional pace, the way they had trained themselves to be.

If things are wrong, you have to do something about it. Well, yes.

Her drink arrived and she took a large swallow from it — too large, and the bubbles went up her nose and made her sneeze. She laughed, groping in her bag for a handkerchief.

"Here," David said, "take mine, it's clean."

"Thanks."

She blew her nose. She felt as if she were going to cry, but she was sure it was just the effect of the bubbles still fizzing in her sinuses.

"It would be a big step, going to Israel," she said. "Would you — would you stay, if you did go?"

"Oh, yes. I'd have to stay. Otherwise it would be — I don't know. Frivolous."

"That's a strange word to use."

"Is it?"

He took a sip from his pint.

"You have a cream mustache," Phoebe said.

He wiped away the froth with his fingers. They were both smiling. Soon David's smile faded, however, and he turned his face away from her again.

"That's the point about Israel," he said. "It's a serious project. You can't just drift in and then drift out again. It requires commitment."

"Yes," Phoebe said. "Commitment. I understand."

"Do you?" He still wasn't looking at her.

"I think I do." She paused. "Do you think I'm frivolous?"

She had asked it without rancor, as a real question, and he pondered it as such.

"No, I don't," he said. "The word wouldn't apply to you. Your place is here, your people are here. This is your project, for better or worse. This girl Lisa Smith: she asks you for help and you help her. You wouldn't dream of not doing it. But the people who need my help are far away."

"Do you feel that, always? I mean, do you feel guilty, being here, and not there?"

"Guilty? No. But — I don't know. Dissatisfied, maybe. No, that's not the word either. Unfulfilled? It sounds ridiculous, I know."

"It doesn't."

He reached across and laid a hand over hers.

"You're very kind, Phoebe," he said. "You're a kind person, do you know that?"

She laughed. "Kind? Maybe I am, I don't know. It doesn't make me sound very exciting, though, does it. Not like the people on the kibbutz. I imagine being kind doesn't arise there. It would be all work, and duty, and commitment. All those stern things."

His fingers closed tightly around hers.

"You know I couldn't ask you to come with me," he said.

"Couldn't you?" Her voice had a tiny crack in it. "Why not?"

"You know it wouldn't work."

"Because I'm not Jewish? Or because I'm too kind and wishy-washy? Because I'm not *stern* enough?"

She drew her hand slowly from under his.

"I'm sorry," he said, so softly she almost didn't hear.

She blew her nose into his handkerchief again. "*I'm* sorry," she said, laughing. "I've ruined your hankie!"

"Phoebe," he said.

She shook her head, her lips pressed tight, and got down from the stool. She wasn't looking at him; she couldn't look at him. "I must go," she said. "I'll keep your handkerchief. I'll wash it for you. It'll be a reason for us to meet again."

He reached out and tried to take her hand. She pretended not to notice, and began to move away, clutching her handbag against her stomach. She felt as if she might be sick.

"Don't go," David said, pleadingly. "Not like this."

She turned to him, suddenly angry. "How, then? How do you want me to go?"

"I don't."

"Yes, you do, David," she said, her voice slowing. "You do."

And she walked away quickly, her head down.

19

The sun was gone from the sky, but the streets were still hot and the atmosphere itself seemed weary after the long day of heat. Hackett walked the few dozen yards from his office to Mooney's, across the road, and by the time he got there he was in a sweat. When he took his hat off he thought his head must surely be steaming. He mopped his forehead. The back of his neck felt gritty. The weather would have to break soon; if it didn't, there would be riots.

Inside the pub it was a little cooler than in the streets, but only a little. He nodded to the barman and slipped into the dark brown snug. All afternoon he'd been looking forward to this moment. He ordered a pint of Smithwick's and downed a third of it in the first swallow. This beer, too, had a washed, soapy texture, but it had more body than Bass. He leaned back on the dusty plush of the bench seat and lit a cigarette.

For the next few minutes he was going to relax. Years of police work had taught him to divide his mind into a number of more or less sealed compartments, so that he could shut away for necessary periods the things he didn't want to think about.

He was considering ordering a second pint when Quirke arrived. He sat down and put his straw hat on the table.

"What will you have?" Hackett asked.

"I don't know. What do you drink in this heat?"

"Something cool and refreshing, like the adverts say."

"I'll have a tonic water with ice and lemon."

Hackett smiled. "Are you still off the hard liquor?"

"Most of the time."

He went to the bar and rapped on it with a coin, and after a minute the barman came and glanced around the partition. Hackett ordered the tonic water for Quirke and another pint for himself, then sat down again.

"I shouldn't be drinking this stuff," he said, gazing gloomily at the puddle of suds in the bottom of his glass. "It gives me heartburn." He studied Quirke. "You're in good spirits," he said.

"Am I?"

"You have the look of a man that's had a spring put in his step. Did you win the football pools?"

Quirke smiled. "What have you to tell me?" he said.

The barman appeared again, and Hackett got up to take the drinks from him and handed over a ten-shilling note. Receiving his change, he returned to his seat. Above the hat line his high forehead was moistly pink.

"I went to see a fellow yesterday that I know," he said. "In the Civil Service. One of the head bottle washers there."

"Oh, yes?" Quirke was lighting a cigarette. "What did you go to see him about?"

"To ask him to do a bit of checking on young Corless."

"And?"

Hackett leaned forward and stubbed out his cigarette, rotating it slowly back and forth in the bottom of the ashtray. He was not a man to be hurried. "Oh, that reminds me, by the way," he said. "I got the full report back from the boys in forensics."

"And what did they find?"

Hackett made a contemptuous face. "Bugger all, as usual. They're a useless shower, so they are. They *think* Corless's car might have been pushed rather than driven from the road onto the grass slope, they *think* it might have had petrol poured over it and set alight, they *think* there were traces of footprints in the grass but they couldn't be sure since the Fire Brigade had tramped all over the place in their ten-league boots. Et cetera, et cetera." If he hadn't been indoors, he would have spat. "Useless — worse than useless."

"As a matter of fact, I have some news for you," Quirke said.

"I hope it's good," Hackett replied dourly.

Quirke took out his wallet. "This was delivered to Phoebe in a parcel of laundry." He unfolded Lisa Smith's note and laid it on the table. Hackett picked it up and read it, moving his lips silently. Then he put it down on the table again, nodding.

"The Mother of Mercy Laundry rears its ugly head again," he said.

"I've arranged for someone to go up there and make inquiries."

Hackett looked at him in surprise. "Who?"

"Maisie Coughlan — do you remember her?"

"Maisie that's working for Dr. Griffin now? Oh, aye, I remember her. I didn't think she'd be up to setting foot in that place ever again."

"She took a bit of persuading, all right."

"How's she going to manage to get in? That place is like Fort Knox."

"There's a nun that she knows there, a decent one, she says, who was nice to her. She's going to pay her a visit and find out about Lisa Smith. And if she is there, which she must be, I'm going to go up and see about getting her out."

Hackett formed his lips into a silent whistle. "That won't be easy."

"No. But I'm going to do it, all the same."

Hackett shook his head in amusement. "You're a fierce man, when you set your mind to a thing," he said.

They drank their drinks. They could hear the noise of the traffic outside. Now and then a waft of exhaust smoke came in at the open doorway and made its way even into the snug, where they were seated.

"Dr. Griffin is very ill," Quirke said.

Hackett turned to him. "Is that so?"

"Yes. He's dying."

"Ah, is he, now. I'm sorry to hear that. He's a decent man. That will be a great shock for his wife. For you and your daughter, too. I know" — he coughed — "I know Miss Phoebe was very close to him."

"Yes, she was. Still is."

"Does she know he's dying?"

"She does. I told her."

Hackett clicked his tongue. "Ah, that's very sad."

Quirke stood up, pointing to Hackett's empty glass. "Can I get you another?"

"I hate drinking on my own."

"I'll have something with you."

"Good man! I'll take a ball of malt, so."

Quirke went to the bar and when the barman came he ordered two small Jamesons. He waited for the drinks to be poured, paid for them, set them on the table, and sat down. For a minute neither man touched his glass. Quirke gazed at the whiskey with the air of a man standing on the edge of a cliff and trying to gauge how deep the drop would be. Hackett watched him sidelong, and said nothing. At last Quirke picked up his glass and sniffed at the whiskey. "Here's to life," he said.

"While we have it," Hackett answered.

And they drank.

"So," Quirke said, leaning back against the plush, "what did your civil servant have to say?"

"A lot, as it happens. It seems our young Mr. Corless was off on a frolic of his own, gathering information about a project that would not be unfamiliar to you and me."

"Don't tell me," Quirke said. "Babies, and

what to do with them."

Hackett nodded. "It seems, according to my informant, that the scheme Judge Garret Griffin and his associates used to run, taking babies from unmarried mothers, or mothers they deemed unfit for motherhood, and smuggling them to America and other parts is still going strong. Only now it's being carried out on a financial footing."

"What does that mean?"

"The people running it are making a fortune. Babies are being sold to rich American families for two, three thousand dollars apiece. That's a lot of money, for a scrap of a child, wouldn't you say, Doctor?"

In times to come, Quirke thought, people will look back and say, How could it happen? The future never understands the past. He and Hackett had tried to destroy the network that Garret Griffin operated, in collusion with Rose Griffin's first husband, Josh Crawford, but they had failed, overruled and overborne by the forces ranged against them — the Archbishop, the Knights of St. Patrick, and all the other shadowy figures of power, wealth, and influence who knew how the world should be run and ran it according to their own, unwritten laws. He picked up the whiskey glass. Could he have done more? Should he have persevered, should he have carried the fight into the belly of the beast itself? Pathetic notion. The beast would have belched him out and turned its back and slouched off about its beastly business.

This, at least, is what he told himself; and he was half convinced.

Drink the whiskey, and then order another. That had always been a solution to his doubt and his dread.

He set the glass down on the table.

"Come on," he said, "let's go for a walk."

Hackett looked at him, startled. "You haven't finished your drink."

"No," Quirke said. "I haven't, have I."

They strolled by the river in the gathering dusk, under a lavish mackerel sky. The tide was low. Couples passed them by, hand in hand, the young men with their shirt collars turned up fashionably at the back, the girls in sandals, with cardigans draped over their shoulders. The world is not what it seems, Quirke reflected. However tranquil the scene before us, beneath our feet another world is thrashing in helpless agony. How can we live up here, knowing what goes on down there? How can we know and not know, at the same time? He would never understand it. Had Joe Costigan been there, he would have been able to explain it to him, as he had done before, though the lesson hadn't sunk in.

They had not spoken since they left the pub. At Capel Street Bridge Hackett stopped, and leaned on the embankment wall, and looked down at the river, a trickle of quicksilver meandering through the mud.

"Do you know who's in charge of the undertaking now?" he said. "Have a guess."

Quirke didn't have to guess. "Costigan," he said.

"Right first time!" Hackett cried. "Give that man the prize money!" He chuckled. "Yes, the same Joseph Costigan, the fixer of fixers. And he's getting fat on the proceeds. Oh, fat as a spring pig. He has a new house out in Monkstown, among the quality, and a big American car with two fins on the back of it that would frighten a shark. His eldest daughter recently had a wedding in the Shelbourne that was the talk of the town for weeks."

"It's not like him," Quirke said, "to flaunt his money."

"They always get careless," Hackett said complacently, "even the most cautious of them."

Outside a pub on the other side of the quay, two young men were engaged in a drunken fight. At the sound of it, Hackett turned and contemplated the scene. They swung their arms wildly, capering like monkeys, and cursed and grunted, then grappled clumsily and fell over, rolling on the pavement.

"Where are the Guards when they're needed?" Hackett muttered sardonically.

Now a third young man appeared, also drunk, and began indiscriminately kicking the pair on the ground. A small crowd was gathering, enjoying the spectacle. Quirke and Hackett walked on.

"Do you ever think of leaving the city," Quirke asked, "and going back to the country?"

"I do, when I see the likes of that," Hackett said, jerking a thumb over his shoulder in the direction of the fight. "But May wouldn't have it. What would she do without Switzers department store and the tram out to Howth on Sunday afternoons?"

They crossed the bridge and turned right and walked back along the other side of the river in the direction they had come from. Why are smoky summer evenings like this always so sad? Quirke wondered.

"So what are we going to do?" he said.

"What are we going to do about what?"

Hackett inquired mildly, with lifted eyebrows.

There were times when Quirke felt a deep sympathy for the long-suffering Mrs. Hackett.

"About," he said patiently, "Leon Corless and what he found out regarding Costigan and his American money. What did your civil servant panjandrum say, exactly?"

"Well now," Hackett said with a laugh, "the man is a civil servant, so there's not much chance of him saying anything *exactly.* It seems Corless had a bee in his bonnet about Costigan and this thing he's carrying on with the babies. I don't know how he heard about it in the first place, but when he did he made it his business to record every scrap of information he could lay his hands on."

"And what became of it, all this information?"

"Ah, that's the question. If I were to guess, I'd say it's likely to have been mislaid by now, or it might even have disappeared, mysteriously. Costigan and his pals tend to be thorough, where incriminating documentation is concerned."

They were silent for some paces; then Quirke spoke. "You know what we're talking about here," he said. "We're talking about the distinct possibility — in fact, the distinct probability — that Joe Costigan was behind the murder of Leon Corless."

Hackett had begun nodding while Quirke was still speaking.

"Yes," he said, "that is what we're talking about, Dr. Quirke."

They walked on in somber silence. Gulls were wheeling above the river, ghostlike in the twilit air. Why, Quirke wondered, do they go silent as night approaches? Making no sound, they seemed even more eerie.

"I've just realized something," he said.

"What's that?"

"I'm tired of this country, of its secrets and its lies."

"That's easily understood. But tell me this, Doctor: where is there a place with no secrets, and where people all tell the truth?"

Faint wisps of music came to them on the breeze. "It's the dance band in the ballroom in Jury's Hotel, over on Dame Street," Hackett said. "Did you ever go to a dance there, in the day when you were sowing your wild oats? Wild stuff, it is — shoe salesmen and solicitors' clerks, and nurses from the Mater and the Rotunda, looking for a husband."

Quirke tried to picture the detective, younger, slimmer, in a sharp suit and a loud tie, gliding round and round the dance floor, in the spangled light and the blare of the band, with a girl in his arms.

"What's funny?" Hackett asked.

"Oh, nothing," Quirke said.

He wanted another whiskey. He *craved* another whiskey. Why hadn't he finished the one he had?

In fact, he recalled, he had been to one of those dances in Jury's, a long time ago. And it was a nurse he had gone with, on a date. He tried to remember her. Tall, with dyed black hair. Her hand cool and damp in his. When he stepped on her toes — he was always a terrible dancer — she put on a brave face and said it was all right, that he was not to worry, that she was used to farmers' sons walking all over her at harvest festival dances, when she went home for the weekend to — to where? Where had home been? Somewhere down the country. That was where home was for most of them, the women he had known in those early days. The nurse that night had explained to him, as they sat at the bar, that for a girl like her there were three choices: be a wife, be a nun, or be a nurse. The first and third options were not mutually exclusive, except that of course you couldn't be both at the same time; either you worked and looked after your patients, or you stayed at home and looked after your man. The nunnery she hadn't fancied. In the taxi back to the nurses' hostel she had let him put his hand on her leg, above her stocking, but that had been the limit.

He thought of Evelyn Blake. *I want to swallow you, all of you, into me.*

"The thing is," Hackett said, breaking in on his thoughts, "I'm not sure at all that there's much we can do. I could bring in Costigan and question him, but on what grounds? And then think of the ructions he'd kick up, afterwards. The Commissioner, by the way, is a Knight of St. Patrick. It's a thing to keep in mind."

"Maybe the girl, Lisa Smith, will know something, if we can get her out of that damn place. She was Leon Corless's girl, after all, and she's going to have his baby."

They came to O'Connell Bridge. It was night now, yet still the sky retained a delicate glimmer above the western rooftops.

"Aye, maybe she'll be able to help us," Hackett said. He sighed. "I can tell you, Doctor, you're not the only one tired of this place."

They had stopped on the corner by the bridge. Crowds were going home after the pictures, and there were long queues at the bus stops. Somewhere unseen a drunk was singing "Boolavogue" in a quavery, tearful wail. "Will you come for a nightcap?" Hackett asked. "There's a good twenty minutes to go before closing."

"No, thanks," Quirke said. "I have an early postmortem in the morning."

"Right, so. Good night to you, Doctor. Oh, and let me know how that young one, Maisie, gets on at the Mother of Mercy."

They turned from each other and went their separate ways.

Quirke, on Westmoreland Street, thought again of Evelyn, of her pale smooth flesh and huge dark eyes, of her lovely, mismatched breasts. Was he making a mistake? Probably. He didn't care. How often again in his life would he be offered love?

The postmortem proved difficult, he wasn't sure why. Some were like that. The corpse was that of a girl of nineteen, a shop assistant in Lipton's, who had been taken ill behind the counter and was rushed to the Holy Family but was dead on arrival. He searched first for the likeliest causes of death, an embolism or a cerebral hemorrhage, but found neither. Sinclair, assisting him, was puzzled too. At last they decided on ventricular fibrillation — the poor girl's heart had stopped, for reasons unknown to reason.

"Maybe she was crossed in love," Sinclair said.

Quirke gave him a searching look, to see if this had been meant as a joke. But Sinclair's face, as usual, gave nothing away.

Afterwards they went up to the canteen and drank mugs of bitter tea sweetened with too much sugar, and sat in silence for a long time. Then Sinclair began to talk of his plan to go to Israel. Quirke was only half listening.

"Israel?" he said vaguely, as if he had never heard of the place. "How long would you stay? Haven't you used up all your holidays for this year?"

"I'm not talking about a holiday," Sinclair said, making patterns with the tip of his cigarette in the ash in the ashtray.

"What, then?" Quirke asked, trying to seem interested.

The Tannoy speaker in the corner of the ceiling behind them crackled into life, summoning Quirke to the telephone. He groaned. "Christ," he said, "what now?"

He stubbed out his cigarette and went down the stairs to his office, taking his time. He didn't feel like talking to anyone. Then it occurred to him that it might be Evelyn, and he quickened his pace. He shut the office door behind himself and sat down at his desk and picked up the phone. The new girl at Reception hadn't got the hang of how to transfer calls, and he had to wait for fully a minute before at last he heard Phoebe's voice. She sounded breathless.

"What is it?" he said. "What's wrong?"

"Nothing, nothing," she said. "I just spoke to Maisie. She went to the laundry."

"Oh, yes? And what happened?"

"She saw her friendly nun. She didn't know of any Lisa Smith." Quirke began to say something, but she interrupted him. "No, listen. There is a Lisa there, but she's not Lisa Smith."

"Then who is she?"

There was a rattling noise on the line and he didn't catch her answer, and had to ask her to repeat it.

"Her name is Costigan," Phoebe said. "Elizabeth Costigan."

20

In the end it was decided that Phoebe should go with Quirke to the Mother of Mercy Laundry, since it was she who knew or at least had seen Lisa Smith, or Elizabeth Costigan, as they now knew her to be. Quirke and Phoebe had come to the house on Ailesbury Road to talk to Maisie. Mal and Rose met them, and they went, the four of them, and sat in the conservatory, at the little metal table in front of the somehow lost-looking miniature palm. It was cooler today, and now and then a breeze would wander in from the garden through the open French doors. Maisie was summoned, and repeated her account of her meeting with Sister Agnes. She had nothing to add to what she had already related to Phoebe, and Rose told her she could go.

"Costigan has a daughter called Elizabeth," Quirke said. "I checked. She's the youngest of three." He turned to Phoebe.

"There was an Elizabeth Costigan on the list of names from the secretarial course. It has to be your Lisa Smith."

"I was sure Smith wasn't her real name," Phoebe said.

Mal took off his glasses and pressed a finger to the bridge of his nose. He was pale, and his eyes had a slightly stupefied look, as if he been straining for a long time to see something too far off to be made out. "You say she's pregnant?" he asked.

"Yes," Phoebe answered.

Mal nodded. "So that's why she's in the laundry."

"Costigan would have put her there," Quirke said.

"Yes, one of the parents would have had to bring her in." Mal glanced at Quirke. "It's usually the father who does it."

There was a brief silence.

"What will we say?" Phoebe asked. "How will we go about getting in to see her?"

"I don't know," Quirke said. "You should be the one to call the laundry. Maybe pretend you're a relative. You could even say you're Lisa's sister."

"Why should we lie? It's not a prison, after all. I'll tell them I'm her friend and insist on seeing her."

Yes, Quirke thought, it might work. The

Griffin name would carry significant weight in the Mother of Mercy Laundry. But it would be he who would have to do the talking. He had been to the laundry before, he knew what it was like, he knew the obstacles.

Rose stood up. "Anyone care for a drink?" she asked. "It's practically lunchtime. No? Well, I'll leave you conspirators to hatch your plans. I'm going to fix myself something tall and cool."

She walked off, into the house. Somehow Rose's departure from a room was always followed by an uneasy silence, as if the people she had left behind were convinced that if they spoke she would still be able to hear them.

Mal was fiddling with his spectacles again. "Joseph Costigan," he said musingly. "How that man has haunted my life." He turned to Phoebe. "You know, don't you, that your grandfather did many bad things?" Phoebe, with a quick glance in Quirke's direction, nodded. "Joe Costigan was his right-hand man — or left-hand, I should say. A sinister person."

"Why isn't something done about him?" Phoebe asked. "Why isn't he in jail?"

Mal smiled sadly. "Why not, indeed. Because he has powerful friends, who protect him. Indeed, I used to be one of his protectors. Does that shock you, my dear?"

Phoebe only looked at her hands and frowned. She knew the ways in which Mal had helped shield his father and his associates from being called to account for their misdeeds; she knew more than anyone imagined she knew.

"You can't blame yourself for looking after Grandfather," she said, still with her eyes cast down. "He was your father, after all."

"Ah, yes," Mal said, "that fine excuse." He turned to Quirke. "You know they'll resist you, at the laundry."

"Yes," Quirke said, "I know that."

Mal was regarding him keenly. "And then there's Joe Costigan. He's very dangerous, though you hardly need me to tell you that."

"Yes, I know," Quirke said. "But maybe this time he's gone too far. Locking his daughter away in that place is one thing. Murder is another."

Mal shook his head. "You know Costigan. If he was responsible for that young man's death, you won't trace it back to him. And even if you do, his friends will pull the usual strings. The Joe Costigans of this world can indeed get away with murder."

Quirke turned to Phoebe. "Go and make the phone call," he said. "Don't say that I'll be with you. We'll just turn up. They won't be able to send us away."

Phoebe rose and went into the house. When she had gone, Mal and Quirke sat for a time in a strained silence. Mortal illness, Quirke reflected, is always, at some level, an embarrassment. "How are you feeling?" he asked.

"Oh, I'm all right," Mal answered. "Terrified, of course, terrified all the time. It's an odd sensation. I feel as if I'm floating, as if there's a balloon inside me, filled with hot air, buoying me up. Breathless, too, as if I'm constantly running away from something." He smiled. "Which, of course, I am."

"Is there anything I can do?"

"For me? No. Come round of an evening and talk to Rose. This is hard on her. First Josh, now me. It's less than fair."

Quirke got to his feet. "I'd better go," he said.

"Yes. And take care, Quirke." Mal turned to look out at the garden. "It seems so strange, doesn't it, talking about these things, while the world goes on as if nothing mattered."

"We'll get Costigan this time," Quirke said. "I promise you."

Mal looked up at him. "Maybe you will," he said. "It won't change the past. I used to believe in redemption. Not anymore."

"It's too big a word, Mal. Let's aim for something more modest."

Mal stood up, and together they walked through the house. They met Rose in the front hall, with a glass in her hand. She gave Quirke a sardonic smile. "Off you go, Sir Galahad," she said. "Watch out for dragons."

Quirke had met Sister Dominic before. He could still see, and he had seen then, the distaste she felt for him. They faced each other across the broad expanse of her desk, while Phoebe sat off to the side — put in her place, as she had ruefully to acknowledge. Sister Dominic was tall and gaunt and strikingly handsome. She wore a floor-length habit, with an outsized set of wooden rosary beads knotted loosely around her waist. She had piercing eyes of bird's-egg blue, and long, bloodless hands, the slender fingers of which were rarely still. The close-fitting black wimple gave her the look of a compellingly lifelike statue peering out of a niche. Despite the warmth of the day she looked cold, and the tip of her nose was bone-white.

"So, Dr. Quirke," she said, "this is an unexpected pleasure. What can I do for you?"

Quirke was lighting a cigarette; deliberately he had not asked the nun's permission. "I'm told, Sister, that there's a young woman in the laundry by the name of Elizabeth Costigan. She would have come here recently."

Sister Dominic blinked, her eyelids dropping slowly and slowly rising again, like the shutter of a camera set to a long exposure. She looked down at the desk and moved a pencil an inch to one side and straightened a leather-bound blotter.

"Elizabeth Costigan," she said, isolating and, as it were, examining closely each syllable of the name. "I'm not sure that I know her. She came to us recently, you say?"

"Yes. Sometime in the past week. Perhaps you haven't had the opportunity to meet her yet."

Sister Dominic's faint smile was condescending. "I know all my girls, Dr. Quirke, be assured of that."

"Good," Quirke said blandly. "Then you must know of Miss Costigan."

"She calls herself Lisa," Phoebe said. "Perhaps that's the name you know her by."

Sister Dominic did not even glance in her direction. Her eyes were still fixed on Quirke. He could almost hear the delicate mechanism of her brain at work as she calculated how much he might know about Lisa Costigan and to what extent he might be bluffing. Then she came to a decision.

"Ah, yes," she said. "Of course. Lisa. Yes."

There was a long pause. Quirke went on gazing at the nun, putting on an expectant look, one eyebrow cocked.

"I'd like to see her," he said. "Do you think that would be possible?"

Sister Dominic again touched the pencil and the blotter, lightly, with the tips of her unquiet fingers. How they must torment her, those fingers, Quirke thought; she had spent her life shedding all signs of inner conflict and agitation, yet here, at the very extremities of her hands, she still betrayed herself.

"May I ask," she said, "what it is you want to see her about?"

"Well, she's a friend of Miss Griffin's, you see. We thought we'd come up and see her, have a word with her, you know."

"I'm told you're not the first one to ask after her," the nun said. "One of our former girls, Maisie Coughlan, was here, making inquiries, asking questions. Did you know that?" she turned to Phoebe. "Maisie works at your — at Dr. Griffin's house now, doesn't she?"

"Yes, she does," Phoebe said. "It was she

who told us that Lisa was here."

Again there was a silence; again Quirke could almost hear the nun's brain busy at its calculations.

"We all wonder how she's getting on, you see," Quirke said.

"I can tell you that she's getting on very well," the nun snapped back at him. "All our girls get on well."

"I'm sure they do, Sister, I'm sure they do. But I'm sure also that she'd welcome a visit from Phoebe. Everyone, always, likes a visit, don't you find? Especially when they're cut off from the outside world, as you all are here, at the laundry."

"I'd hardly put it that way," Sister Dominic said frostily.

"Wouldn't you?" Quirke smiled.

Sister Dominic looked over the desk again, like a general surveying a set of campaign maps, eyeing in turn each of the things that were on it: the pencil, the blotter, an inkwell, a box of paper clips, a big black telephone, the cut-glass ashtray, into which at intervals Quirke insouciantly flicked his ash, to her obvious, tight-lipped irritation. Sister Dominic was not a tolerant woman. She had her standards. Her church was the Church Militant; not for her those pale, languishing saints, the ones clutching lilies and prayer books, their eyes cast upwards in meek devotion, their pink little mouths open in adoration and awe, to whom so many of her fellow nuns had dedicated themselves. No, give her vigor and certitude. Her favorite passage in all of Scripture was the one in which Christ made a whip of cords and drove the money lenders out of the Temple.

"The thing is, Dr. Quirke," she said, "we don't really welcome — that's to say, we can't really accommodate unannounced visits. Our day here is highly structured, as it must be. You'll know that from your own work, at the hospital. Institutions have their rules, which must be observed."

"I appreciate that, of course," Quirke said with a show of bland urbanity. "And yet, since we've come all this way, I do feel I can ask you to bend the rules, a little, just this once?"

Somewhere in the building a machine switched itself off, adjusting the silence in the room.

"I wonder, Dr. Quirke," the nun said slowly, "if you are aware of who Lisa is. More to the point, I wonder if you know that her father is Joseph Costigan. You'll remember Mr. Costigan?" She turned to Phoebe again. "He was a close associate of your grandfather's."

"Oh, yes," Quirke said brightly, "I know Mr. Costigan, I know him well. He's a formidable man — I know that, too."

"And do you know that it was Mr. Costigan himself who brought Lisa to us, who gave her into our care?"

"Yes, I would have guessed as much."

Phoebe was sitting on the edge of her chair; her palms, she found, were damp.

"Dr. Quirke," Sister Dominic said, with the resigned air of a person compelled against her will to make a frank disclosure, "I have to tell you that Lisa Costigan is in a rather disturbed state."

"I know that she's pregnant," Quirke said flatly.

Again the nun did that slow, mechanical blink.

"Yes," she said, "as it happens, Lisa is, to her great misfortune, expecting a child. That's why she's here, of course."

"Of course?" Quirke said softly. "But this is a laundry, Sister, not a lying-in hospital. As I understand it." The nun was about to speak, but he cut her off. "There's something that perhaps *you* don't know, Sister," he said, letting his voice harden a little. "Her boyfriend, Lisa's boyfriend, the father of her child, died in the early hours of last

Friday morning. He was found in his car, crashed against a tree in the Phoenix Park. The Gardaí, I have to tell you, suspect that his death may not have been an accident. In fact, they think he may have been — well, murdered."

The nun fixed him with a level look. It seemed to Phoebe that her pale features had grown paler. Her fingers were doing an agitated little dance on the blotter.

"I knew the young man was dead, yes," she said. "I heard nothing of any suspicious circumstances surrounding his death."

"Well, there you are," Quirke said, lifting both hands and letting them fall again. "The fact of the matter is that Leon Corless — that was the young man's name, if you didn't know it — is dead, murdered perhaps, and his pregnant girlfriend is here, under your care."

Sister Dominic drew her narrow shoulders upwards. "Are you suggesting, Doctor, that there's a link of some kind between this so-called suspicious death and Lisa Costigan's presence here with us?"

Quirke gave all the signs of pondering this carefully. "Yes," he said at last, "I think that is what I'm suggesting."

Phoebe watched him intently. He, in turn, did not take his eyes from the nun's face.

They could both hear the nun breathing.

"And what," she asked, "could this link be?"

"I don't know. That's one of the things I'd like to have a word with Lisa about. In fact" — he drew his chair an inch or two closer to the desk — "in fact, Sister, what I would suggest is that Lisa should collect her things and come away with us, with Phoebe and me, today. Now."

"That's out of the question," the nun said, with a dismissive little laugh. "Her father expressly —"

"Yes, I'm sure her father insisted that she should see no one, talk to no one, and certainly not leave the laundry, without his permission."

"Exactly."

"But I, Sister Dominic, I'm here to — how shall I put it? — I'm here to countermand his orders. I'm here to fetch Lisa and take her away, to a place of safety."

"Safety?" the nun said, in a deepened voice. "Are you implying that she's in some kind of danger here?"

"I believe," Quirke said slowly, "that she's in danger generally. I can't say exactly what kind of danger. But let me put it this way: I know her father, I know the kind of man he is. *He* is a danger. And he's not to be trusted with the safekeeping of his daughter, nor" — he tapped the desk with the tip of his middle finger — "with the care of her unborn child."

The nun sat back in her chair, her mouth set in a thin line and her eyes narrowed.

"Dr. Quirke," she said very softly, "these are outrageous charges."

"Yes," Quirke said calmly, "they are, aren't they. But so are the circumstances. I know as well as you do what goes on here, Sister. Therefore I suggest that you do as I say, and tell Lisa that I'm here, that Phoebe is here, and that we've come to take her away."

"This is ridiculous, I can't possibly —"

"Yes, you can, Sister. And you will."

Phoebe felt a thrill of excitement rising in her breast. The nun took a deep breath, controlling herself.

"I'll phone the girl's father," she said, picking up the receiver. "I'll phone him now and tell him the scandalous accusations you've made against him and —"

She stopped, watching, as if mesmerized, Quirke's hand as it slowly approached and slowly took the receiver from her and replaced it gently on its cradle.

"You will call no one," he said in a calm, low voice. "Instead, you'll tell one of the sisters to fetch Lisa Costigan here, with her belongings." The nun's pale blue eyes were wide. "Believe me, Sister, this is the best course to follow, for all concerned. In fact, it's the only course open to you."

"How do you judge that?"

Quirke smiled his gentle little smile. "Sister Dominic," he said, "I know you value the privacy and seclusion that you depend on for your work here in the laundry. Imagine the publicity it would attract if the Guards were to arrive at your door and demand that you hand over a material witness to what was most probably the deliberate killing of a young man. Lisa, you see, was in the park the night her boyfriend died. I know that Inspector Hackett, of Pearse Street Garda Station, is actively seeking the whereabouts of Miss Costigan. Wouldn't it be better if she came with us now? Wouldn't that be better than that Inspector Hackett and his men should come to you?"

Lisa Costigan hadn't changed out of the dark blue housecoat that all the laundry's inmates wore. She was carrying a small pigskin suitcase. She seemed to be in shock. Her cheeks were hollow and she walked with her shoulders hunched. She kept glancing to and fro, anxious and disoriented. Phoebe gave a little cry and ran to her and made to embrace her, but the young woman drew back, staring dully. She had a shocked, empty look, as if she had been incarcerated for years, and now could not believe that she was free.

"Are you all right?" Phoebe asked.

"Yes," Lisa murmured. "Yes, I'm all right." She tried to smile. "I didn't think you'd come."

Suddenly she began to cry, weakly and without sound, from weariness, it seemed, more than anything else. Phoebe put an arm around her shoulders and led her forward. "It's all right, Lisa," she said. "You're free, now. You're safe."

Quirke and Phoebe walked with her between them down the drive, to where the taxi they had come in was still waiting for them.

At the gate Lisa stopped and drew back. "Where's my father?" she asked, eyeing the taxi. "Is he here?"

"No, he's not," Quirke said.

She gazed into his face. "He's not?"

"No."

It was hot, in the sun. The taxi's engine was running, and there was a smell of exhaust smoke on the air.

"Where are you taking me?" the young woman asked.

"To a place where you'll be safe," Quirke said.

Lisa turned to Phoebe. "I didn't know if you'd get my note. I took a chance."

"Yes, you did," Phoebe said, "and it worked."

In the taxi Quirke sat in the front, beside the driver, and Phoebe and Lisa Costigan got into the back seat. Lisa asked for a cigarette. Quirke gave her one from his case, and held the lighter for her. She was trembling.

She turned to Phoebe again.

"I lost the baby," she said.

21

May Hackett was excited, she couldn't deny it, though it made her feel a little foolish. When she was at school, years ago, her class was told one day that a new girl would be joining them, all the way from South Africa. For a week before the girl's arrival, May and her classmates could talk of nothing else. What would she be like? May had never seen a black person before, except in the pictures, like *Gone with the Wind* and *Show Boat.* They had been told she spoke English, but would they understand her accent? And who would be chosen to share a desk with her? The week went slowly, and at last the girl arrived. To everyone's surprise, and secret disappointment, she wasn't black at all. In fact, she had ash-blond hair and blue eyes. Her name was Johanna de Kuyper, and she was Afrikaans, which was what the Dutch settlers in South Africa called themselves. After she got over an initial shyness,

Johanna turned out to be quite ordinary, except when she talked about things like snakes, and the lovely white beaches there were around Cape Town, and the number of servants her family had — all black, of course — and how lazy they were, and how they stole things.

In her heart May knew it would probably be the same with the daughter of that blackguard Joe Costigan. And yet, all morning, she had been fizzing with anticipation. She had cleaned the house twice, and lost count of the number of times she had gone up to check the spare back bedroom and make sure that everything was ready for the guest's arrival. She changed her clothes a number of times, too. First she had put on her blue frock, and even a string of pearls. Then she caught sight of herself in the mirror and saw how ridiculous she looked in such a fancy getup. So she took off the frock and the pearls and put on an old tweed skirt and the brown housecoat she wore when she was doing the cleaning. She went to the mirror again. This time she looked like a priest's housekeeper, so it was back upstairs again for another desperate search through the wardrobe and the chest of drawers. In the end she shut her eyes and chose a dress at random — she only had three or four outfits, so the choice wasn't wide — and when at last she heard the squad car pulling up outside she was glad to think that she looked her usual self. Hackett, when he had phoned, had warned her the girl was in a bad way with her nerves, and that it would be best not to make a fuss.

When Lisa Costigan came in, May saw that her husband had been right — the girl was in an awful state, pale as a ghost and trembling all over as if she had been struck by lightning.

"You're very welcome," May said, and took the suitcase from the girl and led her into the living room.

Dr. Quirke was there, and his daughter, whose name for the minute May couldn't recall. Phyllis, was it?

Hackett, coming in behind the others, had a sheepish look, and wouldn't meet her eye; she supposed he felt awkward, having to let the great Dr. Quirke see where he lived.

She hadn't met Quirke before, though she had seen his picture in the papers. But her husband had talked about him so much over the years that she felt she knew him. He was grave and polite, and even made a little bow when they shook hands. She knew the type; her own father had been that way, wary and secretive. Hackett had told her

Quirke was a drinker, just like her father.

"This is very good of you, Mrs. Hackett," Quirke said, keeping her hand in his for longer than politeness required.

"Oh, you're very welcome, Doctor," she said. She was flustered, and felt herself blushing a little, to her annoyance. "Any Christian would do the same."

The Quirke girl hung back, smiling vaguely, her hands together at her waist. She was pretty, in a severe sort of way. She had something of the look of her father, but not much. The black dress with the white lace collar suited her too well. It had been a hard life for her, up to now — Hackett had told her the girl's history — and by the look of her, things wouldn't be much easier in the future.

She turned her attention back to Lisa. Who would have thought it? Joe Costigan's daughter, staying here in this house, a virtual fugitive. There was that to be said for being married to Hackett: life was never dull for long.

They went upstairs together, the girl holding on to the banister rail as if she were afraid she might fall, and May behind her, carrying her case. In the room the girl sat down on the side of the bed with her knees pressed together and her hands in her lap and her eyes flickering here and there, taking in everything in the room. She was like a creature brought in from the wild.

"Will you be all right, now?" May said.

Lisa looked up at her and tried to smile.

"Yes," she said, "yes, I'll be fine. I'm just a bit —"

"I know, dear, I know. Maybe you'd like to lie down and have a rest? You can unpack later. I'll leave your suitcase here, look, at the end of the bed. There's the wardrobe there, and you can use any of those drawers for your things. The bathroom is across the landing." She smiled. "I'll leave you, so, and let you get your bearings. If you want anything, just give a call down the stairs and I'll come up."

She went out and closed the door softly behind herself. She was halfway down the stairs when she heard the girl's sobs. She debated with herself whether to go back up again, but decided against it.

The three of them, Hackett, Quirke, and his daughter, were much as she had left them, standing ill at ease in the living room, Dr. Quirke with his hat in his hands and Hackett gazing vacantly at the floor. It was, she thought, like one of those occasions when people come to call at Christmas, and everyone feels awkward and doesn't know

378

what to say.

"Well," she said brightly, "will I make tea?"

The Quirke girl had followed her into the kitchen, offering to help. May suggested she might set up a tray with the tea things, and showed her where they were stored. She wished she could remember her name. Philomena? No, something fancier than that.

She put the kettle on to boil. The sun was shining in the window above the sink, and there was an identical star of light on the curve of each of the two brass taps.

"Your friend will be grand, here," she said.

"Oh, yes, yes, I'm sure she will. My name is Phoebe, by the way." She smiled. "I don't think anyone introduced us."

May wiped her hands on her apron. "I'm very pleased to meet you. My husband often mentions you. He's very fond of your father."

"Yes," Phoebe said, "I know he is."

They stood smiling at each other.

"He's very hard on himself, your father, I think," May ventured.

Phoebe raised her eyebrows. "Do you think so?"

"Oh, it's just that he has the look of it." What was she saying? The day was topsy-turvy. "I'm sorry. It's no business of mine."

Phoebe didn't seem to be paying attention; instead she stood thinking.

"He's not used to kindness," she said at last. "I think that's the problem. If he seems rude, you mustn't pay any attention. It's just the way he is — it means nothing." She turned back to the tea tray. "Where's the sugar?" she asked.

"Here it is, on the shelf."

Phoebe took down the sugar bowl, then paused. She was smiling again, to herself. "As a matter of fact," she said, "he's just fallen in love."

May felt the blood rushing up from her throat. What sort of a thing was that for a daughter to say to someone she had only just met? And about her father, too. Hackett had told her they were a queer lot, Dr. Quirke and his daughter and the Griffins, and it seemed he was right.

"That's very — that's very nice," she said, stammering. "Is it somebody he just met?"

"Yes. Actually, she's my boss. Dr. Evelyn Blake. I work for her, in Fitzwilliam Square. She's a psychiatrist. Isn't it mad? I mean, isn't it mad my father should fall for her? I couldn't be happier for him." May Hackett stood gazing at her, her mouth open a little way and her eyes slightly glazed. "I think the kettle is boiling," Phoebe said. "Will I bring in the tray?"

May spooned the tea into the pot and poured on the water. And to think she had expected Johanna de Kuyper to be exotic.

On the way back in the squad car, Quirke asked to be dropped off at Ailesbury Road. Phoebe went on to Fitzwilliam Square and Dr. Blake's office, and Hackett returned to Pearse Street to sit at his desk with his feet up, picking his teeth with a matchstick, and brooding. It had been a long and eventful day.

When Quirke turned in at the gate he saw Rose Griffin standing in the big bay window to the left of the front door. She was smoking a cigarette, with one arm folded across her midriff. She looked down at him without expression. The day was clouding over, and there was a warm wind blowing, drawing up eddies of dust in shadowed corners.

Rose opened the door to him herself.

"Mal is in his room," she said, turning away. "I'm not going to disturb him."

"I don't want you to." He followed her into the drawing room. "I just came to let you know about the girl."

Rose went and stood again in the bay of the window, looking out, her back turned resolutely against him.

"I don't know what it is I've done to make you angry," he said.

She didn't turn. "What makes you think I'm angry?"

Quirke sighed. "Don't pretend, Rose, it doesn't suit you."

She said nothing for a while, then turned from the window, seeming not angry now, only tired and dispirited.

"Have a drink with me, Quirke," she said.

She made gin and tonics for them both. Quirke had asked for a tonic only but she ignored him. She handed him the glass, and knocked her own against the rim of it. "Here's to chivalry," she said.

They carried their drinks across to the sofa and sat down. The day outside was darker now, and they could hear the wind blowing along the street.

"I'm not angry at you, Quirke," Rose said. "Or I am, but not especially. I'm mad as hell at everything, and you just happen to be standing in the way." She picked a thread from the sleeve of her blouse. "It's the damnedest thing," she said. "I was fond of Josh, but when he died what I felt was mostly relief." She glanced at him and smiled. "Are you shocked? You should be. I was sort of shocked myself. But Mal, poor Mal, he's another thing altogether. I'm going to grieve for him — I'm grieving for him already. I guess" — she took a drink from her glass — "I guess I must love him. It's funny, I don't think I ever loved anyone, before. Thought I did, but I'm thinking now I was wrong." She leaned forward and tapped him on the knee. "I even imagined for a while I was in love with you, Quirke. Fancy that. I was jealous, the way you kept following Sarah around like some poor lovesick hound when the moon is full. I could hear you howling, even though you didn't make a sound."

"I never knew what I wanted, Rose. That was always my trouble."

She nodded dismissively. "But you know what you want now, don't you."

"Do I?"

"I can see it in your eyes. You're not doing that silent howl anymore. I'm glad for you, but I can't say I didn't prefer you the old way." She sipped her drink, studying him. "You going to tell me about her?"

He knew she meant Evelyn. He shook his head.

"Oh, well. I guess you will, in time." She ran a hand through her hair. "Tell me about the girl, then."

"She's staying at Inspector Hackett's house."

"What happened to her?"

"Her father had somebody watching her, a fellow by the unlikely name of Abercrombie. He followed Phoebe and her down to Ballytubber, with a couple of his heavies, and took Lisa from the house and brought her to the Mother of Mercy Laundry."

"What a name that place has," Rose said. "How did you get her out? Beat some poor nun into submission, did you?"

"Something like that. I don't think you realize what those places are like, Rose, that Mal's father and your first husband set up."

"Yes, they were a pair of rascals, weren't they, Garret and old Josh. They thought they ruled the world on direct instructions from the good Lord above." She had finished her own drink, and now she took the glass from his hand and drank from it, and gave it back. "Sorry," she said, "lipstick yet again."

He took out his cigarette case and lit two cigarettes and gave one to Rose. She watched him, amused. "You see too many movies," she said. "You think you're Cary Grant."

They smoked in silence for a while, companionably. Something in the dimmed light outside communicated itself to them, a sense of loss and sweet melancholy.

"What will you do?" he asked.

"You mean, after Mal is gone?" A thrush was whistling somewhere outside, a limpid, liquid warbling. "Maybe I'll go back to the States," she said. She waved a hand at the room. "I'm sure as hell going to get rid of this white elephant. Can't think why I bought it in the first place. Delusions of grandeur, I guess. I liked the idea of a girl from the backwoods living amongst so much gilt." She laughed, then said, "The girl's father, Costigan — he was Garret's bagman, if I remember rightly?"

"Among other things."

"Why did he put her away? Because she was going to have a child?"

"That, and the fact that she'd found out about some things he was up to, and told her boyfriend, and her boyfriend started poking around, and ended up in a burning car with his head bashed in."

She nodded. "That sounds like Costigan, all right." She took his glass, which was empty now, and went to the sideboard and made new drinks for them both. "So what are you going to do?" she asked over her shoulder. "You and that detective friend of yours going to put old Joe in the slammer? If that's your plan, you better have all your ducks lined up in a nice neat row. Joe is a

slippery customer. You too could find yourself in a burning car with a bump on your
head the size of an egg." She came back,
and handed him his glass, and sat down.
"What about Phoebe?" she said. "You think
Costigan might go after her?"

"He might."

"She really should come here, stay with
us, like you suggested. I'll hire in some serious people to look after her. Costigan is not
the only person with contacts."

He shook his head. "No good. When I
tried to persuade her to come here she
laughed, and then got annoyed. She has her
mother's spirit — her stubbornness, too."

"She's a damn fool," Rose said mildly. She
stirred her drink with an index finger. "So
how are you going to protect her?"

"I don't know."

"Are you worried? I mean, are you seriously worried?"

"You said yourself, Costigan is a dangerous man. He'll want his daughter back."

"But you, and your detective, you're not
going to give her back, right?"

"No, we're not."

She sat and gazed at him, smiling to
herself, then leaned forward suddenly and
put a hand against his cheek, as she so often
did.

"Oh, Quirke," she said, "you're just hopeless, ain't you. You're like a little boy in the playground, saving some girl you're sweet on from the school bully."

Quirke sipped his drink. "According to Costigan," he said, "there are two worlds, the fantasy one where people like me live and the real one, where he carries on his business. He's right, of course. But being realistic is a great excuse for doing all the bad deeds you want to do and then saying it's a result of the way things are, the way things *really* are."

"Oh, phooey," Rose said. "You think you can choose how to live? So does Mal, or he used to, anyway, until recent developments showed him how wrong he was. We drift, Quirke. You know that yellow foam at the edge of the waves at the seashore, that stuff that looks like tobacco spit mixed with soda water? That's us. The wave rolls in, the wave rolls out" — she demonstrated, moving a hand languidly back and forth in front of her — "and we roll with it. I bet that yellow stuff, too, thinks it's moving itself about, just like you do."

She stood up, stretching. "Ah! My back aches," she said. "I'm getting old." She drained the last of her drink and took an ice cube into her mouth and cracked it between her teeth. She looked down at him, still crunching. "Only one thing to be done with the Joe Costigans of this world, Quirke," she said. "And you know what that is, just as well as I do. Now I'm going up to check on my poor Mal. One thing I hate to see is a man dying. You want to have some lunch with me when I come down?"

Quirke stood up. "Thank you, no," he said.

"You have things to do?"

"Yes," he said, "yes, I have things to do."

She drew close to him, looking up into his face. "Kiss me," she said, "will you, Quirke, for old times' sake?"

She put her arms around him. They were both holding empty glasses. Her lips were cold, from the ice. She drew her head back, smiling. "We did love each other, a little, didn't we, Quirke? Say we did. Lie, if you have to, I don't care."

He said nothing, but kissed her cold lips again, lightly, then stepped away from her, and put his empty glass down on the mantelpiece and walked out of the room. She stood for a moment, gazing at the floor, then went to the bay window. Big drops of rain had begun to fall.

Quirke was already on the front steps. She watched him all the way to the gate. He didn't look back.

■ ■ ■ ■

At the hospital he went to his office and shut the door and sat down behind his desk and picked up the phone and dialed the girl at Reception and asked her to find Sam Corless's number for him. He waited, drumming his fingers on the desk.

Corless, when he came on, was hoarse and sounded exhausted. Faintly in the background there was the sound of dance band music. "You have to put up with that all day long?" Quirke asked.

"All day," Corless said grimly, and coughed. "What can I do for you?"

"I was just calling to see how you're faring."

There was a brief silence; then Corless coughed again. "No, you weren't," he said. "But I'm doing all right, I suppose."

With his free hand Quirke fumbled a cigarette out of his case, fitted it in the corner of his mouth, and lit it. "I have some information that will interest you," he said.

"Oh? What sort of information?"

"I believe I know who murdered your son."

22

Coming up the stairs to his flat he brushed at the raindrops on the shoulders of his jacket. The bottoms of his trouser legs were wet, too, and his feet felt damp. When he got to the door he saw at once where the wood was splintered beside the lock, and when he put a hand against the door it swung open easily. He smelled cigarette smoke, not his brand. He wasn't surprised, and yet he hesitated. It was interesting, how calm he felt, and how little afraid he was. He knew he shouldn't be calm; he knew he should be afraid. He could turn and walk quietly back down the stairs, he could go to the phone box at the corner and call Hackett, and Hackett would send a squad car, or come himself with Jenkins and a couple of uniformed Guards. Instead he took two or three slow, shallow breaths, and stepped inside.

Costigan was standing by the window,

looking out into the rain. He wore a dark blue suit, with all three buttons of the jacket fastened, so that the flap at the back rode high. He was smoking a cigarette. There was a scattering of ash on the floor at his feet. He was a big man — Quirke always forgot how big he was — with a big square head and a broad forehead and a nose like a stone axe. His hair was thick and oiled and swept back smoothly from his brow. His glasses were heavy black horn-rims. He didn't turn at the sound of Quirke's step behind him.

"Where is she?" he said.

"Where's who?"

Costigan took a deep drag from his cigarette.

"I had people here with me," he said. "They're the ones I needed to get the door open. I could have kept them, they could still be here. Instead, it's just me." He glanced over his shoulder. "You can't say I'm not a reasonable man."

"No," Quirke said, "I suppose I can't."

Costigan had turned to the window again. "So in all reasonableness, I'll ask you again: where is she?"

Quirke took his cigarette case from the pocket of his jacket and freed one of the neat row of cigarettes from under the elastic strap holding them in place and put it between his lips and lit it. His fingers were steady, he was glad to see.

"You could say," he said, "that she's in the hands of the law."

"What's that supposed to mean?"

"Mr. Costigan, you don't really think I'm going to tell you where she is, do you? What would have been the point of getting her out of the laundry in the first place, if I was going to hand her over to you?"

Rain whispered against the window.

"You know I'll find her, sooner or later," Costigan said. "We could behave like civilized men and sort this out between us, here and now. Don't you think that would be the best thing to do, the simplest thing? What's the point of fuss and bother and all the rest of it?"

"Why don't we sit down?" Quirke said.

Costigan still had his eye on the street. "I'd rather stand," he said.

"Suit yourself. I'm going to have a drink. Do you want one? Oh, I forgot — you never touch the stuff."

He went into the kitchen, taking his time, and reached up for the bottle of Jameson at the back of the wall cupboard beside the window. As he did, he glanced down into the street. He was sure Costigan was lying; his men were bound to be down there somewhere, waiting for word from their boss to come clattering back up the stairs, carrying whatever it was they had used to break open the door. He could see no one, however, and there were no cars parked at the curb.

He took a tumbler from the draining board and polished it with a tea towel. He had balanced his cigarette on the edge of the sink. Why, he wondered, did cigarettes always seem to send up a thicker stream of smoke when they were set down on something cold, like the porcelain of the sink, or a marble shelf? Or was it just something he imagined? The world was full of things he didn't know the reason for.

Costigan appeared in the doorway and stood there with his hands in his pockets. Quirke poured himself a tot of whiskey, measuring it carefully.

"Watching your intake, are you?" Costigan said. "Have you been back to St. John of the Cross since we last ran into each other?"

"I don't think so. When did we meet last?"

"Oh, I see you about, frequently."

"Do you?" Quirke took a sip of his drink. The sharpness of the whiskey burned his tongue pleasantly. "I don't see you."

"No, you wouldn't."

Quirke turned with the glass in his hand. "So you're keeping watch on me, are you?"

"I keep a watch on a lot of people."

"I'm sure you do. Look, Costigan, you've asked what you came to ask, and I've given you my answer. I'm tired."

"I can believe it. You've had a busy day."

Quirke sat down at the table by the window. Costigan hesitated, then came forward and pulled out a chair and sat too.

"How are we going to resolve this, Quirke?"

"I'm not sure we are going to resolve it. For a start, I don't know what you're talking about. What kind of resolution could there be?"

Costigan ran his fingers over the smooth plastic top of the table. "You know, I could have you charged with removing my daughter from a place where she was legally residing."

Quirke laughed. "Go ahead. Besides, I didn't remove her. She came of her own free will, despite the best efforts of Sister what's-her-name."

"Dominic," Costigan said darkly. "Sister Dominic. Who'll shortly be on her way to the mission fields in the Congo." He paused, his jaw working. "How's Malachy?" he asked.

"He's not well."

"Is that so? I heard something, all right. Is he bad?"

"Yes, he's bad."

"Sorry to hear it." Costigan set both fists on the table now. "Come on, Quirke, where's my daughter, what did you do with her? Was that bastard Hackett with you when you went to the laundry?"

Quirke took another, sparing sip of his drink and sat back in his chair, crossing an ankle on a knee. He felt slightly light-headed; he supposed he must be afraid, after all. Yet still there was that strange calm inside him. He could feel the whiskey doing its work on him.

"I know what it was that Leon Corless found out about you and what you're up to," he said.

The lenses of Costigan's spectacles caught the light from the window and turned opaque; they looked like two coins placed over his eyes. "Is that so?" he said. "What am I up to, then?"

"I know about the money you're making in America. When Garret Griffin and Josh Crawford were running the thing, at least they weren't in it for profit."

"Profit? What profit? Have you any idea

what the overheads are in an operation like this?"

Quirke laughed again. "The overheads! Jesus, Costigan." He stopped laughing, and leaned forward across the table, lowering his voice to almost a whisper: "Tell me, did you have Leon Corless murdered?"

"What do you mean, murdered? The young pup was at a party and got drunk and ran his car into a tree."

"No, he didn't. He was dead, or unconscious at least, before he got anywhere near that tree." Those glossy lenses flashed at him. "What happened, Costigan? Was it another one of those mistakes your people are prone to making? Did you send some of your boys to frighten him, to rough him up a bit, maybe, and warn him to stay away from your business and keep his mouth shut about the things Lisa had told him and the other things that he found out for himself? And then it all went wrong?"

Costigan leaned away from him, putting his head far back.

"You have some imagination, Quirke," he said.

Quirke lifted the whiskey glass and was surprised to see that it was empty. Should he have another? He looked at his watch. Ten minutes; he would wait ten minutes.

He still felt slightly dizzy. Someone was calling to him, a voice in his head. He shut his eyes for a moment. He seemed to feel a finger against his lips. *Not speakable.* He opened his eyes and looked about himself, and for a second he didn't know where he was.

"What's the matter with you?" Costigan growled.

"What?"

"Are you sick too, like Malachy?" He gave a low laugh. "Jesus, if I wait long enough you'll both be gone and out of my hair."

Quirke went to the sink and took up the whiskey bottle and poured a measure into his glass. He must hold on; he mustn't let the dizziness overcome him. He willed the voice in his head to be silent. Whose voice was it, anyway? Evelyn, yes, it was Evelyn's voice, wasn't it? That was all right. She would speak to him; she would tell him things.

He returned to the table. A thought occurred to him. "Where's Lisa's mother, Costigan?" he said. "What does she think of all this?"

"My wife is dead," Costigan said.

"Ah. Sorry."

"You don't sound sorry." Costigan was sweating, and his spectacles had slipped down the moist bridge of his nose. He pushed them back into place with a fingertip. "She died when Lisa was seven. Lisa never got over it. That's her trouble." He looked up at the window. "You know what it's like, Quirke, worrying about a daughter, watching over her and worrying about her."

"Oh, yes, I know," Quirke said. "But I would never have been worried enough to put my daughter into the Mother of Mercy Laundry."

Costigan's look hardened. "I knew what I was doing," he said. "She was going to have that fellow's bastard. Bad enough he was getting ready to try to destroy me, he had to ruin my daughter, too."

"Your reputation, your daughter. Would you have sold her child to the Americans, when the time came, along with all the other ones?"

Costigan brought the side of his fist down hard on the table, making Quirke's whiskey glass jump.

"No damn Commie's son was going to dirty my family's reputation!" he snarled. "You think I'd let that get out, that Sam Corless's whelp had got my daughter in the family way? You think I'd allow that? No, by Christ. No Corless was going to destroy Joe Costigan, that's for sure."

Quirke retrieved his glass from the table, where Costigan's white-knuckled fist was still braced. "I know you had him killed, Costigan. Your people followed him that night, and stopped him, and hit him on the head and doused the car with petrol and set it on fire and then ran it into a tree to make it look like an accident, or a suicide. Abercrombie, was that who you sent? If so, he botched the job. It didn't look like an accident. It didn't look like anything other than what it was. My second-in-command at the hospital spotted straightaway that before he died Corless was unconscious from a blow to the head. That's part of your trouble — you're careless, and the people you hire to do your dirty work are more careless still."

Costigan was smiling. "It's what I say, Quirke: you have some imagination." He lit another cigarette and blew smoke up at the window. Then he sat thinking for a while. "We were always disappointed in you, Quirke," he said, "your father and I."

"What father?"

" 'What father?' he asks." Costigan's smile widened. "As if you didn't know." Quirke stared at him for a moment, then lifted his glass and threw back his head and gulped down the last of the whiskey. Costigan nodded, grinning, those lenses flashing reflected rainlight from the window. "That's right," he said, "have another drink — maybe you'll forget all the things you'd rather not know." He chuckled contemptuously. " 'What father?' " he said again.

Quirke felt dizzy, and his head swam, but not from the alcohol. Something had given way, like the bulkhead of a ship. He had kept it all from himself for so long, for so many years, the known thing that he refused to know. Now, suddenly, as he gazed into Costigan's grinning face, the barrier was breached, and the truth surged in, and at last he acknowledged to himself his true origins, his true identity.

Costigan was speaking again, in a low, urgent, menacing voice: "Now listen to me, Quirke, and listen carefully. You have a daughter, just like I have. You're going to return mine to me, from wherever you've hidden her. And I'd better get her back, if you want your girl safe. You know me, Quirke. You know the lengths I'll go to." He sat back, and took a drag at his cigarette, and expelled two slow streams of smoke from his nostrils. "So," he said, "I'm asking you for the last time. Where is she?"

23

Abercrombie's battered blue Ford nosed its way around the corner from Baggot Street into Herbert Place and pulled up under the dripping trees on the canal side of the road, opposite No. 12, which was where Costigan had told him Phoebe lived. It was still afternoon but the rain made it seem like twilight. He turned off the motor and peered out through the rain-streaked windscreen.

He had two men with him, hard cases who had worked for him before, and he knew he could trust them. One of them, Hynes, tall and thin, with a crew cut, had got out of Mountjoy only the week before. He had wanted to lie low and stay out of trouble for a while, but he owed Crombie a big favor — there was a fellow who'd been sniffing round his missus while he was inside, and Crombie had made him disappear — and so he had no choice but to come with him

401

on this job.

The other one, Ross, sitting in the back seat smoking a cigarette, was a kid of sixteen with a little pinched white face and a widow's peak. He looked like he wouldn't hurt a fly, but he'd already done time for maiming a tinker his ma had been shacked up with and who'd been in the habit of giving her a beating every Saturday night. It was Ross who had gone down with Abercrombie that night to Wicklow to get Costigan's daughter.

"What house is it?" Hynes asked.

"That one," Abercrombie said, pointing. "The black door."

"Is she in there?"

"Whether she is or not, we're going in. If she's not there, we wait. She has to come home sometime." He turned to Ross. "You stay here, keep an eye out. We'll watch from the window. You see her coming, tip us the nod."

"How will I do that?"

"Open your window and wave, you stupid little fuck!"

"Can I not go in with you?" Ross said, disappointed. His voice was a nasal whine that always set Abercrombie's teeth on edge.

"Why don't *I* stay?" Hynes said. "Let him go. He's good with locks." He turned in the seat. "Aren't you, Rossie?"

Ross only looked at him. Ross's eyes were funny; they turned up at the outer corners, like a Chinaman's. Hynes always wanted to ask him if his ma had done it with a Chink, only he was afraid to. He'd never come across anyone like Ross; Ross had no fear, no fear at all. It was uncanny.

"I told you," Abercrombie said to Ross. "Keep your trap shut and your eyes open. Right?"

Hynes got out of the car and held the door for Abercrombie, and together they set off across the road. Abercrombie pulled the collar of his jacket tight around his neck. "Fucking weather," he said. "Sun splitting the trees for weeks on end but today it had to rain."

Hynes had lit a cigarette but it was sodden by the time they reached the other side of the road. He threw it into the gutter and swore.

They went up the granite steps to the front door. Hynes kept watch while Abercrombie worked on the lock. It gave him no trouble, and within seconds they were inside.

Ross saw them go in, and leaned his head back on the seat and settled down to wait. He was angry that Crombie had chosen

Hynes to go in. Crombie had shown him a picture of the girl; he'd have liked to have a bit of fun with her, before they took her away.

Inside the house, the two men crept up the stairs. The place was silent, the people who lived in the other flats probably all off at work. Maybe she was, too. It didn't matter; they could wait.

They reached the second-floor landing and stood outside the door, looking at each other, listening. No sound. Abercrombie nodded, and got to work on the lock.

The car, coming up from the Mount Street direction, had no markings, but as soon as Ross saw it he sat up. It was moving slowly, the tires throwing up little waves of rainwater on either side. Ross watched it, his eyes narrowed. Then he wriggled sideways through the gap in the seats and got behind the wheel. Crombie, the fucker, had taken the key with him. He looked out at the car again, trying to see who was in it. There were four of them, two in the front and two in the back. He couldn't make them out; the rain was coming down too heavily. The car didn't stop, and he relaxed.

Abercrombie and Hynes were in the flat now. They put their heads into the kitchen. Nobody. Then they walked into the living

404

room, and stopped. Hynes turned immediately and tried to make a break for it, but when he got to the door he met two plainclothes detectives coming up the stairs. Abercrombie, standing in the doorway, heard the scuffle outside, and Hynes cursing and then giving a gasp of pain. Hackett was sitting in an armchair by the fireplace, with his hat on his knee. There were two more detectives by the window, one of them on either side. Hackett stood up.

"Well now," he said, "if it isn't Mr. Abercrombie. Come in, come in."

Down in the street the car with the four men in it did a rapid U-turn, its tires squealing. Ross was already out of the Ford, sprinting along the pavement, under the dripping trees. The car pulled up and the four doors flew open and the men inside, all wearing hats and gabardine raincoats, scrambled out. Ross dodged through a gap in the railings and ran along the towpath, head back, his elbows sawing and his knees going like pistons.

And Crombie had called him a stupid fuck. He didn't have the breath to laugh, as he ran. Behind him there were shouts. Too late, boys, too slow.

He raced on.

■ ■ ■ ■

When the phone rang, Quirke smiled at Costigan. They were still sitting at the table, and Quirke had poured himself another whiskey. It was his third, but all three measures had been small, and the dizziness was gone and his head was clear. Costigan was watching him suspiciously, his black-framed glasses riding high on his nose. The telephone kept ringing.

"Are you going to answer it?" Costigan said.

Quirke stood up and went into the living room.

Costigan sat motionless, listening. He heard Quirke pick up the receiver and speak a word or two that he couldn't catch. Then Quirke came back and stopped in the doorway.

"It's for you, Costigan," he said. "Inspector Hackett would like a word."

24

Dr. Blake gave a dinner party, a very small one. She invited Quirke, her nephew, Paul Viertel, and Phoebe. The doctor lived in a tiny mews house in a lane behind Northumberland Road that she had bought and moved into after her husband's death. Inside, the little house had the sequestered atmosphere of a well-appointed and comfortable underground den. This impression was compounded by the tremendous summer storm that had been threatening for days and that finally broke over the city on the evening of the dinner. It was a windless night and the rain was an incessant and thrilling drumbeat on the roof. Rolling thunderclaps made the windowpanes buzz, and flickers of lightning left a whiff of sulfur in the crepitant air. There were repeated brief power failures, until, sometime after nine o'clock, the lights went out and stayed out, and the rest of the dinner took place by candlelight.

Luckily the house had a gas cooker. They ate clear chicken soup and poached salmon and asparagus, followed by ice cream with raspberry sauce. Quirke was careful with the wine, and drank moderately. Paul Viertel and Phoebe talked together a great deal, and the two older people were happy to sit for long periods in silence, glancing at each other now and then through the glitter and flash of the candle flames and exchanging secret smiles.

This was Quirke's first time in the house. The furniture was sparse, and what there was of it was discreetly elegant. Evelyn collected primitive art, and savage wooden heads and fierce-looking masks were set on tables and on windowsills, or lurked menacingly in gaps among the books on the bookshelves. The room where they ate was dominated by an Egon Schiele drawing, startling in its anatomical frankness, of an emaciated and naked young woman seated on the ground, languorously leaning back and supporting herself on her elbows, with one leg flexed and the other slackly splayed. There was an upright piano, on which stood an assortment of framed photographs. Evelyn showed Quirke a miniature of her late husband in an oval frame — "He was young then, you would not have known him" — and some blurred snapshots of her family taken in the 1930s. There was a photograph too of her son, Hanno, who had died in childhood; Quirke gazed at the slightly out-of-focus image of the boy, soft of face and sad-eyed like his mother.

"He looks like you," Quirke said.

"Do you think so? He was such a sweet child."

"What happened —"

She lifted an admonishing finger. "Ssh," she said softly. "Perhaps another time. Not now, not tonight."

When they had finished their salmon, the two women cleared away the plates, and Quirke and Paul Viertel talked about Paul's studies. His field was immunology. He intended, when qualified, to go to Africa and and work there.

"Malaria," he said, "river blindness, even smallpox — these things can be eradicated, I am convinced of it. All that's required is funding, and personnel."

"It's an ambitious program," Quirke said. "I can't see it being carried out in my lifetime."

"No," Paul said, and smiled, "but perhaps in mine."

After dinner they settled into pairs, Paul

and Phoebe remaining at the table, deep in conversation about Cold War politics — Paul was radically of the left — while Quirke and Evelyn sat beside each other on the sofa, balancing coffee cups on their knees.

"I've made a discovery," Quirke said.

"Yes, I thought there was something."

He glanced at her sharply. "What sort of something?"

"Something momentous."

Quirke nodded to himself. "*Momentous*, yes, I suppose that's the word." He took a sip of his coffee. "What it was," he said, "was that I realized who my parents were."

"You realized?"

"Acknowledged. I've known it for a long time, I think." He smiled. "Strange, isn't it, how you can know something and not know it at the same time?"

"Not so strange," Evelyn said. "Many people are capable of it — whole nations are. What happened?"

Quirke shook his head in puzzled wonderment. "It was strange," he repeated. "A man came to my flat — broke into my flat, in fact — a man who knew my father. A very wicked man. A kind of devil."

"Ah, yes. It is usually the Devil who whispers momentous things into our ears." She touched a finger to his wrist. "Do you want to tell me who they were, your parents?"

A beat of silence passed. "My father was a judge," Quirke said. "Judge Garret Griffin."

"I know the name."

"Oh, he was a power in the land. He's dead now." He turned his head aside, frowning. "He adopted me, but I think at some level I knew he was my father."

Evelyn was watching him, her dark eyes darker and larger than ever. "And your mother?"

"I think she was a servant in the Judge's house, a maid who used to work for him and his wife. Moran was her name. Dolores Moran."

"And where is she now?"

"Dead, too. She was murdered. In fact" — he leaned forward suddenly, as if he had felt a stab of pain — "in fact, the man who came to my flat, Joseph Costigan, he was responsible for her death. Him, and Judge Griffin."

Now Evelyn put a hand over his. "This is a terrible story," she said.

"Yes," Quirke said, "yes, it is, it is terrible."

"Your father knew she had been murdered? Did he mean it to happen?"

"He swore to me it was all Costigan's fault, that it was the fault of the men Costigan sent to her house to get something from her, a diary. There was another girl, another of the Judge's girls, also a maid in the house, like Dolly Moran. Her name was Christine Falls. She died in childbirth."

"This child was also the Judge's?"

"Yes, and Dolly Moran had kept a record of it, and that's why she was murdered."

"Were they caught, the people who killed her?"

"No," Quirke said. "The police knew who they were, but they could do nothing. The Judge was a very powerful man, with very powerful friends, in the church and in the government. He was untouchable. Costigan, too — all of them were untouchable."

Phoebe and Paul Viertel were arguing in friendly fashion about Israel and the Palestinians. Quirke watched them, smiling. He had not seen such a light in Phoebe's eyes for a very long time.

"You must be in pain now, yes?" Evelyn said.

"No," Quirke answered, "*pain* isn't the word. What I mostly feel is relief, or something like it. And sadness, of course, for Dolly Moran, for poor Christine Falls."

"And for yourself?"

He thought about it. "No," he said, "I don't feel sad for myself. I think I'm cured of that. It's as if I had been walking through what seemed an endless night and suddenly the dawn has come up behind me. Not a very welcome dawn, but dawn nevertheless."

"And will it show you the path to follow, from now on? It seems to me you have much work to do."

"You mean, I should embark on the talking cure? Will you take me on?"

She only smiled.

Later, the two of them were in the kitchen, and she said, "Phoebe, I think, is falling a little in love with my Paul."

"Do you think so?"

"Yes, of course." She was at the stove, making another round of coffee, while he leaned against the sink, smoking a cigarette. A single, tall candle stood on the draining board. "Do you like him?" she asked.

"Paul? He seems a decent fellow."

"Decent. Hmm. That is a good word. Am I decent, would you say?"

She turned to him, and he took her in his arms. "You know that *I'm* falling a little in love with *you*? More than a little."

"Ah. That's good. I like that."

The flame under the percolator was too high and the coffee began to overflow the lid. She stepped away from him, and turned down the gas.

"Why don't you marry me?" he said.

She threw him a sidelong glance. "How funny you are," she said.

"I didn't mean to be."

She took the percolator off the stove and put it to stand on a cork mat on the table. "Let me tell you my joke," she said. "It is the only one I know, but it is such a good joke I don't need to know any others. The *schlemiel* — you know what is a *schlemiel*?"

"I think so."

"Well, the *schlemiel* is having his breakfast. He butters a slice of toast, which he accidentally lets drop to the floor. It falls with the buttered side up — up, you understand? *'Oy vay,'* the *schlemiel* says, 'I must have buttered the wrong side!' " She smiled. "Is good, yes? But you're not laughing."

"Is that me," he said, "am I the *schlemiel*?"

"A little bit, sometimes. But it doesn't matter. The dawn is coming up, remember, behind you. Here, carry the coffee for me."

He didn't move. They stood facing each other. They could hear the rain beating on the little garden outside. Thunder muttered in the distance — the storm was moving away. Neither spoke. A plume of steam rose from the spout of the coffeepot. In the other room, Phoebe and Paul Viertel were debating the future of mankind. Evelyn put out her hand, and Quirke took it in his. The candle flame wavered and then was still again, a glowing, yellow teardrop.

When his taxi came he offered Phoebe a lift, but Paul had said he would walk her home, and the two set out together in the glistening darkness. When they had gone, Evelyn stood with Quirke at the front door for a minute, amid the damp odors of the night. The taxi waited, exhaust smoke trickling out at the rear and its windows stippled with raindrops. Quirke had wanted to stay, but they had become suddenly shy of each other again, and now Evelyn kissed him, brushing her lips lightly against his, and stepped away from him, back into the house. They had agreed they would meet tomorrow for lunch. They would talk about everything, everything. The taxi man revved his engine impatiently.

It was midnight when Quirke got to his flat. He didn't switch on the lights, but stood at the window in the darkness, smoking a cigarette.

Father. Mother. He spoke the words aloud, testing them. They fell from him with a dead sound.

The phone rang, making Quirke jump. It

was Sergeant Jenkins with a message from Hackett, summoning him to the Phoenix Park.

He saw the squad cars stopped at the side of the road and the ambulance with its back doors wide open, shedding a cold white light on the scene. Vague figures stood about, as if idly waiting for something to happen. He got out of the taxi and made his way down the grassy slope. The drenched grass was slippery and the ground underneath was still awash and he had to take care not to lose his footing. Hackett was standing with his hands in his pockets and his hat pushed to the back of his head. He greeted Quirke with a nod. They looked down at the body of Joseph Costigan, his black horn-rimmed spectacles snapped at the bridge and twisted askew.

"Broken neck," Hackett said. He pulled at his lower lip with a finger and thumb. "Expertly done, too."

Costigan's suit was soaked from the rain, and there was mud on his face. He lay somewhat on his side, his legs drawn up and one arm flung wide. There was a leaf in his hair. The light from the ambulance gleamed on the lenses of his broken spectacles. His eyes were open and so was his mouth, as if he had died in amazement. This was the man, Quirke reflected, who years before had sent men to beat him up as a warning against interfering in the business of exporting babies to America, and then had sent the same men to torture Dolly Moran to death because she knew too much. Costigan, the ultimate fixer, had represented, for Quirke, all the vileness and cruelty of life, and now he was dead, and Quirke felt nothing, nothing at all. He wondered if his indifference, like his acknowledgment at last of who his parents had been, was perhaps a sign that "something momentous" had indeed occurred. Was change possible, radical change? He had never believed it before. Now it was as if a door that had long been wedged shut had opened a crack and let in a narrow chink of light.

The bark of the lower part of the big tree under which they stood was badly charred and the branches above were blackened and bare. The night's rain had brought out a rank, acrid smell of burnt foliage, petrol, and scorched metal.

"Is this where Leon Corless was killed?" Quirke asked, peering into the surrounding darkness. Everywhere there was the sound of dripping leaves.

"The very spot," Hackett said. "Some co-

417

incidence, eh?"

The two men looked at each other.

"Yes," Quirke said. "Some coincidence."

Sergeant Jenkins appeared, carrying a walkie-talkie handset the size of a brick. "Forensics are on their way," he said.

"Oh, they are, are they," Hackett said with disdain, turning away. "Tell the supersleuths to report to me tomorrow."

Quirke and he made their way with difficulty up the muddy slope. At one point Hackett slipped and almost fell and had to grab at Quirke's arm for support. They reached the road.

"Bloody rain," Hackett said. "The farmers got the answer to their prayers, anyhow." He peered down in disgust at the sodden legs of his trousers and his muddy shoes. "The missus will murder me," he said, and sighed.

There were still mutterings of thunder far off, and now and then the horizon flashed white, as if there were a battle going on in the distance.

"When did you hear?" Quirke asked.

"About our friend there?" Hackett said, glancing back in the direction of what remained of Joe Costigan, crumpled at the foot of the charred tree. "Anonymous call, made from a phone box. No leads, nothing.

I'd say" — he sniffed — "I'd say, Dr. Quirke, this'll be one of those unsolved ones."

Quirke nodded, avoiding his eye. "You think so?"

"I have that feeling."

Hackett fumbled in his pockets for his cigarettes, offered the packet to Quirke, and took one himself. Then he brought out a lighter, and flipped up the lid and flicked the roller with his thumb, and at once the wick caught. "A handy thing, the Zippo," he said, hefting the lighter in his palm. "Lying there in the grass for God knows how long this evening, in the rain, and still it works." He dropped the lighter into his pocket. "Can I give you a lift, Doctor?" he said.

"No, thanks, I told the taxi to wait."

"Ah. Right. I'll be off, so." He started to move away, then stopped. "Did you ever hear," he said, "of the Battle of Jarama, and the heights of Pingarrón? No? Spain, you know, the civil war. Remind me to tell you about it, sometime. Sam Corless was in it," he added.

Quirke was stony-faced. "Was he?"

"Aye. A fierce scrap, it was, men killing each other with their bare hands." He glanced back to where Costigan's corpse was being transferred into the ambulance. "A terrible thing, having to learn how to break a neck." He studied Quirke's impassive features. "Wouldn't you say, Doctor?"

Quirke said nothing, and the detective tipped a finger to the brim of his hat, and was gone.

Quirke stirred himself. "Good night, Inspector," he called into the glistening darkness, but no response came back.

ABOUT THE AUTHOR

Benjamin Black is the pen name of the Man Booker Prize–winning novelist John Banville. The author of the bestselling and critically acclaimed series of Quirke novels — as well as *The Black-Eyed Blonde,* a Philip Marlowe novel — he lives in Dublin.